FATAL SECRETS

ANITA WALLER

Boldwood

First published in Great Britain in 2023 by Boldwood Books Ltd.

A CIP catalogue record for this book is available from the British Library.

Paperback ISBN 978-1-80415-317-8

Large Print ISBN 978-1-80415-318-5

Hardback ISBN 978-1-80415-316-1

Ebook ISBN 978-1-80415-320-8

Kindle ISBN 978-1-80415-319-2

Audio CD ISBN 978-1-80415-311-6

MP3 CD ISBN 978-1-80415-312-3

Digital audio download ISBN 978-1-80415-314-7

Boldwood Books Ltd
23 Bowerdean Street
London SW6 3TN
www.boldwoodbooks.com

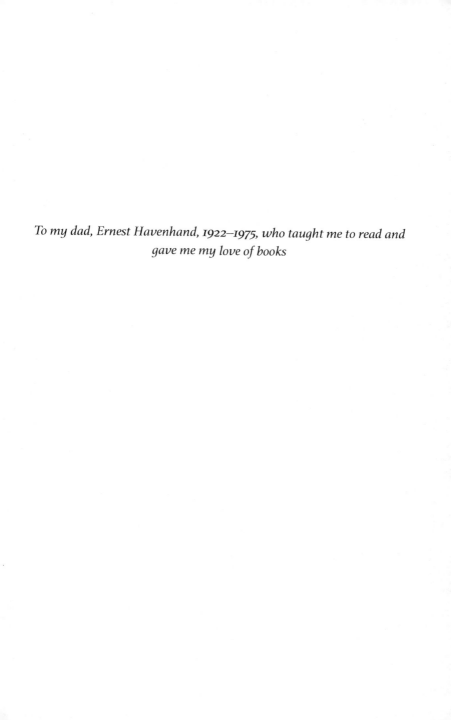

To my dad, Ernest Havenhand, 1922–1975, who taught me to read and gave me my love of books

If you prick us, do we not bleed? If you tickle us, do we not laugh? If you poison us, do we not die? And if you wrong us, shall we not revenge?

— *THE MERCHANT OF VENICE*, ACT 3 SCENE 1,

SHYLOCK

PROLOGUE

JANUARY 2013, A LAYBY ON THE A57

DI Dave Forrester's radio crackled into life.

'Mondeo pulled into layby just before M1 slip road. Shall we carry on?' He knew the two occupants of the squad car had been the first to catch sight of the Mondeo, but he didn't want inexperience causing problems. They were foot soldiers, not CID.

'Thanks, lads,' was his swift response. 'Just drive past him and wait up near the roundabout; we're one minute away. I'll pull in behind him in the layby. Keep your eyes open and follow him if he drives off and passes you; we can't lose this bastard.'

Dave increased his speed, and DS Johnny Keane grabbed onto the door handle. 'We've got him.' His words were full of the anger they both felt whenever Andy Beardow's name cropped up – Andy Beardow who had been in hiding since he had killed one of their own by beating her to death. DC Cathy Adams would never be forgotten, any more than Andy Beardow would.

A tip-off that they only half-believed had led them to this stage in the hunt for the man who had killed just for the hell of it, who had never considered the woman he was hitting with a hammer would have a husband and a child at home; a three-year-old girl who cried every night for her mummy to read her a story.

Cathy had spotted him dealing one night while out on patrol and had pulled the car over to arrest him while she waited for back-up. The back-up arrived too late to save her and it had catapulted Andy Beardow to Sheffield's most wanted in the blink of an eye.

The tip-off earlier that evening had come via an anonymous telephone call. The caller had given details of what car Beardow was driving and as a result of good police surveillance work combined with ANPR, the automatic number plate recognition system, the car had been in their sights as it headed out of Sheffield and either towards the Worksop area or the slip road at Aston for the M1.

Dave Forrester spotted the layby coming up on his left and slowed the car. He didn't want the Mondeo associating a speeding car with plans to trap him; he needed for it to look normal. He pulled in three car lengths behind the silver car and spoke into his radio. 'Confirmed sighting of Mondeo. I am behind it in the layby. Grant, how long before you get here?'

The voice of DC Grant Carney crackled into life. 'Thirty seconds, boss.'

'Okay.' His back-up team all heard him say, 'Let's go get the bastard, Johnny,' and an immediate increase in speed happened in the three cars still to arrive on scene.

'Wait till we're there, boss,' was Carney's taut response.

The two men got out of the car and began to walk towards the Mondeo, both holding Tasers. They had been responsible for the last ten-year incarceration of this man and this time, he was going down for life. Cathy Adams's death would ensure that.

Johnny headed for the passenger side, Dave Forrester taking the driver's side. He felt grateful for the lack of street lighting, hoping the darkness would hide their approach. He reached the driver's door and swiftly tugged on it to open it, but nothing happened.

He peered into the car, shading his eyes to cut out any reflection, and looked across at Johnny.

'It's empty...'

The shot was loud and Dave Forrester slid down the door as he slowly collapsed onto the tarmac, the silver car turning red with his blood. Johnny, too, dropped and moved round to the back of the car, intent on reaching his mate. 'Dave,' he shouted, 'you okay?'

There was no response, and he pulled out his phone.

They saved DI Forrester's life, but at some cost. Andy Beardow disappeared once again, and only the spectacular skills of surgeons helped Dave Forrester through that first week.

When they said he would never walk again, Dave Forrester had felt overwhelming anger, but slowly he began to accept his life as a Detective Inspector was over; his son would now hopefully be the one to fulfil his hopes and dreams of promotion within South Yorkshire Police, and he had no choice but to retire.

1

NINE YEARS LATER

That Saturday in March 2022, the twelfth to be exact, was memorable for many reasons.

Cambridge United had travelled up the A1 for a League One match against Sheffield Wednesday, and DI Matt Forrester and his sister Hermia had both managed to make use of their season tickets without work interfering to stop them; their seats were adjoining on the Hillsborough Kop, and he hoped it would be an excellent game.

Hillsborough stadium looked magnificent as always, and Matt turned with a smile on his face as he sensed Hermia's arrival.

'Hey, sis, cut it a bit fine.'

She gave a slight nod and lowered her seat. 'Dropped some flowers off at the memorial first.'

He should have known. She brought flowers to every home match she managed to attend. There hadn't been so many games this year, he realised. More responsibility for both of them at work meant football had to take a back seat; not a good state of affairs, he sometimes thought.

He studied her face for a moment. At twenty-six, she was beautiful, her long blonde hair swept up into a ponytail, held in place by a Sheffield Wednesday scrunchie. The blue of the team colours in her shirt and scarf brought out the vivid blue of her eyes, and the hint of pink on her lips made any man catching sight of her do a double take.

'Looking tired, sis.'

'Not just looking it. I am tired. This lot had better play well today, or I might just nod off.'

'You due a holiday?'

She laughed. 'What's a holiday? I don't work for the police, you know. I don't get four weeks' annual paid leave, a pension, a uniform, have people touch their forelocks as I walk by...'

'Yes, you do get several weeks' leave. You just don't take them.' He grinned. 'We could book a couple of weeks in Crete or one of the other islands. It's only you saying you can't go on holiday, not the university. And nobody touches their forelocks to me, not sure I'd know what to do if they did. Most I get is being called boss when they're being polite. God knows what they call me when I balls things up.'

'But I've got a team. I can't just up and leave them to go on a drunken two-week break in the sun with my brother! Oh, look, they're coming out...'

The entire Kop rose as one and the strains of 'Hi Ho Sheffield Wednesday' filled the air.

Smiles automatically appeared on the faces of Matt and Hermia, and after the initial start of game introductions, everyone sat back down, but not for long. An unfortunate own goal provided by the visitors gave Wednesday a one-nil lead, and it was during the uproar around this bonus goal that Matt felt his phone vibrate in his pocket.

'For fuck's sake,' he growled, and Hermia glanced at him.

'Problem?'

'It means Russian oligarchs have taken over the Town Hall if this is the station ringing me. I told them where I was going and that would be the only thing that I would accept as a valid reason for a phone call.'

He looked at the screen before answering. 'Shit... it's Dad.'

'But Dad knows...'

'Exactly.' He pressed the green button. 'Dad?'

'Need help.' The voice was weak, nothing like the strident tones usually evident in the older man's voice. 'Need...'

And there was silence.

Matt put his phone away and stood, folding his six-foot frame over as he pushed his way past fellow supporters. Hermia followed, hoping he would explain when they were away from the crowds.

They left Hillsborough in Matt's car, as it was the first one they reached, and they sped across the city heading for Gleadless, where their father lived and worked. An ex-policeman himself, Dave Forrester now owned the Forrester Investigation Agency, based in a shop he had converted to accommodate his wheelchair.

Hermia rang her father's phone again, but there was no answer. 'Had he got something special on? Some job he was worried about?' she asked, glancing sideways at Matt.

'Not that I know of. As you know, he's kind of morphed into dealing with forensic accountancy, and Johnny, being the more mobile of them, deals with the odd case of adultery and missing persons. Dad did say he was extra busy, but he seemed happy enough. And where's Johnny? He's always in the office, even if he's not got much on with his own cases.'

Johnny Keane was their dad's oldest friend, going back to

schooldays, and had hardly left Dave's side since the accident. Once it became clear Dave would never work again, Johnny put in his papers and retired alongside his friend. He'd been there when Dave had taken the decision to buy the shop with the upstairs living accommodation, and he did any legwork required so that Dave didn't have to do much other than the clever stuff. Making the final decision to move into Dave's spare bedroom was a no-brainer, and the friends became inseparable. Again, the thought flashed across Matt's mind. Where's Johnny?

Matt manoeuvred smartly around two lorries, and put his foot down. He felt sick at the thought of what could possibly be wrong – his father was a strong man, both mentally and physically, but limited by his lack of mobility. He laughingly called himself 'two steps Dave', because he could manage to throw himself that distance to get from the chair to the bed at night, and Matt felt panicked at the thought that he might have attempted more than that and now couldn't move at all.

He pulled up outside the double-fronted shop, and was a second behind Hermia as they dashed across the wide parking area to the shop door. The right-hand door was always locked, and he opened the left. The scene was chaotic.

Hermia spotted the wheelchair on its side, and the bottom half of her father lying on the floor.

'Oh, Dad,' she said and moved swiftly towards him. Then stopped. She dropped to her knees, and reached for his neck, checking for the pulse that she knew would be non-existent.

Matt pulled out his phone and put the call in for an ambulance and back-up, a forensic team, and bobbies to control any nosy parkers.

He went to join his sister, who had managed to roll her father onto his back, where she was attempting CPR. There was so much blood, splashed up his desk, puddled on the floor, his phone lying in the middle of it all from his attempt at getting help. He was only guessing, but he reckoned his dad didn't last long enough to call 999 after ringing him.

And then he saw Johnny, mainly hidden by his desk, only his feet visible. 'I'll see to Johnny.'

Hermia nodded. 'Dad's gone, Matt. But I'm not giving up.' Unchecked tears were rolling down her cheeks.

Johnny Keane was crumpled into a foetal position, bleeding heavily from a head wound. Matt checked his pulse; faint, thready. There was a lot of blood, and Matt took his scarf from around his neck and held it to the wound.

Both brother and sister were truly grateful to hear the siren sounds of approaching emergency services.

* * *

Matt pulled Hermia closer to him as they watched their father being zipped into a black bag, and Rosanna Masters, the pathologist, moved towards them. 'I'll take care of him, don't worry. And, Matt, you'll have my initial report by tomorrow. I'm going back with him now.'

Matt dropped his head in acknowledgement of her words. 'Thanks, Rosie. I'm going to get Hermia back to her car, and leave forensics to do what they have to do here. I'll ring the hospital later to see how Johnny is, see when I can talk to him. Hopefully by tomorrow I can get in here and start the investigation.'

'You told Harry yet?'

Matt visibly flinched at the thought of telling his ten-year-old son that his grandfather, his idolised grandfather, had died. It would have to be a joint effort between him and Becky, giving out such immense news.

'No, I haven't told Becky either. I'll go across to their home tonight, hope Dickhead isn't in, and tell them both at the same time.'

'Does Superintendent Davis know he's referred to as Dickhead?' Rosie risked a smile.

'He's probably guessed. Possibly around the time I caught him in bed with my wife, when Harry and I had to go home early from the match due to Harry throwing up everywhere.'

'Water under the bridge,' Hermia murmured, then stepped forward to touch the body bag as it was wheeled from the office, prior to being lifted into the coroner's van.

The photographer then took extra pictures of the site where Dave Forrester had lain, and eventually packed up his camera equipment. 'I'm off,' he said. 'Never in a million years would I have wanted this job, Matt. You need anything, just ask.'

Matt nodded his thanks, and walked him to the door.

The forensic team were busy with fingerprint powder, and Matt stood for a few minutes, watching everything they did. Hermia stood with him, until she eventually said, 'We have to go.'

'I know. I shouldn't be here. I'll take you to your car.'

'Can I go with you? Stay at yours tonight?'

'You don't usually ask; you just crash whenever you feel like being in a different place to your flat.' He smiled down into her tear-stained face.

'I know. Maybe I need a garden to walk around.'

'Then sell the flat, and buy a house.'

'It's up for sale. Got a few viewings over the next couple of weeks. I just don't want to be on my own tonight...'

'That's fine. Let me just check they have some keys to lock up this place, although I know there'll be a couple of bobbies outside all night.'

He was reassured they had keys, and he took Hermia's hand to lead her around the room away from the bloodstains, stepping carefully on the blocks laid down by the people gathering information about the crime scene.

He stopped outside to speak to the two officers on crowd control and asked them to ring him if there was anything to report throughout the night, before opening his car passenger door for Hermia to climb in.

'Boss,' one of the PCs said, 'you want the Wednesday score?'

'Not if they lost.'

'They didn't. Finished two minutes ago, won six-nil.'

2

Matt's house was within a five-minute drive of his father's office, but first he had to head back to Hillsborough to get Hermia's car.

Most of the traffic was heading towards them as football fans returned home, so fifteen minutes saw him pulling up behind Hermia's Porsche Cayman.

'See you back at mine,' he said. 'You got your key?'

She nodded. 'Always on my keyring. First there puts the kettle on.'

He had to trust she was in safe mode, and would drive carefully. She needed to put the horrific scene at Gleadless to the back of her mind for the moment.

* * *

Hermia was pouring the boiling water into mugs when Matt arrived home.

'Slowcoach,' she said, turning her head away so he didn't see the tears.

'I rang Becky, arranged to go over tonight to see Harry. She said she'd make sure Dickhead wouldn't be there.'

'Using those words?'

'No, she called him Brian. You know, Herms, in my job I've had to tell lots of people about the death of a relative, but this will be the hardest of them all. And I've to do it tonight before it's made public knowledge. She was upset...'

'Becky?'

He nodded. 'She thought a lot of our dad. In fact, she got on a lot better with him than she did with me. We drifted apart a couple of years after Harry was born, and it was Dad she talked to. She helped him a lot when he came out of hospital, but I was too busy being a copper, building my career. We're telling Harry together.'

'So Dickhead didn't tell her?'

'He didn't know. He's been playing golf all afternoon.'

Hermia handed Matt a cup. 'Get this down you. You want something to eat?'

He shook his head. 'I'd be sick. After I've spoken to Harry, I'm heading round to the hospital, see how Johnny is doing. There's more than half a chance we'll lose both of them. He lost a lot of blood.'

'Let's hope he remembers something, if he comes through this. I've rung my boss, told him I won't be in for two weeks. I think I need to be involved, somehow. Not sure how I can help, but I'm here if you need me for anything. I'll head home tomorrow, try and spruce the flat up a bit, ready for the viewing next week.'

The front door banged open and Steve Rowlands, Matt's closest friend, confidant and ex-landlord barged in, down the hall and into the kitchen. 'Matt, what the fuck's happened at your dad's place?' He stared in horror when he realised Hermia was there. 'Sorry, Herms, wouldn't have used language if I'd known. Matt? What's happened?'

'Best sit down, Steve. Coffee?'

'Thanks.' Steve sat at the table, followed by Hermia, cradling her cup. 'I'll explain, Matt,' she said gently. She turned to Steve. 'Dad was killed today, and Johnny is in a critical condition, head injuries. He's in hospital. We don't know any more than that; forensics are still doing their job. Matt will be back there tomorrow once they've done everything they need to do.' She allowed the tears to roll unchecked down her cheeks, and Steve stood and walked round the table, pulling her up into his arms.

This was where he'd always wanted his mate's sister, but not under these circumstances. He felt her head drop to his chest and not for a million pounds would he have moved.

Eventually she pulled away from him and he waited until she was seated before taking his coffee from Matt. The three of them sat in momentary silence, each lost in thoughts of Dave Forrester, and what he had meant to all of them.

'You busy tonight, Steve?'

Steve shook his head and sipped at his drink. 'You need me for something?'

'Stay here with Hermia while I nip over to the Northern General?'

'Of course.'

Hermia interrupted. 'I don't need babysitting.'

'You need company,' Matt said. 'I'm the expert in crime, don't forget, and I say I'm not leaving you on your own. I can't take you with me because I'm pretty sure the hospital won't allow you in, but they will allow my warrant card in.'

'Hey, no arguments,' Steve said. 'I'll nip next door and have a shower; it's been a hard day and I'm filthy, so give me half an hour?'

* * *

Harry sobbed, and both Matt and Becky held him tightly as they explained what had happened. Matt left after half an hour, promising to either ring or call round the next day, and he felt tears prick his eyes when he looked back and saw Harry and Becky standing in the front doorway, their arms around each other, both crying.

* * *

So late at night, Matt easily found a parking space near the entrance to the massive hospital, and headed towards A&E reception, keen to find out where Johnny had been taken. He finally reached Critical Care and had a word with the PC on duty before flashing his warrant card as proof of his identity. The nurse smiled at him and said she knew him, he was such a frequent visitor.

She led him towards a bay where Johnny lay, assorted tubes and wires connected to him, and a breathing tube performing its necessary function.

'He's not opened his eyes?'

She shook her head. 'Not for a second, but he's under sedation to rest his brain. It was a hell of a smack he took. God knows what he was hit with, but it worked. Try not to worry, he's doing as well as can be expected.'

'Bit of a cliché.' Matt smiled and reached across to touch Johnny's hand. 'Is it okay if I stay for a bit? He's not just a victim of crime, he's a close family friend.'

'Of course. I'm here all the time anyway – he gets one-on-one nursing until he starts to come out of the induced coma. Then we can ease off a little, because when he surfaces, it's the start of his recovery.'

* * *

Matt stayed for an hour, his mind racing as he stared at the face of the man who had been a brother in everything but name to Dave Forrester. Johnny would be devastated by Dave's death, and Matt knew he would have to be the one to break the news to him.

The nurse was constantly checking his vital signs and expressing satisfaction that all was as it should be, until eventually Matt stood. He needed to go home, get some sleep and be at the station gathering the closer members of his team for a trip back to the shop. All forensics should be checked by now, so they could be in the shop and working by eight, with a team out on the streets door-knocking with questions to be asked of residents about anything in the slightest suspicious that had happened the day before, or even in the few days prior to the attack. He suspected he wouldn't be allowed to be on the case for too long, so he wanted to take full advantage of everything until somebody said stop.

He gave Johnny's hand a gentle squeeze, but there was still no reaction, and after thanking the nurse for her care, he left the ward and headed downstairs towards the car park.

He sat for a moment in his car before starting the engine, wondering just who the hell could attack a disabled sixty-year-old man in a wheelchair, and an even older man with a gentle sort of frailty about him. He felt his anger build inside him, and he knew they would pay, whoever they were.

And the first place he would start looking would be the last known haunts of Andy Beardow, the man who had seemingly disappeared from the known universe since the shooting of the man now lying in the morgue, Dave Forrester. There was nothing to link the nine-year-old case with this one, but he couldn't ignore it. It needed ruling out, so they could move on.

If he had come back to finish off the job he had started in 2013, Matt would find him. If he was in this country, he would find it impossible to hide; his picture would be on every television news station, in every newspaper, and he would become public enemy number one all over again.

The difference now was that he wouldn't survive. Because now he wasn't dealing with Dave Forrester, he was going to eventually face Matt Forrester, a whole new ball game.

Matt turned his ignition on, slipped his car into drive and headed out of the hospital grounds, down Barnsley Road and towards the city centre. He drove on autopilot, hardly seeing traffic lights, lost in deep and dark thoughts.

He called into West Bar police station, handed in a request for some files, and was promised them by early morning. The night-time sergeant had been a huge fan of Dave Forrester, and whatever he could do to help he would do as quickly as possible.

'Check your emails in the morning, lad, it'll all be there for you.'

* * *

Steve was still in his lounge, waiting for him.

'I've made Hermia go to bed,' he said quietly. 'I've given her a sleeping tablet – out of date, but it seems to have worked.'

'Thanks, pal,' Matt sighed. 'I'll take over now; see you tomorrow?'

'I'm here for whatever you need, you know that?'

'I do,' he said. 'I do.'

3

Matt had always been able to rely on Steve.

On the afternoon he had found Becky in bed with his superior officer, Matt had headed immediately to Steve's cottage at the top end of Ridgeway, one of two cottages bought by his friend at a knock-down price because they literally needed knocking down.

But Steve hadn't done that; he had rebuilt the old place, and had started rebuilding the second one with a view to letting it, providing a valuable income when retirement eventually arrived. But the person who arrived before retirement did was his best mate in dire need of a home, and two weeks later, after what felt like twenty hours a day from both of them, the second cottage was habitable enough to move into.

Harry continued to live with his mother, and after many recriminations, arguments and finally acknowledgement that their marriage wasn't worth saving, Becky and Matt separated, then divorced.

And Matt bought his cottage from Steve.

* * *

He headed up the stairs that night, carefully avoiding the third tread because it creaked, and listened at Hermia's door. There were no sounds, so he hoped the out-of-date sleeping tablets were working, and she would get a good night's rest, because he suspected it was going to get much worse before it got better.

The cottage had originally had three bedrooms, although it had no bathroom, so the first rejig of the layout, done while staying with Steve in his cottage, had been to turn the smallest bedroom into a bathroom, and install a downstairs shower room at the same time. Part of the smallest bedroom had been utilised to make his bedroom into something resembling a ballroom; overnight, it became the largest room in the cottage. The other bedroom was turned into Harry's room, until the day he'd taken Harry up into the loft space. The loft space had become his biggest project of them all, and Matt and Steve had worked many hours converting it into two bedrooms, one fit for a little boy who was learning to live between two homes, the other a 'just in case' room for friends who might be in need of a bed at some point in their life, just as he had been that long ago afternoon.

By half past four, Matt was wishing he'd taken an out-of-date sleeping tablet. His own eyes hadn't even closed, because when they did, he saw his father lying half in and half out of his wheelchair, blood pooling beneath him.

He gave in at five and got up, showered, and after leaving a note for Hermia, headed into work.

* * *

The nightshift officers were still on duty, and they all said good morning, somewhat awkwardly in most cases, but one or two said how sorry they were to hear the news. The older members of the force had known Dave, and a few spoke of some incident concerning him that had stayed in their memories. It was obvious there was a great deal of affection for ex-DI Dave Forrester.

Matt began to set up the murder board in the briefing room, knowing it was only the beginning. There would be so much more to add later when the investigation kicked in a little more intensely, but for now, his father's picture stared back at him. He listed the priorities required of his team, starting with a flooding of the area with officers asking questions about seeing anything unusual, any strange cars...

Moving back to his desk, he opened up his laptop and checked his emails, knowing that the files he had requested would be there waiting for him. He forwarded the email to his own personal address, then archived the information. He knew he would need all information on his home computer as well as at work; this case wouldn't be any sort of nine-to-five job.

His team started to arrive from around half past six, all aware today would be a long day, and eager to get on with it. DS Karen Nelson arrived bearing two takeaway coffees, handing one to him. 'Thought you might need this, boss,' she said, her Yorkshire accent obvious in the confines of her workplace, but not in evidence at all when she spoke to anyone of senior rank, or at least higher than her boss.

'Thanks, Karen. I need this.'

'Didn't sleep much?'

'Didn't sleep at all.'

'We going to the shop?'

'We are. I contacted everybody by text last night, so hopefully they'll be in by seven, and we can have a briefing without having very much at all to brief about. We need to get into Dad's files, but we also need feet out on the streets of Gleadless, checking CCTV, knocking on doors, simply observing. And talking to people. Anybody who walks past, that sort of thing.'

She smiled at him. 'All the usual investigative stuff, you mean?'

He smiled back at her. 'Sorry, no sleep and being wound up like a spring is probably making me stupid. Yes, we follow the rules until there are no rules to follow, that's the way this team works, but we don't ignore instincts.'

She stared at him. 'You have one?'

He shrugged. 'I don't know. Andy Beardow...'

'We have permanent alarms set up for his return to this country, don't we? He'd be picked up as soon as he set foot off a plane or a boat, or a train.'

He watched as Karen sipped at her coffee. 'And what if he never left the country? What if he changed his appearance? Easy to do by shaving his head, removing his beard, coloured contact lenses, that sort of thing. He just disappeared altogether after the shooting, and nobody has heard from him since. I've never been convinced he left the country, because we closed every available escape route within two hours.'

'So you think he's resurfaced from wherever he's been?'

'It's possible. We have a letter locked away in the storage facility that he sent, saying he was glad Dave Forrester was dead, he had completed his mission in life by killing him, and he'd try for Johnny Keane next time. It arrived the day after the shooting when he thought he'd killed Dad, but it had a postmark for the day itself, so he was very confident he was going to kill him. He must have been so pissed off when Dad survived, and continued to live a good life, albeit outside the force. And now Dad's dead, and Johnny is alive but currently non-responsive to everything. I asked the CC unit to let me know if he showed signs of waking up, but I got the impression we could be a few days away from anything like that happening.'

The office door opened and the four remaining members of his regular team arrived together, not chatting, carrying Starbucks cardboard coffee cups, and almost in a state of apprehension as they thought of what the day would reveal to them.

DC Kev Potter and DC Phil Newton crossed to their own desks, removing their coats before heading towards Matt and Karen. The two PCs, who had been part of the team for six months and working towards ultimately being DCs themselves, headed straight towards their boss.

'This is shit, boss,' PC Jaime Hanover said, screwing her blonde hair into the ponytail that had started to unravel since leaving home. PC Ian Jameson nodded his head in agreement of her statement. 'Tell us what to do,' he said.

Matt glanced at his watch. 'Briefing at seven sharp. I need the foot soldiers here first, or I'll be repeating myself. The six of us will be concentrating on the immediate locale of Dad's shop, but I want a team of officers out on the streets. I don't care if it's Sunday, and I'm damn sure killers don't either.'

They could hear the clatter of feet coming up the stairs, and Karen laughed. 'I shouldn't imagine for one minute that anybody thought *but tomorrow's Sunday* when you summoned everybody in for seven this morning. Sounds as if the cavalry is arriving.'

Matt sighed. 'I'm being an overwrought idiot, aren't I?'

'You are,' Karen agreed. 'Now calm down, tell them what you want of them, particularly today, and let's get out there and do it.'

The next half hour was spent giving out detailed instructions; Karen made a phone call to check they wouldn't be jumping on anybody's toes in the forensics department, and finally people began to leave the room, organising who was going in which car, with DC Kev Potter handing out hurriedly concocted lists of roads, in an attempt to ensure work wasn't duplicated. Knowing it was too early for his boss to be in, Matt sent a quick email to Superintendent Carl Granger, giving him the bare facts of the actions he had undertaken, and finishing by telling him he would give him a full report in person later.

It was a cool morning, yet refreshing, and the teams of door-knockers breathed a sigh of relief that rain hadn't been promised. There was a small car park adjacent to Dave Forrester's office premises, and the police cars soon filled it, putting off anybody else who might have wanted to park there; better that the police didn't get too close a look at tyres and suchlike seemed to be the general consensus of the drivers who approached their usual Sunday parking area, before quickly driving off in the opposite direction.

Matt had a word with everybody before watching them walk away. There were no smiles. This was the murder of one of their own, albeit a retired one of their own. And their DI's dad.

Matt turned and walked towards the doorway, inserted his key into the lock and opened the left side door. He stood for a moment, surveying the scene, the blood now congealed to a dark, almost black mess, and he drew in a breath. *Calm*, he said to himself, *stay calm*.

'Where do we start, boss?' Karen's tone was gentle, knowing how hard this was going to be for him.

'Okay, I'm not really sure. Let me just explain the layout to all of you. As you can see, the small door off to the side is a lift, which connects this downstairs office to the private quarters upstairs. It leads directly into the lounge. The first door leading off the lounge is Dad's bedroom.' He paused. 'Was Dad's bedroom. The second door is Johnny's room, and has a connecting speaker system with Dad's room, so that if Dad fell at any point, he could quickly get help. The door opposite Johnny's room is the bathroom he uses. Dad has a disabled en suite in his room. The kitchen is the next door, and that's pretty much it. Compact enough for two men who spend most of the day in this office, or, in Johnny's case, out on surveillance or visiting people to interview them. When this office opened, it was opened as an investigation agency, but over the years, it has changed into something much bigger. They now have a couple of part-time employees, somebody who sees to all their IT requirements, that sort of thing. I know Johnny's skill was in following men and women, seeking to spot them with people they shouldn't be with. He's the reason for many divorces in this area.'

He moved across to Dave Forrester's desk. 'This was Dad's desk, and the other one is Johnny's. Dad had full control of all the cases, and Johnny filtered his reports through to Dad to be added to the case files, keeping all cases under one banner, so to speak. It was Dad's business, officially, even though Johnny did most of the physical work. Through the door directly behind me is the office kitchen, complete with a sofa, a very comfortable sofa. I've spent a fair few nights on it in my time. We talked Dad into getting it in case the lift broke down and he had to sleep down here. There are stairs connecting to the living quarters, so Johnny is fine, but Dad couldn't get upstairs without that lift.'

Matt looked up as he heard the shop door open. He felt the blood rush to his face as he recognised the person standing with the light behind him, turning him into a silhouette.

'Sir? You need something?'

'I certainly do,' Superintendent Brian Davis said. 'I need an explanation for why you think it's okay to work this case, without consulting a superior officer first.'

4

For a split second, Matt's mind went blank. He stared at Davis and gave a slight cough before speaking. 'With respect, sir,' then he hesitated as he realised he'd used the word respect, 'it's my job. I'm SIO in murder cases, and we definitely have one death here, with the possibility of that increasing to two, so, as I said, it's my job.'

'Not when you're the son of the deceased.'

Matt fixed his eyes on Brian Davis with what he hoped was a death stare, but knew deep down this wasn't going to end well. He had thought he might get two or three days before somebody put the brakes on his involvement in the case, but it seemed Davis had accelerated the rules.

'I know more about Dad's business than anyone. It makes sense for me to be SIO.'

'How did you get into the premises?'

'I used my keys. It's Dad's home as well as his business, so I have a full set of his keys.'

Davis held out his hand. 'I'll take them. You can, of course, have them back when the investigation is finished.'

Matt felt the anger begin to grow, and knew he couldn't win. He didn't hesitate. He put his hand in his pocket, removed the keys and removed his warrant card.

'I resign.' He dropped both items onto his father's desk.

There was a deathly silence in the room, until he heard Karen's whispered, 'No!'

'That's not necessary,' Superintendent Davis said, picking up the warrant card and handing it back. 'There are other cases you can be working on, just not this one.'

'I thought I made it clear. I resign. You'll get my official resignation letter later today. Can I ask why you're here?' He hesitated before adding, 'Sir?'

'Superintendent Granger was admitted to hospital last night. I have been asked to step into the breach until he's fit to resume his duties, so Central area and the South East have me for all reports.'

There was silence in the room, then Matt moved towards the door. 'This business in part now belongs to me, and if you remove anything at all, even a biro, I want a receipt for it. And start with my keys on that list.'

He walked out and across to his car. The officers on watch duty were standing by their squad car, and moved towards him. 'You need anything, boss?'

'I need you to stop calling me boss.' He grinned. 'From now on, it's Matt. I'm going home. I'd appreciate hearing about anything that's going off here, but if you feel you can't...'

The younger of the two officers stared at him. 'You've finished? With the force?'

'As of now.' He handed them his business card. 'My personal mobile number is on that, but I won't be offended if you feel you can't pass anything on.'

'But...'

'I know. This wasn't on the cards when I came in this morning, but neither was having Superintendent Davis overseeing our operation. So, I'm off. If I can't investigate my father's death from the inside, then I'll do it from the outside.'

He lifted his hand towards them as he walked away, and both PCs added his number to their phones.

* * *

There was a numbness inside the shop, and Davis clapped his hands to get their attention. 'Okay, let's start with checking everything down here. We'll take all the files in the filing cabinet away with us, plus his computer and any other tech stuff we come across. We'll tackle upstairs when we've finished down here. DS Nelson?'

'Yes, sir.'

'You're in charge and I want a full report by the end of the day. Let's get this cleared up quickly. Oh, and please remember Matthew Forrester is no longer a member of this team, so I expect you all to respect his decision to leave, and I hope you won't feel inclined to have any contact with him from now on.'

He turned and walked out, crossing to his car where the driver jumped out to open the door for him.

Karen watched him go, and nobody moved.

'What the fuck just happened?' DC Kevin Potter spoke quietly. He voiced what everyone else was thinking.

* * *

Matt drove his Land Rover onto the gravelled parking area of his cottage and sat, deep in thought, for a couple of minutes before opening the door. He stepped out and the aroma of bacon wafted around him.

The gravel continued down the side of the house, separating

the two cottages, and the crunch as he walked filled him with deep satisfaction. The sound meant he was home from work. This time, it felt pretty permanent.

He opened the kitchen door and stepped inside. Steve was on his feet in the split second his brain registered someone was coming through the door, but he returned to his seated position when he realised it was Matt.

'Didn't know I had any bacon,' Matt said. 'Enough left for me to have a sarnie?'

'I brought it from mine,' Steve responded. 'I knew you wouldn't have any, and I also knew Herms wouldn't feel like eating, so here I am, feeding all of us apparently. Why are you here?'

'I handed my warrant card in.'

Hermia's head lifted with a jerk. 'You're on compassionate leave? I don't believe it...'

'Not compassionate, more permanent.'

Steve stood and moved to the cooker. 'Is this a two breadcake decision, or one?'

'Steve!' Hermia's shock at registering her brother's words was evident in that one word. 'Don't encourage him. Matt, what do you mean?'

Matt pulled out a chair and took hold of his sister's hand. 'This morning, shortly after the team had arrived in Dad's shop, Dick-head Davis turned up. It seems that our own Super got himself admitted to hospital last night, so Superintendent Davis is temporarily covering his own Central patch, plus the South East patch. He immediately stopped everything, told me I couldn't work on the case because of my close connection to the deceased. Asked for my keys, so I gave them to him along with my warrant card, and I'm going in after I've had my bacon sandwiches with my official letter of resignation and a big box to bring my personal stuff home.

So, sister dear, I'm going to need the set of keys Dad gave you, so I can get a new set cut.'

Steve flipped over the bacon and began to butter the breadcakes. 'The breadcakes are mine as well,' he said in a casual tone. 'Will it make sense for me to get extra food in now my best mate has no income, no pension, no job prospects?'

'It'll make perfect sense.' Matt grinned. 'And Hermia will be here as well for the foreseeable. Mind you, she's not walked away from her job, so she's not quite as destitute as me...'

'Hang on,' Hermia interrupted, putting down her now empty coffee cup. 'I'm not staying here for any foreseeable. I've got a viewing of my flat this week, for a start. And I need to be looking round for a new house, so I'm going home this afternoon.'

'No.' Both men spoke together, then looked at each other.

'Herms.' Matt tried to speak gently, in a negotiating sort of way. 'I have no idea yet why Dad was killed yesterday, but I sure as hell intend finding out. I can't do that if I'm having to constantly be worrying about you being on your own. It's all very well immediately jumping to the conclusion that it's the bastard who put him in the wheelchair, but even I can see that's a long shot. Beardow hasn't poked his head above any parapets in this country since the day he shot Dad. It doesn't make sense that he would come back and risk his liberty when he's been free for all these years. I'm guessing Davis will be leaning towards that conclusion, that it's the return of Andy Beardow, and he'll be steering the team towards finding him. I'm just grateful I had a smart dad who emailed me every night with a back-up of all his files.'

'You're changing the subject, Matt. Why can't I go home? You haven't given me a logical reason for staying here yet.'

'Thanks to Steve, I have a cracker of a garden that I know you love. That's reason number one. Number two is Steve is here. That's pretty important in my book. Number three is I need you to be safe and until I've an inkling of what we're dealing with, I think you're safer here.'

'But I've a viewing this week and several next week. I've told the estate agent I want to take them myself, but the first one isn't through them, anyway.'

'Either Steve or I will take you. We'll wait in the car, leave you to do the viewing, then bring you back here. Herms, I'm not asking you to live here forever – heaven forbid – I'm just asking that you do it until we find out who killed Dad and put Johnny into a coma.'

Hermia stared at her brother. It was obvious that independent woman was battling caring man, and she gave in. 'Do I need somebody to accompany me to Sainsbury's because we clearly can't live anywhere without food?'

Steve's guffaw of laughter broke the tension. 'I'll go with you, Herms; I need to restock on bacon and breadcakes, and probably lagers and wine now somebody is out of a job.' He passed the plate containing the bacon sandwiches across to his friend. 'Get these inside you, and think about what's happened this morning. I'm sure they'd accept an apology, a bit of a grovel, and a promise to behave in future if that's what you want, but if you don't, go into the station, get your stuff and leave that bloody letter for whoever is higher than Dickhead. Don't leave it for that bastard. In fact, do you want me to compose it for you?'

Matt gave a genuine laugh for the first time since seeing Dave Forrester's body. 'Good lord, no. I'd probably end up in a cell. These are good,' he said, indicating the sandwiches. 'The resignation letter will be short and sweet, and it will be effective immediately. I'll pack my stuff first, then hand everything in that needs to be handed in. After that, I'll come back here and get on my laptop, find out what the fuck Dad was involved with.'

Hermia sighed. 'Are you absolutely sure about this? You're giving up your career, and it's really all about him, not about you. If another superior officer had told you it was against the rules to work on this case, would you have reacted in the same way?'

'Probably not. And I knew it was against the rules, I just hoped I might have a bit of a crack at it before I was stopped, but he was in there straight away. And at some point, I'd have had to make decisions anyway, wouldn't I? I just didn't expect to have to make them at this moment in my life. Don't forget, sweet sister of mine, we have just become joint owners of a thriving detective agency, despite not knowing anything about any of the cases, anything about forensic accountancy, or even how to keep a fridge stocked.'

It took him a mere five minutes to end his career, and he folded the letter carefully before sliding it into an envelope. He slipped it into the inside pocket of his jacket, and sighed.

5

Steve's Audi accelerated away, and suddenly his world felt brighter, all because he was going to Sainsbury's with Hermia sitting in his passenger seat.

He could see the tail-lights of Matt's Land Rover some distance in front, and hoped the instant decision to quit the force wouldn't cause regrets six months down the line. It had been sudden. Matt hadn't expressed dissatisfaction with his job – nothing beyond saying he wished he could work at gardening for a living every time he helped out on any of the jobs that required two men with muscles.

If he'd thought for one minute that Matt was serious about quitting the force, he would have brought him into his business as a full partner, giving him the opportunity to expand in the way he planned to eventually grow, but doing it five years earlier.

He pulled into Sainsbury's car park, aching at the sight of the sadness on Hermia's face. He squeezed her hand. 'Come on, let's go feed that brother of yours. And we'll go grab a coffee when we're done here, and talk about Dave.'

She raised a half smile. 'You know me so well.'

* * *

Matt dropped the keys in at the little market shop in Crystal Peaks, asked for two copies of each key, and said he would be back within the hour. He got the usual Sheffield shaking of the head, and *Oh, I dunno if I can do it that quick*, and responded with, *I'm sure you can. You've a good reputation, mate.* He'd guaranteed the keys would be ready on his return with that short phrase.

He pulled out of Crystal Peaks, drove for a minute and turned into the police station car park.

Everyone in the briefing room looked towards him as he walked through the door. He raised a hand in salute, then entered his own small office. He placed the cardboard box on the table and began to clear his desk. He was surprised at how little emotion he felt. This had been his life for so long, and to achieve the giddy heights of having his own office had been such an amazing feeling. Now it was over, and he felt a calm acceptance.

His chocolate drawer seemed sadly depleted – one Mars bar and a Crunchie, so he left them for one of the others to steal when they were hungry. He glanced up as his door opened.

'You're serious then?' Karen Nelson stood in the opening.

'I am. I can't work under that prick, anyway, but taking me off the case was the worst thing he could have done. So, I'm back on the case but on my own terms now.'

She quietly stepped further into the room and closed the door. 'Move over and make it look as though I'm helping you pack,' she said quietly. 'Okay, I'm going to book out your keys to go back to your dad's place. Is there a key-cutting shop anywhere at Gleadless?'

'Doesn't matter,' he said, his voice low. 'Hermia had a set. They are currently in Crystal Peaks market being duplicated. Two sets, in case he catches me there, and takes another set off me.'

'Smart arse,' she said. 'Sir.'

'Not sir any more. From now on, it's Matt.'

'I just want you to know that I think this is so wrong. You have the best clear-up rate, and he was wrong to take you off this, no matter what the rules say. What I'm saying is, general consensus of opinion seems to be what we find out, you find out. I'll be your point of contact, but basically you still have a team of six watching your back. Nobody queried it, nobody argued it was against the rules, they're all pretty pissed off about losing you. Sir.'

Matt picked up the photograph of his dad, with himself and Hermia on either side of him, stared at it for a moment, then placed it into his box. He turned to Karen. 'Thanks for your help. I'll be in touch, and all of you have my number. Don't be strangers now I've morphed into an entrepreneur in my own right.'

She stared. 'God, I never thought of that. You're taking over your dad's business?'

He grinned. 'Too bloody right I am. It's called Forrester's and it will remain Forrester's. Unless Dad changed his mind and left it to the Dogs' Home for Unwanted Mutts, Hermia and I inherit equally. I can't imagine for one minute she will want to give up her career at the university, so I can see me having to buy her out, but all that is in the future. For now, I need to sort out Dad's cases, see if anything in there could have led to what happened yesterday.'

He picked up the box, and Karen held the door open for him. 'Take care, Matt,' she said quietly, as he headed for the corridor leading to Superintendent Davis's temporary office. He turned and looked at her.

'Every Friday evening, Dad sent me an email attaching every file on his computer. He once accidentally wiped something out and we couldn't get it back, so this was his system for backing up his work. He had an external hard drive which he backed up every night as well. I've never had to open one of these emails until now, but Dad felt happier knowing they were there if necessary. He then deleted the email from his Sent Emails folder, because he always said he didn't want me implicated in any queries that might arise. So I will be going home now, and opening last Friday's email...'

'And presumably I'm the only one who knows about this? It stays with me, Matt.'

He nodded, continued down the corridor, and ended his police career.

* * *

He said many goodbyes, accepted far too many condolences, and finally left the station car park to return to Crystal Peaks. He parked in the doctor's car park this time, not wanting to be the recipient of a parking fine for having returned too soon to the official car park, and walked down the slight incline towards the shopping mall.

He collected the keys, bought two key rings to hold them securely as two separate sets, and rang Steve's phone.

He discovered they were in a small coffee shop eating Danish pastries, and asked that they order the same for him, along with a flat white. 'I'll be there in ten minutes. I'll have to stick to speed limits now I'm a civilian.'

'You've done it then?' Matt could sense the shock in Steve's voice.

'I have.'

'You okay?'

'No. I'll be there in ten,' and he disconnected.

* * *

'So we have a plan?' Steve had waited until Matt took his first bite of the Danish pastry before trying to discover where his friend's future lay.

'We? What's this we? Last time I heard anything, you've a busy landscaping business and Herms has a career in God knows what at the uni.'

Steve looked at Hermia and she gave a slight nod.

'We've been talking. I know it's March and starting to get busy, but for heaven's sake, I've five lads working for me, all good lads, and I've put Rob in temporary charge while I take a month off. While I was organising that, Hermia was contacting her boss, who, it turns out, is the head top dog at the uni, to sort out taking a month's leave. What we're trying to say is that you're not on your own. Dave was so important to all of us, he treated me like a son for all of my life, and if I can't take time out to help him now, I'm not much of a son, am I?' Steve brushed away a recalcitrant tear, and Hermia leaned across, touching his arm lightly.

Matt swallowed his mouthful of pastry. 'I feel like the third musketeer.'

'Good. One for all, and all that. But seriously, mate, Herms and I are with you on this. How have your team taken the news you've definitely gone?'

'Exactly as I expected them to take it. They're all going to report to me if there's anything to report, and I think we can expect Karen to be a frequent visitor.' He felt ridiculously upbeat at that statement.

Hermia sipped at her coffee. 'So what's the next step?'

Matt fished around in his pocket and handed her the keys he had borrowed. 'To return these. I've had two sets cut, so once I've sorted them and attached them to key rings, I'll give you one set, Steve – that's a sort of back-up against anybody else taking them – and I'll have the other set. We have to wait a couple of days before attempting to get back into the shop, because even though the surveillance bobbies would be quite happy to let me go in, they'd also have to report it. I'll not put them under that pressure, so we'll wait until it's no longer a crime scene, and then we'll turn it into our own crime scene.'

His phone pealed out. 'Rosie? You have news for me?'

The pathologist hesitated for a heartbeat. 'I have the post-mortem results. I understand you've resigned…'

'I have. And I understand if you can no longer discuss the results with me.'

'I've sent it to Superintendent Davis, but also to your DS. Karen has very kindly given me your personal email. Are you with me?'

'I am, and thank you. Be careful, Rosie. Davis is not a friend of mine, as you know.'

'I know, and that's exactly why I've emailed you. Good luck, Matt, and stay safe.'

They broke the connection, and Matt checked his emails. He forwarded Rosie's to a second email address he held that wasn't in everyday usage, trying to ensure nothing would happen to the precious report before he had a chance to print it and read it carefully. His dinosaur attitude towards technology led him to a preference for reading the printed word.

'We have Dad's PM report,' he said, sipping slowly at his drink, enjoying the heat of the coffee.

'Did she say anything?'

Matt shook his head. 'No, she already knew I'm no longer SIO, so she played by the rules and didn't give me a verbal report. Karen presumably has that, but Karen gave her my personal email address.'

Hermia finished her coffee and leaned back. 'We have to go home and decide what happens next, don't we?'

Matt nodded. 'We'll set everything up in my dining room, until such a point comes when we can use Dad's premises. That could be as soon as a couple of days' time. We'll let the forensics team do their jobs thoroughly, then we'll go in and do it the way we want it to be done. I don't want anything happening there until we get those keys back from Davis, then there'll be no comeback. What the fuck did Becky see in him?'

'Maybe he didn't put work before his family,' Hermia said, the sarcasm in her voice evident to all three sitting around the table.

'Ouch,' Matt responded. 'Say it like it is, why don't you?'

'If I'd said it when I could see it happening, maybe the situation would have been different, but you're ever so slightly pigheaded, sweet brother of mine, and you wouldn't have believed me, anyway!'

6

Hermia returned home with Steve, leaving Matt to return on his own, but via the Forrester office at Gleadless. The crime scene tape was still around the entire frontage of the shop, and he briefly wondered if that meant he could get in via the back door without causing issues further down the line, but he decided to leave it. There was a squad car still parked outside, but with only one occupant to keep an eye on things. Matt waited a minute, trying to see who it was. His light bulb moment came as the officer's head turned slightly and he recognised Ray Ledger, someone who had been with the force seemingly forever, but always doing the menial jobs such as surveillance; he had never progressed beyond the PC level, never wanted to progress beyond that.

Matt exited his Land Rover and walked towards the squad car, but he didn't have a chance to knock on the window. The glass rolled down, and PC Ray Ledger leaned across from the driver's seat.

'Afternoon, sir.'

'Afternoon, Ray. And it's not sir any longer. You'll hear when you get back, but I've resigned.'

Ray looked suitably nonplussed. 'Resigned? You serious?'

'Couldn't be more serious. Has anybody been around? Anybody to cause the hairs on the back of your neck to tickle?'

'Not particularly, but if they've been in my line of sight, I've made a note of their car reg numbers. I can see anybody who comes past the shop, but I can also see anybody who approaches along that little service road, and if they've come up this end, anywhere near this shop, they've gone onto my sheet.'

'Anybody said how long they're keeping surveillance on it?'

'Think this is the last day, unless something shows up in the meantime. They don't keep us at crime scenes for very long.'

'I know. Most of the criminals around South Yorkshire know that as well,' Matt said with a smile.

'So sorry to hear about your dad, and to hear Johnny's taken a bit of a battering as well. I worked with them both, was on the detail chasing bloody Andy Beardow around the country. You reckon he's back?'

'Could be, but he's never been spotted since he shot Dad, so if I'm being honest, no, I don't think this is him. It may be connected to him. He must have had a real grudge against Dad in the first place to shoot him. He would have assumed he'd killed him, only to find out later Dad had recovered. It made headlines in the papers, so he must have known. But no, I don't think this is him. Too long since the shooting. This is probably more to do with one of Dad's cases.'

'You going in to have a look round? I might have to walk across the road to that sandwich shop to use their toilet.'

'Not today. I just wanted to drop by, be here, take it in. Can't imagine life without him, don't want to imagine it, but it's happened.'

Ray nodded. 'Couldn't agree more. I used to drop in occasionally, share a sandwich with him or a cuppa. Good times. I'll miss him.'

'Well, don't let Dad not being here stop you in the future. I'll be here, or Hermia, my sister. A lot depends on what the will says, what she wants to do, but I'm set on carrying on the business. This agency holds the key to what happened and why. I'll not keep you from your job any longer; thanks for talking, Ray.'

'Here,' Ray responded, and handed him a sheet of car registrations. 'If I hand this in at the station, I don't think for one minute anybody will act on it. But you will. If anything else crops up today, can I get in touch with you? All of these are in my police notebook, so I'll write them out again when I get to the station and nobody will know I've handed them to you.'

Matt passed him his personal card. 'Any time,' he said. 'And thanks for the trust.'

* * *

He reached home to find his cupboard and the fridge stocked with food that was remarkably fresh and tasty, nothing like the odd bit of cheese or couple of eggs that were normally part of his diet.

'Has anybody fed Oliver?'

'Well, you're a bit late thinking about him,' Hermia said. 'I fed him first thing this morning, and he disappeared as soon as he'd eaten. It strikes me that he's a remarkably self-reliant cat, is Oliver.'

'Has to be,' Matt said. 'I didn't ask him to come live with me, don't forget. He just turned up here one day and expected me to have food for him. He's been doing me the favour of living here ever since.'

'My god, Matt Forrester, anybody would think you didn't love him to bits to hear you talk.'

He shrugged. 'Well, maybe I'd miss him if he took off.'

'Good job he's got me as back-up,' Hermia said. 'So what's your plan now? For today, I mean?'

'I've got some things to do – I've just accidentally acquired a list of car registrations that have been in the vicinity of the shop today. I'm also going to print off the PM report.'

'You can read it on screen, you know, Mr Dinosaur.'

'I might want to make notes on it, ask questions. I'd rather do that with a pen in my hand.'

She sighed. 'Okay. Listen, I have a viewing on Tuesday, so I need to go down to the flat at some point, just for a quick tidy up. There's a casserole I put in the oven ready for me to heat up after the match – God, that seems a lifetime ago now, doesn't it? When I put that casserole in the oven, I had a dad. And I need to get that casserole out of the oven and into a bin before it leaves an unhealthy pong around the place.'

He pulled her close. 'We still have a dad, he's just not with us in the physical form any more, but he's always with us. He's led us through life to this point, and if we go by the "What Would Dad Do?" mantra he taught us years ago, I'm sure he'll live on in us.'

She nodded, her nose buried in his chest. 'Have you heard anything about Johnny?'

'Not yet. I'm going over to the hospital once I've looked at this PM report. They'll not tell me anything if I just ring and ask, but I might find out some of the truth if I turn up, especially while they still think I'm DI Forrester.'

His phone pinged to tell him he had a text, and Hermia stepped away from him. He took the phone from his pocket, murmured, 'Karen,' and walked through to the dining room, now known as the info room. He had already moved his laptop and printer to the dining table, and stuck three long strips of old wallpaper to the wall with Blu Tack, wrong side out so he could write on them.

Karen's message, sent from her personal number, was brief yet to the point.

No CCTV of any use. Outside camera smashed, inside camera sprayed with black paint. Chasing up CCTV from adjoining properties now. Will keep you informed. Delete this and any future texts. Xx

He stared at the kisses for a moment, wishing... then pulled a notebook towards him, a small one that could be easily hidden. He copied the text word for word, before deleting it from his phone. He supposed it could be recalled if anybody really wanted to prove something against him, but for now, he could keep the words manually. He hesitated before adding the kisses, but then did so. Right now, he needed all the affection he could get, even if it was two simple kisses on the end of a text from a married woman.

He replied with *Thank you*, hesitated, then added *xx*. He deleted his response.

* * *

Matt was on his way to the hospital when he received the phone call.

'DI Forrester? It's Critical Care at the Northern General. You asked me to call to let you know if Mr Keane showed signs of surfacing from his coma. He opened his eyes ten minutes ago, and we're pleased with the general signs he's displaying. It's good news, we believe.'

'Thank you so much, I'm on my way there at the moment. I should be there in the next ten minutes. Take care of him for me.'

He disconnected and a smile flashed across his face. Finally, something to give him hope. He didn't think it would have been bearable to lose both his dad and the man he regarded as dad number two.

He easily found a parking place and used the back entrance of the hospital to reach the Critical Care Unit; the door was buzzed open for him as soon as he said, 'Matt Forrester to see John Keane.'

A nurse, Laura according to her name tab, was leaning over him, using what looked like a lollipop to dampen his lips.

'He's not capable of drinking for himself yet, so I'm just applying water to make him feel better in his mouth. His eyes opened a couple of minutes ago, but only for seconds. He's gone back to sleep again now, but it's good that he's starting to come round. Everything else is looking good, the doctor was here half an hour ago, and there is nothing of any immediacy that's of concern; he needs time to recover. We don't know yet if the head wound has caused any brain damage, and won't know until he surfaces enough to speak, but he's responded well to all the treatment and surgery he's had.'

The bed was quite high so that doctors and nurses could easily deal with whatever needed doing, so Matt chose not to sit by the bed, but to stand. He took hold of Johnny's hand, careful not to go near the canula inserted into the back of it, and squeezed his fingers gently.

'You're doing well, Johnny,' he whispered. 'I need you to wake up so I can go get the half-human who did this to you. I need you to tell me what happened, and I need you to come home with us as soon as you can. Hermia and I will take care of you until you're well enough to take care of yourself, and she sends all her love, as does Steve.'

'Keep talking to him,' Laura advised. 'With head injuries, we never have any idea when they will come out of it, and only gently reduce his sedation so that if he becomes distressed at any point, we can put him back where he feels safe, asleep. But we do know with certainty that they hear what is told to them. So many patients, when they come round, repeat what they heard while we assumed they were unconscious, so keep talking, DI Forrester.'

'Okay, Johnny, here's what you missed yesterday. Wednesday won six-nil. It was a good day for all the Bs in the team – one from Bannan, one from Byers and a hat trick from Berahino. The first goal was an own goal from the other side. Great match, I understand; we just missed it 'cos our two favourite old codgers had visitors to their office. I've recorded it for you, so when you get back home, we'll sit and watch it.'

Matt felt a slight squeeze to his hand, and he said, 'Laura! He just squeezed my fingers.'

She laughed. 'You'd be surprised how many of our patients in comas start to respond to football talk. Don't bring up what happened to him, just talk of mundane things that are important to him. And don't give up on him, he's a fighter.'

7

Matt felt marginally better about things as he drove to Ridgeway that Sunday evening, knowing he had taken control of his life. His plan for arriving home was to have whatever Hermia had deemed to be good nutritious food as opposed to the takeaways he usually had, then print off three copies of the PM report. He would give Hermia a choice of whether she wanted to read it or not, but knowing his sister, he guessed she would want to see it. Then she would want to kill whoever had done that to her father.

As he entered the front door, he heard laughter from the kitchen, and he knew Steve was winning in his attempts to restore Hermia's normal joie de vivre. He headed through to the sound of their voices, and saw Hermia dabbing her eyes.

'Onions,' she said. 'We're having spag bol.'

Steve was stirring the minced beef. 'I got the easy job,' he said with a grin. 'It'll not be long, we'll be enjoying this within the next half hour, I reckon. Everything okay?'

'With Johnny? I'm hopeful, but that's all I can say really. He's still heavily sedated, although I'm sure I felt him squeeze my hand.'

Steve's head swivelled round. 'He's going to live?'

'Nobody's saying that yet, but they also aren't saying prepare for the worst. He looks very pale, but that's to be expected, I suppose. They still think I'm DI Forrester, so they'll ring if there's any news. I'm off to print Dad's PM report in the dining room, so we'll look at it after we've eaten?'

Steve nodded. 'You fancy beer or wine?'

'Water. I'll keep off alcohol for the short-term future, just until I know I'll not have to belt over to the NGH if it becomes dodgy with Johnny. And if he does come round, I'll be shooting off over there; we need to know if he recognised who did it, and I've also got to tell him about Dad. That won't be easy.'

The printer noisily churned out three copies of the report, and for the millionth time, he thought he might have to invest in a new one; one that didn't drink ink as if it was whisky. He made a mental note to close the dining room door while printing in future, because if Hermia saw, and heard, what he was still working with, she would simply turn up with a supermodel new printer that he would have to learn how to use.

Steve popped his head around the door and said, 'It's ready.'

The next half hour was a pleasant one, chasing spaghetti around the plate and eating the delicious meal. They chatted amiably, keeping away from uncomfortable topics, until Steve stood to sort out the dishes for the dishwasher.

'Okay, I'll set this going, and make three coffees. You two go into the lounge, we'll read the report and then see where we go from there.'

'We?' Matt said. 'Don't forget I'm under the radar now, so there's just me. I can't involve you two.'

'We are involved,' was Steve's short answer.

* * *

The report told them nothing unexpected. Dave Forrester had died from massive head trauma and blood loss caused by the injury. Hermia read it through twice, desperately trying to hold back the tears; Steve handed her a small glass of whisky, and the tears came. She couldn't take both kindness and overwhelming grief without a dam bursting.

'So what's next?' Steve said, putting his copy on the coffee table. The first read-through had told him enough. And he desperately wanted to hug a sniffling Hermia.

'I have all Dad's files up to and including Friday night. If something happened to affect any of the files on the Saturday morning, I won't know about it. So, tomorrow I start to go through them. That will be Monday taken care of, then Tuesday I'm going back into the shop and upstairs into the flat. There has to be something somewhere that gives us a clue to what caused yesterday afternoon to turn into a bloodbath.'

'Don't forget I have a viewing of my flat on Tuesday,' Hermia said, 'but honestly, I don't need babysitting. I can go on my own; I'm a big girl now.'

'That's the point, Herms, you're not a big girl. You're five feet two inches of slimness, so I repeat, you're not a big girl. One of us will wait outside for you and you'll have the safety net of knowing we can be with you in thirty seconds if there's a problem.'

'Are all brothers like you?'

'Most of them, yes.'

'Steve,' she said, turning to the man who had always been there in her life, 'tell him I'll be fine.'

Steve laughed. 'Oh, you'll be fine all right, because if Matt isn't with you, I will be. Now stop mithering, Herms, and accept you've only limited freedom until Matt solves who's done this to your dad.'

'But I was hoping to go and clean the place tomorrow ready for the viewings.'

'I'll go with you and help,' Steve said. 'Matt won't need me tomorrow if he's going through Dave's files, and we'll not need to be there all day, will we?'

'No, it's clean anyway, I just want to put some flowers around the place, that sort of thing. Make sure it looks welcoming.'

'Okay, we'll go in the morning, get it done, then come back and feed the starving brute that will have been reading Dave's notes all day. That sound okay, Matt?'

'Sounds good. Herms, I know we're being over-cautious, but until we know why Dad was killed, that's the way it will be. If it turns out he was killed just because somebody was pissed off because they'd lost their week's wages on a horse, then we can all go back to living normally, but until I know why he died, then we have to take precautions. All of us.'

Hermia sighed. 'I know. Sorry for being a bitch, but I've looked after myself for a long time now, and it feels strange having anybody looking out for me.'

* * *

Matt slept sporadically. His mind was fixated on his father; the PM report had been heart-breaking to read, and it was running around his mind, preventing deep sleep. Finally, at six o'clock, he threw the bedclothes off, and headed into the shower.

He dressed quickly in a pale blue T-shirt and jeans, and walked quietly downstairs to see what delicious items had been added to his cupboards that might provide some sort of repast. After feeding Oliver, he settled for marmalade on toast for his own breakfast, found the biggest mug in the cupboard for his coffee and went out into the garden, slipping on a jacket before doing so. March in England wasn't warming up very quickly.

Oliver followed him and sat on one of the chairs, cleaning his paws, while Matt repeated the action to get the marmalade from his fingers. He patted his knee and Oliver jumped across, ready for five minutes with the man who fed him every day.

They sat in silence, man and cat, looking at the garden, appreciating the plants already coming into flower; spring bulbs always put on a good show, and Matt had gone to considerable trouble to plan the blue and white swathes of flowers.

It was just after half past seven when Matt placed Oliver back on his own chair, and stood to take in his plate and mug. Hermia had arrived in the kitchen, her hair all over the place, a dressing gown of Matt's tied tightly as she attempted to make it fit her small frame.

'Morning, sis. You want a coffee?'

She nodded. 'Please. Don't talk to me; it's not nine o'clock yet.'

She turned and walked down the hallway, and five minutes later Matt joined her, bearing two coffees. She was curled up on the sofa, her legs tucked beneath her.

'You're crying.'

'I know. I can't believe he's gone. What will we do without him?'

'I don't know, but what we can try to do is find out who took him from us. I'll make a start today with his most recent cases, and work backwards. What time are you and Steve going to your place?'

She shrugged. 'Ten-ish, I think we agreed. I really can do it on my own, you know.'

'Let's not have this argument again. You have names for the people who are coming to view the flat?'

'I do. The chap who's coming tomorrow is the brother of one of my neighbours. She's in Egypt or somewhere at the moment, and he spotted my "for sale" board when he popped over to water her plants. He rang me, told me he'd been looking for something in the area to be nearer to her, and he virtually offered me the full asking price on the strength of that phone call. I persuaded him he needed to see it first, hence he's number one on the viewing list. The next appointment isn't until Monday. I'll write the names down for you, just in case anybody arrives with a gun or something.'

'Don't make light of it, Herms. I know you think I'm being paranoid, but I get to see the worst in people in my job, and I honestly can't think of any reason why Dad and Johnny should have been targeted. They dealt with soft crime, not hardcore stuff. And most of the time, it wasn't crime at all, it was adultery, neighbour disagreements, that sort of thing. And money, of course. It could be that this is all connected to money. In the past few years, Dad has picked up on some fraud within company accounts that has ended up in prison sentences for the perpetrators. That's when it becomes not so soft a crime.'

Hermia sipped at her coffee, occasionally brushing away a tear, and snuggled against Oliver, who had followed Matt inside then discovered a cosy dressing gown wrapped around a supine wearer. He took advantage, and Hermia ran her fingers gently through his fur, unaware of the cat falling asleep.

'If the flat sells quickly, you can stay here as long as you want,'

Matt said. 'In other words, look for the right property, don't go for second best. The reason behind this move is a garden, isn't it? Your balcony is a bit overcrowded with pots – your green fingers are becoming greener every day.'

'Your fault,' she countered. 'Yours and Steve's. I've seen what you've both done here, and I want this. The flat has been fine for five years while I was getting established at the university, but I'm in danger of that becoming my life, and I need something new to focus on. A real house instead of a third-floor flat, a real house with a garden. Thanks for the coffee,' she added, placing it on the coffee table. 'I'm going for a shower, then I'm going to maybe pick one or two flowers from this beautiful garden. That okay?'

'Of course it is. Take as many as you need, I'll send you the bill later.' He laughed at her pained expression, and left the room to go into the dining room. Opening up his laptop, he sat at the table and waited patiently for it to wake up. He really did need new tech stuff, but the thought of it distressed him to quite a considerable extent. He was used to his old equipment, and although not happy to wait for things to work, he knew it would wind up eventually. He'd manage for a bit longer...

Finally, he opened up the last email his father had sent to him on the night before he died. There was no message, simply the files he needed his son to back up.

8

Steve and Hermia left Matt hunched over his laptop, muttering to himself, making almost illegible notes in a large notepad and drinking coffee.

They drove in silence, Steve feeling that Hermia needed time to come to terms with the changes happening in her life. It had been a huge jolt when their mother had died, but nothing like the devastation of Dave Forrester dying. Andrea Chesterton had been living in Spain with her second husband for some time, and meetings between them had been sporadic and difficult, so grief hadn't been an overwhelming issue when Ewan Chesterton had phoned to say she had suffered a stroke from which she didn't recover. They had gone to Spain for the funeral, and that was followed by the huge shock of the amount left to them equally in her will.

Steve pulled up outside the flat that Hermia had decided was right for her when house-hunting for her first home, and helped her get the flowers from the boot.

'This is where I'll park tomorrow. I can see your flat balcony, and I can see the main door.'

She smiled at him. 'Thank you, but honestly, I'm not convinced I need all this care and attention. You'll be bored out of your mind.'

'I'll bring my Kindle.' *As if*, he thought. His eyes would be well and truly trained on what was happening around him. He trusted Matt's instincts, and if Matt felt there was potential danger, then potential danger there was.

They crossed to the entrance and Hermia keyed in the code. The lift was waiting and they entered, immediately filling the small space with the heady perfume of the flowers in their arms.

'He'll think you hide dead bodies in the flat when he turns up tomorrow and gets a whiff of this lot,' Steve said, making a grab as one of his bouquets threatened to fall out of his arms.

'I like flowers,' Hermia said.

He smiled down into her earnest face as the lift doors opened. 'I know. Addictive, aren't they? I run a business that involves flowers seven days a week. And when you find your new home, Matt and I will be your heavy work employees if you want us. We're good at standing on the sidelines and barking out orders.'

'Thanks. Appreciate that.' Hermia took out her key, and opened the door to her flat.

* * *

Three hours later, they were sitting on the balcony, enjoying the tiny bit of warmth emanating from the mid-March sunshine. Hermia had defrosted some breadcakes and made them a sandwich and a latte, and he considered the balcony to be the nicest part of the flat. Yes, the rooms were large, well presented, and definitely Hermia-type rooms, slightly over the top in decorative effects, but welcoming. But the balcony was clearly why she needed a garden. It was a large balcony, with a small table and two chairs. The rest of it was pots, filled with all different sorts of plants. Tiny spring flowers were everywhere, and he could see the imminent addition of tulips joining in the show. The greenery in the foliage plants was healthy, and he knew from having seen it the previous year that it would be a riot of colour throughout the summer months. Yes, she certainly needed a garden.

'You taking these pots with you when you leave?'

'Definitely. They're like my babies. That Pieris that's currently the star of the show was only six inches tall when I was given it, and now look at it. I'm not leaving it here to have somebody potentially kill it. Nope, they're all going with me.'

She sipped at her coffee. 'You think Matt meant it when he said I could stay at his until I find something?'

'Of course he did. Matt doesn't say anything he doesn't mean. And take your time deciding on your next move. It has to be right, not rushed into. I spent two years looking for a doer-upper, and came upon my two cottages that came as a package quite by accident when I took on the landscaping of the house the owner lived in, as you know. And now look at us. Matt was looking for a place after your mum died, and he asked if he could buy my other cottage as he was living in it anyway. Things happen, Herms, so don't rush into anything. You know we'll help, and in my job, I see all sorts of houses, so I'll be keeping my eyes open for you.'

He finished his sandwich and picked up his coffee. 'It's a lovely, sheltered balcony; you'll certainly miss this little oasis. But to sit out like Matt and I can, in gardens created by us, is a different ball game.'

'I've decided not to actively look for anything at the moment; all I can think about is Dad, and what this means for us. We're going to have to make some big decisions in the near future about his business, about Johnny, and generally what comes next. If Dad has left the business to us on an equal shares footing, what will this mean for the two of us? I can't just walk away from the university; it's been a lot of study and pressure to get where I am, and I actually enjoy my work. And I've never considered a career move into the private eye world,' she finished with a laugh.

'I can just see you in a deerstalker hat and a pipe in your mouth,' Steve said. 'Come on, let's get these few pots washed and put away, and then I don't think we can do anything else to make this little palace more palace-like.'

* * *

The phone call from the Northern General to say that Johnny had woken up, but was still sleeping intermittently, saw Matt drop everything and head out to his car. He spent ten minutes finding a parking place then ran up the steep hill and into main reception before forcing himself to walk, knowing that tearing through hospital corridors at breakneck speed would be frowned upon.

He found Johnny being attended to by a nurse, as she gently held a sippy cup to his mouth.

The old man turned his eyes towards Matt as he reached the bedside, and a brief smile flashed across his face. 'Matt.' His voice was a little croaky, but Matt sensed there was a wealth of relief in the one word.

Matt reached for Johnny's hand, which still sported a canula, and squeezed it gently.

'Good to see you awake, Johnny. And no chasing the nurses now you're back with us.'

Johnny gave a slow wink. 'I'll try to be good.' He took another sip of water, then briefly closed his eyes.

Matt looked at the nurse and she explained he kept drifting off, but it was perfectly normal until he was fully out of the sedative-induced coma. 'We'll probably be demoting him tomorrow to the

HDU, and from there he'll go to a general ward until he's well enough to return home.'

'He'll come back to my place for the time being. He's a very close friend, and we'll take care of him until he can go back to the place he shared with my dad. He may not want to go back there, because it's where he was attacked, but we'll sort that out when the time comes. Is it okay if I stay?'

'Of course. He'll be awake again very soon. This is how it works when the coma recedes, but it's a question of waiting for those blue eyes to open.'

* * *

The blue eyes opened an hour later, and his first word to Matt was, 'Dave?'

Matt took a quick breath in, and said, 'I'm sorry, Johnny. He didn't make it.'

The blue eyes glistened. 'I saw him go down. His chair toppled over. Like in slow motion. I yelled out, and both of them turned on me. He wouldn't tell them, Matt, he wouldn't tell them.'

'Tell them what? What did they want, Johnny? What could they have thought Dad could give them, that cost him his life and all this to you?'

'Hermia. They wanted Hermia. Must have been out of their minds to think we'd ever give that lovely child up to them.'

'Herms?' Matt felt his mind reeling. What the hell could they possibly want with her?

'So they said. I didn't know who they were, but they both had a Sheffield accent, that much I'm sure of.' His head sank back further into the pillow and his eyes closed. 'Give me a minute, Matt.'

'Close your eyes, old man. I need to ring Steve, so I'll go get a coffee and be back soon.'

* * *

'Steve? Where are you?'

'Just leaving the flat. Spotless and fragrant, that place is. Why? And you're on loud speaker.'

'Okay. Don't stop for anything, take Herms home and stay with her. Make sure the doors are locked and don't answer the door to anyone. I've got my keys, so I'll be able to get in.'

He heard Hermia's voice cut in. 'Matt, you're scaring me. What's going on?'

'I'm at the hospital, Herms. I've had a small chat with Johnny, who's on the road to recovery, and I've picked up some bits of information. Now don't argue, straight home, batten down the hatches and stay put. Herms... have you started something new at work?'

'Not really. I'm continuing something that was started by Professor Hartner before he died, and I have all his research papers to move his work forward, but it's not new. Fascinating but not new.'

'But new to you?'

'I've been working on it on and off for about six months now.'

'Okay.' He drew the word out slowly. 'Please do as I ask, smart arse sister of mine, and get yourself home. Securely. I'll explain why when I get back; I'm grabbing a coffee and going back to Johnny now. I'm not staying long; I need to be home. Johnny's safe here, and when he's released, he'll be safe with us.'

'He's guarded at the hospital?'

'He is. The PC on duty turned a blind eye when I walked in, even though he knew I'd resigned, but I'm not sure how long that can last, which is why I want to go back up to the ward now. By tomorrow, I may be persona non grata when the staff find out I've lost the DI part of my name.'

'Take care, Matt,' Hermia said softly, and disconnected.

* * *

Matt climbed the stairs, carrying two hot cardboard cups carefully. He could do without burnt fingers at this stage of the game.

He handed one to the PC, who stood as he approached. 'Don't go in, sir,' he said quietly. 'And thank you for this. I'll say a nurse brought it for me if I'm asked.'

'I'm not a sir any longer, I'm Matt. What's wrong? Is Johnny okay?'

'I'm sure he is, but Superintendent Davis is in there. I don't think you'll be welcome. Just giving you a heads up.'

Matt pursed his lips. 'Do me a favour. When Davis goes, can you nip in and tell Johnny why I've gone? And tell him I'll be back tomorrow if he's on HDU, as a normal visitor.'

* * *

Davis stayed by the bedside for half an hour, waiting for some sign of an awakening from the fragile old man in the bed. He needed to ask him things, and hoped he would get some answers as to who the perpetrators were. He sat, he stood, he sat, he stood, and yet Johnny Keane showed no signs of waking.

Eventually, Davis stood for the final time and walked to the door. 'I'll return tomorrow when hopefully Mr Keane will be more alert.'

'I'm sure he will be.' The nurse smiled. 'I'll tell him you were here, Superintendent Davis.'

He had a brief word with the PC outside the door and headed towards the stairs.

Johnny opened his eyes, and whispered, 'Has he gone? Can I have a drink now?'

9

Matt, Steve and Hermia ate their evening meal at the kitchen table, a bottle of white wine shared between them. They raised a glass to Johnny, following the news that he was slowly drifting into recovery mode, and it was agreed that when he returned home, he would move into one of Steve's spare bedrooms.

'I just feel he'll be safer there. Whoever attacked Dad and Johnny possibly, probably, knows of their connection to me, so I'd rather he wasn't in my house, leaving him vulnerable to them. They won't be so aware of his connection to you, Steve, so even if he's only 10 per cent safer with you, I think it's the best place for him. Is that okay with you?'

'Couldn't agree more. Either that or I move in with you, we put Johnny in the second bedroom and Herms moves up into your second spare bedroom in the attic, next to Harry's room. Like a bloody hotel, this cottage, it's got so many rooms. I'm happy to sleep on the sofa in the lounge; it wouldn't be the first time after a night out at the pub that I've collapsed on that particular item of furniture. Very comfy, it is.'

'We could actually utilise Harry's room. I'm going to have a word with Becky, suggest Harry doesn't come to stay over until we've got these scum behind bars. It's not safe, and I don't want him being here if anything turns nasty. So, Johnny on the first floor in the room Herms is currently in, Herms moves up to the second floor in the room at the side of Harry's room, and you in Harry's room, Steve?'

'I'd rather be downstairs, I think.'

Matt thought for a moment. 'Maybe you're right. You'll hear any noises outside by being downstairs. We don't even know if they know where I live, but I'm trying to cover all options. Anyway, let's leave it while we enjoy our meal, and then we'll have a chat in the dining room, so I can put some info on the white board. I didn't get as much done as I'd planned today with Dad's files, because of the call from the hospital, but I can go through whatever I do know.'

The talk turned to Harry's birthday, each of them saying they had no idea what to get him for a gift, and realising it was only three weeks away.

'Let's take him away somewhere for a holiday.' Hermia's suggestion was greeted with a stunned silence.

'It was only Saturday when you were saying you couldn't do holidays, too busy at work. Now you can?'

'Things have changed. Let's book a holiday, Florida or something like that, and make it his birthday present.'

'Count me in,' said Steve. 'I've never been, but it's on my bucket list, that's for sure. The three of us and Harry, brilliant combo.'

'I'll have a chat with him, make sure he wants that, and come up with some explanation as to why he can't come to stay at the moment. He'll not be happy about that.'

Hermia filled the dishwasher and shooed the two men towards the dining room, before joining them.

The part of the day had arrived that Matt had been dreading. It was one thing to tell Steve about the reason Dave had died, but he knew exactly how Hermia would take the news – with pain, shock, and disbelief that she should be the reason behind her father's death. He had died protecting her, keeping her whereabouts a secret. And then the anger would surface.

* * *

Hermia stared in horror as Matt finished speaking. 'You're telling me Dad died because they wanted to know how to get to me? What the bloody hell have I got that they could possibly want?'

She stood and walked to the murder board and stared at the picture of Dave. 'Dad, you should have told them. I can handle myself. It wasn't worth dying for.' She ignored the tears travelling down her face, and touched her lips with her fingers before transferring the kiss to her dad's picture. 'We loved you too much to lose you in this awful way.'

Matt felt as if his own heart was breaking. The only time he could previously remember seeing Hermia cry was when she'd first laid eyes on Harry, and then it had been tears of joy and awe, not this heart-breaking slow cascade of tears that she didn't even realise were there.

'I'm sorry, Herms, but now you know the facts, maybe you will appreciate more just how careful we have to be. I might add that even though I'm going through Dad's files, I'm not convinced they'll tell us anything beyond the work he was doing currently, and the work we have to look at completing. Tomorrow I'm going to make an appointment to see Dad's solicitor, because let's face it, he might have left the whole kit and caboodle to Johnny, and not us. Maybe I shouldn't have eyes on these files, maybe it should be for Johnny's eyes only, but either way, we have to know.'

'What time is the viewing tomorrow, Herms?' Steve spoke in a quiet tone, attempting to soothe Hermia without knowing how the hell to do it. She was clearly distraught in a controlled kind of way, and his instinct was to take her in his arms and hold her, but with her brother in the room, he backed away.

'He said between ten and half past, depending on traffic. He's travelling up from Nottingham.'

Matt looked up. 'And this is the brother of your neighbour?'

'It is. He's from Sheffield originally, he was saying, but moved to Nottingham when he married. Now he's widowed, he wants to move back here and be closer to his sister.'

'You know him?'

'I know she has a brother, but I've never met him. He sounded really nice on the phone...'

'Fred West probably sounded really nice on the phone, Herms.' Matt frowned at her. 'I'd feel much happier if one of us was in that flat with you.'

'Well, I wouldn't. It's like saying I need protection because I'm a woman. And that's simply not true. We'll carry on as arranged. Steve will wait in the car and watch who goes in. Don't forget I've spoken to this man, and he sounded nice. Now, the other viewings have been organised by the estate agent and I've not had any contact with those people, so I might feel a little more wary, but this one I'm quite confident about.'

'Okay, here's the rules. Check through the spyhole on the door to make sure he's alone. Under no circumstances do you open your door if there are two people there. When you get there in the morning, I want you to take a carrier bag of torn up newspaper and stash it somewhere easily accessible on your balcony. Steve will be watching, and if he sees just one piece of paper flutter down, never mind the whole bagful, he'll be running up those stairs to get to you. Just say yes, I understand, Herms.'

'Yes, I understand, Herms,' she said, hiding the smile that tried to appear on her face.

'Hermia!'

'Matt, I hear you, and yes, I will take the carrier bag, but I do have a panic alarm that I can hang round my neck. Wouldn't that be more effective than a carrier bag full of torn up newspaper?'

'I didn't know you had a panic alarm. How come I don't know this about you?'

'Maybe I'm smarter than you think, brother dear.'

'Okay, forget the carrier bag. Just press the bloody panic alarm. And make sure you're wearing it. I want to see it around your neck before you leave here in the morning.'

She shook her head, dried up the last of her tears and looked at the two men in her life. 'I'm a smart, intelligent woman intending to be the next prime minister of this godforsaken country, so stop treating me like a fool who doesn't know how to take care of herself.'

'Herms,' Steve said, trying to keep a straight face, 'would you have said your dad and Johnny were smart, intelligent men? I'm not saying they ever intended being prime minister, but if they had that intention, they'd have had my vote, and they were completely overcome in the attack. Now stop playing the feminist card, and accept you're a five foot two inches ball of womanhood, potentially being attacked by a six foot six male with biceps like tanks. Listen to us. We love you, and we don't want anything to happen to you. I intend standing outside that car all the time you're having that viewing tomorrow, so if you feel there's a problem, get to the balcony. Don't let him see you have a panic alarm; just press it and I'll be there.'

Hermia crumpled before their eyes. 'I'm sorry, I know I'm being difficult. I am so used to being head of everything – my job, my research, everything in my life, and this is making me feel like a weakling. As if I'm not in control of anything any more. I am listening to you, and I'll follow instructions to the letter tomorrow.'

Matt breathed a sigh of relief. He looked at Steve and could see he was feeling the same.

'Look, now we've sorted out tomorrow's viewing for you, if I make an appointment for the solicitors for one day this week, will you be able to attend with me?'

'Yes. My next viewing is Monday, followed by two on Wednesday and one on Thursday. Hopefully one of them will snatch my hand off for the flat, and that will be an end to keeping things tidy.'

Matt stood and walked towards her. 'Good, now let me give you a hug. I'm not trying to control you, but I have much more experience of the criminals around here than you do, and I really don't want to lose you as well as Dad.'

Steve opened up the bed settee and lay watching television for a while. He heard Hermia shout goodnight to both of them, and he was just about to turn off the television when the sound of Matt's bedroom door opening added to the television activities.

'You okay, Matt?' Steve had deliberately left the lounge door open; he needed to be able to hear every movement.

'No. It's going round and round my head that this is connected with Hermia. It occurred to me she didn't say what that professor chap was working on before he died. She just said she continued his research. She said anything to you?'

Steve shook his head. 'No, but we need to know. What exactly is her job?'

'I'm not sure of its title following her promotion, but she writes papers on things like studies that she does on different subjects. I know she worked closely with that professor, but what he was working on when he died is anybody's guess. The last paper she wrote was something to do with high-rise living in Sheffield in the sixties, and how to bring it back without creating the same problems they had back then.'

'And things like that can get people killed?'

'It all depends on what subject she's transferred to now. The research done by her department is used by the council when it comes to decision making for the city.'

There was a slight noise on the stairs, and the two men looked at each other. Another stair creaked, and Hermia's head appeared round the door. 'I can hear what you're saying. I can't sleep either. The research I'm currently working on that Professor Hartner started is going to be in a paper entitled "Gangland culture in the Sheffield, Barnsley and Rotherham areas". I've spent the last two months intermittently interviewing people in Sheffield, as this is the largest place. I've to finish my own project first before I can make Hartner's work fully my next priority. Barnsley comes next, followed by Rotherham. You think this is the issue?'

10

Steve pulled up once more outside the block of flats, and sat in the car watching as Hermia walked across the car park towards the entrance. He had a clear view of both the entrance door and Hermia's third-floor balcony; his plan was to be outside the car as soon as he saw a middle-aged to elderly man approach the entrance sometime between 10 and 10.30.

His unease was off the scale, and not for the first time, he wished he still smoked. A cigarette would have gone some way towards calming him down. He checked his watch every two minutes, feeling angry that time was moving slowly, and he knew he wouldn't feel happy until the morning was over, and the man had departed.

* * *

Hermia put on the coffee percolator, allowing the delicious smell of coffee to move around the flat, and unlocked the sliding doors leading to the balcony. She watered the plants, did a little dead-heading, and staked a couple of the taller ones that seemed to be in danger of turning into beanpoles.

Satisfied that everything looked presentable, she sat on a patio chair and waited, enjoying the sunshine that still didn't have much warmth in it, but was welcome, nevertheless.

She took out her phone to check for messages and wasn't surprised to see one from Matt.

Be careful, love you.

She smiled, and replaced the phone in her jeans pocket, then touched her hand lightly against the panic alarm tucked inside her shirt.

* * *

'Hello, Mr Emily's brother,' she whispered to herself, hearing the doorbell peal at just after quarter past ten. She headed for the door and looked through the tiny spy hole. She saw a man with grey hair, a suntan which spoke of a recent visit to somewhere bathed in hot sunshine, his tall frame clad in a smart grey suit. If she had to guess, she would place him somewhere between fifty and sixty, and definitely fit.

Briefly touching her hand to the panic button, she fixed a smile on her face and opened the door.

'Ms Forrester? I'm Emily's brother. Vincent Walker.' He held out his hand and she shook it.

'Please, come in, Mr Walker. Can I offer you a coffee before I show you the flat?'

'Thank you, that would be good. Milk, no sugar.'

She led him into the lounge, and waited until he was seated before heading into the kitchen. She sent a quick text to Steve,

saying, *Everything okay. He seems smart*, then poured two coffees.
She carried them through to the lounge, where Walker was
standing looking out of the patio doors leading onto the balcony.

'Beautiful view, even better than the one from my sister's place.
And I thought Emily had been lucky with hers, but she'll be
envious of this, I'm sure.'

She handed him his coffee, and they sat either side of the
coffee table.

'Is Emily still away?'

'Due back tomorrow. I don't need to water her plants after
today. I see you like gardening.'

'It's the reason I'm selling up. I need a garden, a proper one, so
I'll be house-hunting.'

'You don't have anywhere yet?'

'Not really looked yet, but it won't affect the sale of this. I can
move in with my brother if I don't have a house before the sale
goes through on this property.'

He gave a gentle smile. 'We brothers do come in handy,
don't we?'

She put down her cup. 'Okay, so this is the lounge. As you
know, the flat has three bedrooms, although I use the smallest one
as an office. It uses underfloor heating, and is always warm, no
matter which room you're in. It's controllable for each room,
though – I only use it in the guest bedroom if I have someone stay
over. One of the pleasures in life is to step out of the shower onto a
warm floor.'

'I currently live in a small cottage that we hesitated to
modernise; it would have spoilt the ambience of the place, but now
my wife is no longer here, I have decided to move back to Sheffield
where I was born, partly because I love this city, but partly because
Emily hasn't been too good, so I need to be near her. There's
another flat for sale not too far away, but this one ticks every box,

the other one doesn't. I'm looking to get away from gardening, so I won't be like you and fill the balcony with pots. I'd probably opt to have a barbecue out there, and an outdoor sofa set.'

Hermia laughed. 'And yet you've travelled backwards and forwards watering Emily's plants for her.'

'I know. As I said earlier, we brothers come in very handy.'

Walker placed his cup on the coffee table, and Hermia stood. 'Okay, let me give you the grand tour. This block is a four-sided block, and as you know, this is the top level. I refer to this flat as the penthouse one, but Matt says I have delusions of grandeur. However, it's a fact there's no other flat over the top of this one. The four sides of the square form a central courtyard. We pay an annual service charge to have it looked after, because there's plants and a grassed area, and wooden picnic tables out there. It's well used in the summer. I was out there when I first met your sister. The kitchen window overlooks the courtyard, so you can always see who's down there. And this is the kitchen,' she said.

He looked around. 'I'm impressed. All these cupboards, and enough room for a table and chairs.'

'There's no formal dining room. In this flat, the kitchen is definitely the hub of the home. I'm in here more than anywhere else. Even though I have an office, I spend more time working on this table than I do my desk.'

'You work from home?'

'About half and half. I work for the university in the research department, and sometimes it's quieter to work from home. It depends where I am in preparing my reports, or the papers I write.'

He walked across to look out of the window. 'A slightly different angle to Emily's view, but basically the same.'

Hermia nodded. 'I'll show you the bathroom and bedrooms.'

Walker followed her down the corridor and inspected each

room without much comment. He took longer in her office, asking a couple of questions that she felt were intrusive in regard to her filing cabinets, what she stored in them, all the time trying to be jokey about it. 'Is there a safe built in anywhere? I have a few documents I'd like to keep secure. Passport and such things,' he asked, looking intently at every wall in the small office. Hermia smiled and admitted she'd never thought about having one fitted. They returned to the hallway, where she showed him the small cloakroom to the right of the front door.

'I use it for storing the vacuum cleaner, sweeping brushes and such like, and I fixed a small set of hooks so that I could hang up my coat. All in all, it's a very convenient flat, easy to live in, excellent parking facilities, and I shall certainly be sorry to leave it. I count buying this place as one of the better decisions I have made, but it's time to move on now. Let's go back into the lounge and I'll introduce you to my favourite place of all, the balcony. All the balconies are a really good size, will easily accommodate a sofa rather than a bistro table and two chairs, which is what I have, but my plants rule the roost out there. They take up a huge amount of the space. I'm staying at my brother's home at the moment, and I have to keep nipping home to make sure they're okay, but I reckon it's time to take a couple of pots a day over to his place, until I've emptied this space. It will be a start towards moving everything out.'

He walked across to the doors and stared out. She reached around him and unlocked the doors, then slid them open.

'Sliding doors. That's a good idea, takes up less space. I thought Emily's doors were French doors.'

'They probably are. I changed them to this type purely because I felt doors that opened in the traditional way took up too much room.'

She stepped onto the balcony and leaned against the railings, with safety glass attached to them. 'It's such a light balcony because it doesn't have a solid wall. I went to look at one place that had concrete-walled balconies, and I knew immediately it wasn't for me, but this one is lovely. It's why the plants thrive so well; the sun reaches them.'

Hermia pulled out a chair and pointed to it. 'Sit down and enjoy the pleasure of this small space. Can I get you another drink?'

'Maybe a water?' He smiled at her, and she gave a quick nod before leaving him to experience what she hoped would be the emotions she felt every time she set foot outside the sliding doors.

* * *

Steve saw the two figures on the balcony and held up his camera in order to zoom in. Everything looked okay, there had been no strident horn emanating from the panic alarm Hermia had shown him before leaving him in the car, and he breathed a sigh of relief. A few more viewings to go and maybe they could all relax a little. He saw Hermia move back inside, and snapped a photograph of the man looking out from the balcony. Steve guessed he was admiring the view, but wished he would simply accept it was worth buying the flat, and leave it at that, exiting from the proximity of Hermia.

He saw Hermia return to the balcony, and bend towards where he knew the table was. He guessed they were probably about to have a drink, and then hopefully today's particular worry would be over.

He remained outside the car; no time to relax until Hermia sent him a text message to say the man had left.

* * *

They sipped at their glasses, enjoying the icy coldness of the water, returning eventually to talking about the property.

'I will, of course, offer the full asking price,' Vincent Walker said.

'Thank you. And if that proves to be the case after you've had a day or so to think about it and confirmed it with the estate agents, I will be happy to take it off the market. This will mean you will be the only one to have seen it, as my next viewing is a few days away. Is that okay with you?'

'It is. This is absolutely perfect. And may I say I have enjoyed your company as well? It's been nice chatting with you. Emily said what a kind person you are. You've certainly made me feel welcome, and I can absolutely move in here and know I need do no decorating, just furnishing. Emily will love coming just across the hallway for a barbecue, I'm sure.'

Hermia stood and took the two empty glasses through to the kitchen then sent a second text to Steve that simply said, *Two minutes*, before returning to her guest, who was now standing and looking out over the balcony towards the distant Derbyshire hills.

'Is there anything else I can show you?' she asked.

'Yes, what's that building over there? I can't see it from Emily's place.'

She stepped forward and he moved out of the way to give her room.

Within seconds, she felt his arms clasp her around her thighs, hoist her up and tip her over the balcony rail. Her scream reverberated around the building and as she fell, the world turned black.

11

Everything happened in a flash, and Steve ran. The scream had been cut off; Steve was dialling 999 as his legs moved faster than they had ever moved before. He saw her inert body lying in the shrubbery, and he touched her neck, searching for a pulse, wanting to cry when he felt one, feeble but there. He gave details to the woman on the other end of the phone, and she asked him to stay on the line while she despatched help. She then came back to him and took down the few details that Steve knew.

Against her wishes, he disconnected and rang Matt. Few words were needed, and he went back to tending to Hermia, still immobile, her right arm and right leg clearly injured quite badly. There was a gash down her cheek, presumably caused by one of the shrubs that had cushioned her fall, and he thanked the lord that underneath her balcony had been a shrubbery, and not concrete slabs. There would have been no pulse to feel if she had landed on any sort of hard surface. His instinct to go after the man was quickly squashed, and he stayed with Hermia, feeling sick with worry.

* * *

The paramedics worked on Hermia for a long time before carefully transporting her to the ambulance. Karen arrived with two of her team, DCs Kevin Potter and Phil Newton, and she took Steve's statement. He told her as much as he knew, detailing the identity of the man who had viewed the flat as neighbour Emily's brother. He showed her the picture he had taken when the man had appeared on the balcony for the first time, but stressing that the man must have already been in the flats when he and Hermia had arrived, because he had been looking out for the man's arrival. Karen immediately rang in the sparse details and requested a fast internet search of the block of flats for a resident with the name of Emily.

Matt spoke briefly to Karen, then drove his car to the hospital, never more than three metres away from the ambulance carrying his sister, cursing that they hadn't treated the situation seriously enough. Steve stayed in case Karen needed anything else from him and to simply observe in order to report back to Matt later in the day.

* * *

The response to Karen's request for a resident going by the name of Emily was fast – Emily George lived across the hall from the victim. They were still waiting outside, unable to gain access to Hermia's flat until forensics had done their jobs, so Karen took the decision to head across to the neighbouring property and work out how to get inside. If Emily George was in Egypt, it meant she had a damn good alibi, but it also meant they would have to wait for her return to see if she had any connection at all to the man claiming to be her brother.

She took Kevin Potter up with her, and knocked on the door. They tried a second time with no luck, and Kevin slipped on nitrile gloves before trying the handle. The door swung inwards, and the two officers looked at each other.

'Do we believe there's a danger to life?' Kevin asked.

'I've no idea, but we're going in anyway.'

Karen stepped into the hallway of the flat, and hesitated for a second. The smell was unmistakeable. She glanced at Kevin and he nodded.

'Yep, I'm thinking the same as you. We're going to need forensics in here as well, aren't we?'

Emily George's body was in the bath, fully clothed and definitely dead. Initial thoughts were that she had been dead for about a week, but confirmation would follow the post-mortem examination. The shower curtain had been pulled across the bath, presumably so the killer could continue to use the toilet without seeing the body of his victim.

'You think he was holed up in here until he could get in to attack the DI's sister?' Kevin asked.

'I'm pretty sure that's how it went. And it's Matt, don't let Superintendent Davis hear you refer to Matt as the DI. We'll have a new one in post next week, so we really have to start thinking of him as Matt instead of boss, or whatever else we called him. I'm sure the killer was staying here, which would explain why Steven Rowlands didn't see anybody approaching the flats. He was already here, waiting out his time until his appointment for the viewing.'

The two of them were once again standing out in the communal hallway, awaiting the arrival of a second forensic team.

Karen was organising additional help for door-knocking, hoping that somebody had seen the man disappear after he had thrown Hermia Forrester over her balcony.

* * *

Steve found Matt in the visitors' room at the hospital, sitting with his head bowed, deep in thought.

'Matt. Here.' He handed a coffee to Matt, who took it without realising what it was he was taking. His thoughts had been totally centred on what was happening to Hermia.

'Oh.' He stared at the cup. 'Thanks, mate.'

'No problem. Any news?'

'She's in theatre. The main thing is there's no obvious head injury, the gash on her face will heal, but they're resetting some bones. I haven't seen her, they wanted her in for scans and stuff pretty quickly, and then into theatre, so I'm sitting here like a spare part. Guess I'd really be off the case now, with two members of my family having been attacked. What the fuck do they want, Steve?'

'Search me. But if Herms hadn't been so pig-headed about not having one of us with her, this wouldn't have happened. Wonder what he would have done if there had been somebody alongside her in that flat?'

'He could have had a gun. Then two people would be dead. Herms is still alive and we can go get him, whoever he is. And we will.'

'Then we start with what we know. They wanted Hermia.' Steve frowned. 'What does she have, or know, that they want? And he obviously didn't get it because...'

'Maybe he did. You went straight to Hermia when she screamed, you stayed with her while you organised help, and me.

And you couldn't see the biggest part of the car park from that angle, because it's round the side of the building. He could have taken whatever he wanted, knowing Hermia going over the balcony would distract everybody. All he had to do was get in the lift and walk out. And of course we're going to find out he's nothing to do with neighbour Emily; she's happily in Egypt, and he's probably been using her flat.'

'Shit, I haven't told you – Emily George is dead. Karen went to speak to her, hoping she was back from Egypt, and they didn't even need a key. He'd left the door unlocked, and they walked in. She was lying in the bath.'

'And Karen is SIO?'

'So she says, for the moment, anyway. They've a new DI starting soon, but until then, Davis has put it all on her shoulders. She said to tell you she'll track you down later, whether it be here or at home. She also said Dave's office has been cleared as a crime scene and she'll bring you your keys back when she sees you.'

Matt smiled. He always smiled when he thought of Karen.

The smile disappeared as the door opened to reveal a doctor in blue scrubs. 'She's out of theatre, Matt. She's been one lucky lady with the way she fell. There's no sign of head trauma, and we've stuck her face back together. That's the minor injury. The scar will fade in time, and she'll be as beautiful as ever. Her right arm is broken in two places, and we've had to sort out her right shoulder. Her right leg is injured, but it's mainly bruising, bad bruising, and deep scratches, so she's on antibiotics to be on the safe side. She'll be on ICU overnight where we can observe her, and if everything looks good in the morning, she'll be transferred to a normal ward for a couple of days. She's young, she'll heal quickly, and if you want to see her, head over to ICU in about half an hour.'

Matt stood and held out his hand. 'Thank you, doctor. She fell from a third-floor balcony...'

'I know. Thank God for whoever decided a shrubbery was needed, and not a car park. You can stop worrying now, she's on the mend, and everything is mendable. She'll be good as new in six weeks, but she'll have to live with a cast on her arm until then.'

Matt waited until the door closed before sitting back down, dropping his head in his hands and saying, 'So there is a god.'

Steve laughed. 'We've both been praying, then. And she's not as smashed up as we feared, and could be home soon. Hallelujah!'

'Now that I'm not a copper, am I allowed to admit I'm going to find this bastard and chuck him over a balcony? And I'll make fucking sure there's no convenient shrubbery underneath him; it'll be concrete.'

'Just tell me when you need a hand to do it. If we take a leg each, he'll fly much higher. Come on, let's go see if Johnny has surfaced yet, then bully our way into Hermia's bit of ICU. It's bloody careless of us to have two close associates in ICU at the same time.'

* * *

The gentle hum of machinery filled the air, and they walked towards Hermia. A nurse was helping her to have a sip of water. They hadn't expected her to be awake, and seeing her brought instant smiles to their faces. The sight of a still comatose Johnny had evoked no smiles, just heartfelt sighs. The nurse had confirmed he had slipped back a little and would be on ICU for the foreseeable future, certainly until he was properly awake.

They waited patiently for Hermia's nurse to finish her checks, then moved to the side of the bed.

Matt lifted his sister's left hand and kissed it. Her eyes didn't open; she had drifted off again. 'Love you, sis. Do as you're told, and we'll have you home in no time.'

He lifted his head to look at the nurse. 'She's doing well?'

'She is. I suggest you get yourselves home and leave her to sleep. The more rest she gets, the quicker she'll heal. She'll probably move to an ordinary ward tomorrow if everything is okay overnight, but I understand she will be in a side ward as she needs protection.'

'There's nobody outside now.'

'Not necessary till she moves on from here. In ICU, no patient is ever on their own. That's what ICU means. Intensive Care. And nobody comes near my patient unless they've got doctor in front of their name.'

She lifted her arms as if to push them towards the door, and they took the hint. They collected two coffees as they left the hospital, surprised at how dark it now was as the afternoon rapidly approached evening, and walked down the steep hill towards the car parks. Matt veered off first to get his car.

'You going straight home?' Steve asked.

Matt hesitated. It was all very well risking his own life, but to drag Steve into it... he needed time to think, to work out how he could keep everyone but himself out of it.

'Matt?' Steve obviously wasn't going to let it go.

'Well, I can hardly go to Hermia's place, that will be locked down for a few days as there's now a dead body involved. And I need to let Karen just get on with it, take on the responsibilities she's more than capable of handling, so for now I'll stay clear.'

'You're hedging and waffling. Where are you going?'

Matt breathed a deep sigh. 'You going to carry on being like this?'

'Yep. Where are you going?'

'Dad's place.'

'I'll meet you there.'

'I don't need a bodyguard. I'm six foot three or thereabouts, built like a tank, and I've had boxing lessons.'

'You're crap at boxing. I'll meet you there.' He lifted a hand in salute, and walked down to a further car park, leaving Matt to shake his head in disbelief. Crap at boxing?

12
———

Matt wasn't surprised to find Steve's car already parked, and Steve standing outside the front door of the shop. Both Steve and Hermia mocked him for the legal speed of his driving, and Steve would have known he only had to break the speed limit but a tiny amount to get there before his friend.

Matt had broken the speed limit earlier on, though, following Steve's frantic phone call. He climbed out of the car, locked it and walked across to the shop.

'Crap at boxing?' he said, and Steve grinned.

'Okay, crappish. That a word?'

'The word would be ouch if I hit you.' He took out his keys and unlocked the door. 'But let's just be clear on this, if anybody tries to have a go at us in here or anywhere else, you let me hit him.'

'Perhaps,' Steve said, and followed him through the door. It was quite dark, and Steve moved across the room looking for the light switch.

'Lights,' Matt said, and smiled at the expression on Steve's face as the overhead lights came on. 'Lamps,' he said, and the two desk lamps illuminated.

'That's brilliant,' Steve said, a touch of awe in his voice. 'Are we okay to be in here now?'

'We are. Forensics are finished with it. Dad had the lighting and other stuff installed to make life a little easier. The blinds work in the same way, but obviously the forensics people didn't know that because they haven't closed them. Probably assumed they were always left slightly open. I did tell them how to turn off the lights, though.'

'I need this! Imagine being able to walk from room to room, working things with just your voice.'

'Idle sod; you've got legs and arms. Dad had it put in because he was in a wheelchair.'

'No, he didn't, he was as big a tech aficionado as me. Loved anything like this. And you telling me those files simply disappeared doesn't sit right with me. The Dave Forrester I knew wouldn't lose files, not even accidentally. He'd know how to retrieve them.'

Matt nodded. 'I know. And he didn't actually think he had. His first reaction was hacking, and the files being removed remotely. He immediately changed all passwords to something like sjth-Yrs2Bnh and actually gave me a handwritten piece of paper with them all noted, so that nothing went through his computer. Then he started sending me a weekly email with his files on it to cover for anything like it happening again. He had all sorts of back-up stuff going on, way beyond anything I understand, but I'm glad he did, because everything on my computer is bang up to date up to the night before he died.'

'Do you trust me, Matt?'

A frown flashed across Matt's face. 'Do I trust you? I'd trust you with my life. I did trust you with my life. I was in a bad place after the Becky/Dickhead fiasco blew up, and you rescued me. You saved me. Of course I trust you.'

'Then let me look at what your dad has sent. I'm not outstandingly brilliant on computers, but I'm a darn sight better than you. Something may just hit me as unusual that you would gloss over because you don't know any better.'

'And here's me thinking you'd never ask. I'll keep you fed and watered, you find me some answers. Deal?'

'Deal. Now let's go home, get us a pizza ordered, and I'll make a start on the files he sent you. You still got that piece of paper with Dave's passwords on? Hopefully we'll get Dave's laptop back soon, and we can check other things.'

'I have. It's taped to the back of that picture of the Hope Valley. I'll try to untape it after I've ordered.'

'We can come back here tomorrow when we're not so stressed, and take the place apart if necessary. Meanwhile, I'll see what we can find in the last email Dave sent.'

* * *

Matt ordered two large pizzas, leaving Steve to get to work on his laptop. He poured them both a beer, and was lifting a couple of plates down from the kitchen cupboard when he heard the sound of the doorbell.

He opened the door, reaching out a hand for the pizza, then took a step back in surprise. 'Karen! Does Davis know you're here?'

'No, he bloody doesn't,' Karen Nelson said, a smile flashing across her face.

'Then you must have sensed we'd be having pizza.'

'No. I came to see you.'

He stepped back, and she walked through to the kitchen. 'Steve here?'

'In the dining room. He's going through Dad's files because he says he's brighter than me. He could be right.'

'He could indeed.'

He stared at the woman who had been his DS for some time, sensing something different about her. 'What's wrong, Karen?'

Her shoulders dropped. 'Everything. Nothing. I...'

He waited.

'It's crap without you.' The words spilled from her mouth, desperation evident in her tone.

'And it's just as crap for me without my team, but Davis left me no choice, did he?'

'You don't understand, Matt. I could bear everything while you were there by my side, working with me every day, I could keep control of my thoughts, my feelings, but now you're not there, and I miss you.'

She lifted her hands, pulled his head down and kissed him.

The doorbell pealed, with excellent timing. He stared down into her upturned face. 'Hold that thought,' he said, and headed back towards the front door.

Steve walked out of the dining room, a puzzled expression on his face. 'How many deliveries are we expecting, Matt?'

'Just this one,' Matt said. 'Karen's here.'

'Does she have something to tell us?'

'I don't know. Let's eat in the kitchen, try to be a bit civilised.'

'I'll get my beer,' and Steve returned to the dining room.

Matt placed the pizza boxes on the kitchen side, and turned to Karen. 'Meat feast on one, chicken and mushroom on the other. Wine or beer?'

She hesitated momentarily. 'You have a Coke?'

He reached into the fridge and took a Coke and two further beers from the top shelf, then lifted a third plate down. He waved a hand towards the table, and she sat. He took a seat by her side.

'We'll talk later,' he said quietly, squeezing her hand gently as they heard Steve close the dining room door.

They talked throughout their meal of Karen's results, or lack thereof, from the case so far. No fingerprints or anything else at the Dave Forrester crime scene, nothing from Hermia's crime scene, although Karen did say that if Hermia gave him a drink, then the second glass was missing.

'She would have certainly offered one,' Matt said. 'But he could hardly be in her flat with nitrile gloves on, so my money is on him taking the glass with him when he left. Nothing on CCTV?'

'No,' Karen confirmed. 'He didn't leave via the entrance lobby, and that's where the CCTV is. There is no CCTV one floor down, where the bin room is. And obviously there are double doors leading from the bin room to the outside world. It would have been all too easy for him to just walk away.' She reached across for a piece of meat feast pizza.

'And how are you getting on under the guidance of Davis?'

* * *

Steve headed back to the dining room, grabbing the last slice of chicken and mushroom pizza as he left the kitchen.

Matt and Karen cleared the table, then loaded the dishwasher, both carefully avoiding getting too physically close to each other.

Karen wiped down the side and stepped back. 'I have to go…'

'I know. Let's just pretend it never happened.'

'No!'

'No?'

'I don't want to pretend anything of the sort. I came here tonight because I'm so damned unhappy without you. You must know, must have guessed how I was feeling.'

'Karen, you're married.'

'More to my job than my husband.'

'But I know Finn, we've all been out for drinks together…'

'I know. Crazy, isn't it? But I can't help how I feel about you, and the devastation that washed over me when you resigned wasn't pleasant. So I knew I had to tell you.'

He ran his hand through his hair, unsure what to say or do. He knew what he wanted to say, wanted to do, but couldn't see beyond the fact that if he followed through, he would be wrecking a marriage that he had assumed to be strong.

'Why didn't you tell me?'

She shrugged. 'What difference would it have made? You would have said it couldn't work because we were part of the same team, or you respected me too much to put me in such a position, or you respected Finn too much, or personal partnerships at work rarely work... Oh, I went through all your and my arguments against it, believe me. But none of it mattered against the fact that you made every day happy for me; I loved working with you, just to be near you was enough. But now I'm not working with you, so all bets are off. I want you, Matt. No more DI and DS, this is me, Karen, wanting you in every way possible.'

'God, Karen.'

'He doesn't come into it. This is between me and you. And I know it won't be easy. I'm going home now, leave you to carry on with whatever you and Steve had planned. You have my number, Matt...'

He stepped towards her, at the same time as she stepped towards him, and they were in each other's arms. The kiss deepened, and neither of them heard the kitchen door open. They heard it close however, and moved away from each other.

'This isn't one-sided, Karen.' Matt's voice was husky. 'I've had to fight our relationship ever since you transferred to my team. Never for a minute did I think it would go beyond a working relationship, but I certainly made you my right-hand man... woman.'

She reached up and kissed him again. 'Think about things,

Matt. I'm not asking for a lifetime commitment; in fact, I'm half hoping we discover we don't really want even an affair and I can get you out of my system. That would certainly be the easiest outcome, but I also know that scenario isn't going to happen. I've wanted you and needed you for too long, and a resignation isn't going to keep me from you. As far as work goes, I shall deny having been in contact with you, because if they, meaning Davis, find out I've even spoken with you, they'll take me off the case and I won't be able to pass on anything to you.'

She opened the kitchen door, and headed towards the front door. 'Night, Steve,' she called, and smiled at his response. 'He's a good mate.'

'He is. Keeps me sane.'

'Night, Matt.' She reached up and gave him a final kiss. 'Take care; I couldn't bear to lose you.'

He watched as she climbed into her car, and continued to watch until he could no longer see her taillights. He touched his lips, remembering the feel of hers, and knew he wanted more.

He hesitated outside the dining room, then turned the handle and walked in, sitting down opposite Steve, who looked up without speaking.

'How's it going? Anything indicating anything?'

Steve pushed a piece of paper across to him. 'These are the current cases. I'm concentrating on them because if you're taking over this very profitable little business, then you're going to have to contact every one of those clients as soon as possible. I'm working my way through them, looking at them more in depth now. Karen gone?'

'She has.'

'I went into the kitchen – did I interrupt something?'

Matt laughed. 'Not quite so devastatingly as the pizza man did earlier.'

13

Wednesday dawned with heavy rain bouncing off pavements, and a definite chill in the air. Matt hadn't slept much; he had listened to all the advice from Steve about the mistakes he would be making if he followed his heart, then spent what should have been his sleeping hours discounting everything. The kiss he had longed for had happened, and there was no turning back. He had known Karen for long enough to tell when she was serious, and serious she had been the previous evening.

Steve's last words to him as he had said goodnight had been with an air of resignation. 'Just make sure Finn doesn't find out. That's one complication too many for us, right now.' Steve had clearly accepted the inevitable, as had Matt.

Steve walked into the kitchen, and removed Matt's coffee from his hands.

'I need this more than you,' he said, and sipped at it as he sat down at the table. 'Even my dreams have been about numbers and equations. Clever bloke, our Dave.'

'You only just realised that? He was an accountant before he joined the police, and soon moved on into the forensic accounting section. He liked numbers. You found anything?'

Steve shook his head. 'Not yet. He's got some big clients, though. I'll carry on with it today. You rung the hospital yet?'

'No, I figured they would be busy at this time; it's only seven. I'll give it another hour and I'll ring. They said they would ring if anything changed, so no news, and all that...'

'And Karen?'

'What do you mean?'

'Well, I'm assuming you haven't slept much. No more advice from me, except take care, but whatever happens, I'll have your back. Like always.'

'I can't think about it. Everything about it is wrong, and...'

'And you fancy the pants off her, literally.' Steve's grin lit up his face. 'Maybe it's time to dump Becky out of your head once and for all. You not making yourself a coffee?'

'I did.' Matt turned to the coffee percolator and took down a second mug. He poured one and decided against having milk. Maybe taking it black would wake him up a little quicker. He joined Steve at the table.

'I'm hoping I can go to the hospital this morning, see both of them. This is going on too long with Johnny; I am going to talk to him. A bit of rabbiting in his ear might make him realise he's still got a life to live. When I've seen them both, I'm going to Dad's place. I don't expect to find anything in the office, not really, because Karen said they'd not found anything helpful, but Dad wrote a lot. I was never sure what he was writing, but he called it journaling. Proper sucker for a writing book, was Dad. I just want to make sure the police have checked everywhere, because if there was something worrying Dad, that's where we'd find it.'

Steve put down his cup. 'Journaling? That's strange...'

'What?'

'His case files. He numbers them. Hang on.'

He stood and left the kitchen, turning into the dining room. He returned with a sheaf of handwritten notes. 'I made notes as I went along if any little thing occurred to me. I didn't want to write anything on your dad's files, because we need them intact. That will tell us something one day, just like the word journaling has. Look at these and see if you can tell what I've been seeing, without really seeing it.'

Matt pulled the sheets towards him, and on the third page it hit him. 'All the case numbers begin with JNL. Then there's a number which could refer to...'

'A page number in a journal. It's then followed by the date. Look at that one. It's JNL147221121. Split that down and it's Journal, page 147, date 22 November 2021. Now, we must be looking for a hefty notebook if it's got 147 plus pages in it, and if we can find that, we'll find stuff that he wouldn't commit to computer. Computers can be hacked, but these days, it's highly unlikely anyone would even consider there would be handwritten stuff. What the hell was Dave doing if he had to resort to this? He really did believe he was hacked when that work went missing, didn't he?'

'For fuck's sake. Why didn't he talk to me? He was an ex-copper; he knew I could look at it on the side.'

'He also knew you're useless at anything more than basic computing skills. He could have confided in Hermia, though. She's pretty smart. Or did he think she might be in danger if he did go to her? He'd never cause her any grief, ever. Should we be considering that as a link to what happened? We need to find this journal, see what Dave's put in that.'

'So where is it, this journal? On his bookshelves hidden in plain sight? Could he have been that daft? I'll contact Karen and make sure they didn't find one, but I'm pretty sure she would have told us last night if they had. She talked through the entire case with us, or as much as they have so far.'

'Plus it's an excuse to talk to her,' Steve said.

Matt sipped at his coffee and didn't respond.

'He had his bookshelves specially made so he could reach every book from his wheelchair.'

'They stretch along two walls, don't they?'

'They do. They're like floating bookshelves, start a foot from the top of the skirting board and finish about five feet above that. Brilliant joiner; did everything Dad asked of him. I wonder if Dad requested a hidden cupboard, like a safe built into the wall, behind the bookshelves? I'll ring that chap; I put his name into my phone because Becky and I were going to have him put bookshelves in our house, but I left her instead. Just need to remember his name first.'

He picked up his coffee once again, deep in thought and clearly reciting his way through the alphabet. 'Tony! That's his name.' He picked up his phone, and Steve stopped him.

'Not everybody's up with the larks. It's only just after seven, so leave it a bit. You want a bacon sandwich?'

'Good idea. I'll make a fresh pot of coffee; we might need lots of it.'

* * *

By eight o'clock, Karen had received her first text of the day.

Good morning. Did you find a hand written journal when you took stuff from Dad's place? Xxx

She gently touched the kisses and smiled. She had received

many texts from Matt over the three years she had worked with him, but they had never contained kisses before.

Good morning. No. Took his laptop, iPad and phone, but very little else. Can we meet later? Xxx

He knew he couldn't say no. His sleepless night had been filled with thoughts of the woman whose company he had enjoyed at work for such a long time, but hey, he didn't work there now!

Where? Xxx

My place? Finn away with work for a few days. Xxx

He felt his face grow hot. This was certainly playing with fire.

Text me when you're home. Xxx

* * *

Matt's conversation with Tony the joiner was short – he hadn't built any hidden cupboards behind the shelving; it was oak shelving that had required extra strength supports as they were floating and not freestanding, but apart from that, they were pretty straightforward.

It was only after he disconnected that he realised he still didn't know Tony's surname, but he guessed it didn't really matter, he was contactable as Tony.

He rang the hospital to be told Hermia was awake although still sleeping off the after-effects of the anaesthetic. They would be moving her to a general ward during the afternoon, and would be subject to strict visiting times at that point, so he said he would be there within the hour, and to give Hermia his love. He then asked about Johnny and was told there was no change; he would be on ICU until he woke.

Matt moved into the dining room to fill in Steve on his whereabouts during the next few hours, and Steve dragged his eyes away from the screen. 'You need me to come with you?'

'No, I'm good. It's more important we cover all bases with these files, I think.'

'I'm just a bit concerned that Hermia said she didn't need me with her. That was a load of balls, wasn't it? I don't want you getting into some sort of fix, and having nobody with you.'

'I'm only going to the hospital. Herms is sort of awake, moving to a regular ward this afternoon, Johnny still asleep. Tell you what, I'll ring you as I leave the hospital, and I'll meet you at Dad's. We can spend some time looking for this blessed journal. It'll give you a break from that screen.'

'The police haven't got it, then?'

'No. I'm guessing this means Dad hid it, and hid it for a reason. They've got exactly what we've got, his files. And you can bet your life that we're going to find nothing from them, and neither are the police. I have a list of cars that were near the shop on Saturday, but I think I'm going to have to ask Karen to deal with them. I've no official access now.'

'You regretting the resignation?'

'No. Although, with hindsight, I could have done what Dickhead wanted, and worked some other case. I could have worked on Dad's as a side-line, and through Karen. Then I could have checked out these cars. But what's done is done, and I kind of think there might be other benefits from my resignation.'

He was smiling as he left the dining room, and Steve threw a pencil at him. 'Sex-starved moron,' he called out, but he too was smiling.

* * *

The drive to the hospital seemed to take forever – crossing the city from south to north was never a good idea during the rush hour. The early hour meant he had little difficulty parking his car, and he headed straight for ICU, only to discover Hermia had fallen asleep once more.

He placed a chair by the side of her bed, and took out his phone. He began to text Karen, telling her the good news that Hermia was well enough to move to a general ward, when Hermia woke.

She stared at him, deeply engrossed in his texting, and waited.

"'I frown upon him yet he loves me still.'"

Matt's head jolted upwards. 'Herms! Thank God you're back with us. And do you remember every line of Hermia's?'

'Yep. Mum drilled them into me. It's not just every line of Hermia's, it's every line in *A Midsummer Night's Dream*. I was always going to be named after someone in that play, wasn't I?'

'Thank God she didn't consider Shakespeare names when I was born.' The comment was heartfelt. 'So you're feeling okay?'

'I'm good. I have a magic button.' She pointed to a button on the bed. 'When I press that, it takes away any pain.'

'My sister, the drug addict.' He smiled at her. 'So, did you know him?'

'Ever the policeman, Matt. No. I knew his voice, recognised it from the phone calls, so it gave me no reason to think he wasn't kosher, and he was very pleasant, very chatty. Then he threw me over the balcony.'

'Thank God you're not damaged too much, and everything is mendable.'

'How's Steve?'

'He's good. We both intend being there when we find this chap, and we're going to throw him over a balcony.'

There was a short hiatus before she spoke again. 'I was wrong.'

'I need to record this. I've never heard you admit that before.'

'I should have had one of you with me. I'm sorry. It won't happen again.'

Matt nodded. 'I definitely should have recorded it, because Steve will never believe it either. He never left your side while you were unconscious, stayed with you until they put you in the ambulance. He cares, Herms, he cares. Anyway, I'll shut up about Steve. Couple of questions I need answering... remember when Dad thought he'd been hacked? Did he ask you for help with it? And did you ever talk to Dad about the project you've inherited from your professor?'

She frowned. 'No and no. I knew he'd mislaid some files, but he never said anything about the possibility of hacking, and he never said anything else about them, so I assumed he'd recovered them. And I think the only thing I said about the gangland project was that I had taken it on as my next project. I seem to remember him commenting that it would be interesting, and I'd to take somebody with me when I interviewed any of the thugs.'

'Okay, who can I talk to at your work?'

'Nobody.' She smiled at him. 'You wouldn't get beyond the key fob protected doors; you're no longer a copper, Matt. But that's not the real reason. This is a project that is mine alone, just as it was Eric's project. Our department is quite singular in that we don't interact with each other, we deal with our own reports, et cetera, and nobody knew anything about what I was working on. Before Eric died, he would have known about my work, but once he died, I became him, and I know what the others below my position are doing, but the buck stops with me until it reaches the council, for my work.'

'So trying to bluff my way into your workplace wouldn't help anyway? Have I got that right?'

'You have, but once I'm out of here, I have a lot of stuff I can go through, and target my report towards you. And all my work is in the Cloud, so it's pretty secure. Just take care of my briefcase, everything is in that. You think I'm the key to all of this?'

'I think Hartner was, therefore, I now think you have something Hartner had that they want. Just don't grumble when we talk protection, and don't expect Steve to ever leave your side until we've solved all this.'

'Oh, good,' she said, trying not to laugh.

14

With a side ward empty, the porters arrived half an hour later to take Hermia down to her second bed. Matt went with her, ensured a PC was stationed outside the door, and went back to ICU to see Johnny.

The gentle hum of the various implements helping Johnny on his road to recovery soothed Matt, and he settled once more in an uncomfortable plastic chair. He stroked Johnny's hand, careful to avoid the tube feeding saline into his arm, and began to talk.

He told him they all sent their love, adding that Hermia was currently in the same hospital but everything was fine, and went on to talk about their checking the files and looking for a journal they believed Dave had kept as a back-up away from his computer files. Matt told him of their belief that the police hadn't found it, and that, as he was no longer a member of the police force, he was going to look for it with Steve that afternoon. He talked and talked until he had nothing left to say. As he left, he stopped in the doorway and looked back at the man who had been his father's closest friend. He had no colour in his cheeks, and he was scarcely breathing. Matt felt tears prick in his eyes, and he walked away after ensuring the nurse had his contact details. The PC on guard raised an eyebrow in silent question, and Matt answered with a shrug, equally silently. He simply didn't know what to say.

He sat for a while in the car listening to the tapping of the rain on the roof, wondering what to do. The couple of hours of talking, combined with an almost sleepless night, had left him feeling drained, and the thought of a cool beer when he got to the Forrester Agency encouraged him to turn on the engine. He swiftly messaged Steve to tell him he was heading off to Gleadless, then drove out of the Northern General Hospital, leaving two very precious people still inside the Victorian buildings.

* * *

It was still raining heavily when Matt reached Gleadless. Steve was already there, sitting in his car with his Kindle open.

They reached the door together and Matt quickly unlocked it, leaving Steve to order the lights to come on, but keeping the blinds closed. They didn't want anyone thinking they were open for business.

'Beer, tea or coffee?'

Steve shivered. 'Tea, I think. I feel wet through and cold. I'll have a beer tonight when I'm not having to drive.'

'Me too. I was fancying a beer when I left the hospital, but I've changed my mind. I'll put the kettle on and we'll have a cuppa while we plan how to do this.'

'I've been thinking about it all morning. I think someone killed Dave to shut him up. Whatever he knew got him murdered. But I don't believe they know he wrote stuff down. They asked where Hermia was, so it's probably something Hermia knows about, but possibly doesn't know its importance. If they had known of the existence of the journal, they would have been back for it, leaving evidence of having searched the place. But look at it.' Steve swept his arm around. 'Nobody's been in here except the police forensic team and us.'

Matt filled the kettle and switched it on. 'I agree. God knows what it is Hermia has tucked away, and I don't think she knows either, so this leads me to thinking maybe it's something to do with the work she's inherited from that professor who died, which might go a long way towards explaining why Hermia doesn't know why she's been targeted. The killers probably think that with Dad and Hermia dead, they don't need to worry. What they're not counting on is me.'

'Which makes you next on their list. And once they realise Herms didn't die, they're going to come back for her.'

Matt's mobile phone rang, and he fished it from his back pocket. 'Shit. It's the hospital.'

The conversation was brief, and Steve breathed a sigh of relief when he realised it didn't concern Hermia, and it appeared to be good news about Johnny.

'No, it will be because he would be thinking about Hermia. I told him she was in the same hospital as him. Hermia is a character from Shakespeare's *A Midsummer Night's Dream*, that my mother saw fit to bestow on a one-day-old little girl with no say in the matter. Thank you for letting me know, and when he next opens his eyes for a second, tell him I'll see him soon.'

He disconnected, and returned to making their drinks. He handed one to Steve. 'Johnny opened one eye very briefly, and said a word. The poor nurse was a bit confused and thought she had heard incorrectly. She thought he said "Shakespeare". I had to assure her he would have done, because I had told him about Hermia being a patient, although not why she was there. It's such a relief to know he's showing signs of coming back to us, even if he's done it by saying something daft like Shakespeare. He'd know that by saying that word, he was acknowledging he'd heard what I said when I was talking to him about all sorts of stuff this morning. Christ, I feel so much better just for hearing that one simple word.'

They found some biscuits and sat down for ten minutes, both pairs of eyes looking around the open-plan room for places that would hide a journal of which they had no idea even the colour of the cover.

Matt finished his drink and stood. 'Okay, I'm going through all the hundreds of books on these shelves and seeing if there's one without a title. If we can rule these out, that will be a good start.'

'Okay. Shall I start in Dave's bedroom?'

'Start wherever you want. Knowing Dad, I don't think it's going to be easy finding it, and even if we do, I'm not convinced it will be of any help, but we have to do this, don't we? Let's not forget we're working on hunches, not facts. It's the JNL in front of the file numbers that's led us here, but in actual fact, we haven't a clue what we're doing.'

'You fill me so full of confidence, Matt. Shout out if you find it.' He walked through into the bedroom, and silence descended as they both began to search.

Matt was surprised by the huge collection of crime novels on the shelves. He had always known his dad liked to read, but he had whole collections of certain authors, as well as one-off novels by others.

One shelf was full of true crime, and he realised where Dave had acquired the vast amount of information he always seemed to have about everything. It brought to mind a long conversation he had enjoyed with Dave about Harold Shipman, the doctor who had really enjoyed killing his patients, just because he could. The book on the shelf showed exactly where his dad had learned so much about the serial killer.

He checked every book, taking it out and replacing it in the same spot, just in case his dad had put a dustjacket from another hardback around his journal, in an attempt to disguise it. He reached the end of the first shelf, knowing every book was what it said it was.

The second shelf was a more eclectic mix of books, and included a lot of the classics: *Jane Eyre*, *Northanger Abbey*, and many of Charles Dickens' novels. Most of the dustjackets were missing from them, and most of them were old copies. *Jane Eyre* had a bookmark in it, personalised with the name of the book, and it made Matt smile. He would never forget his father's words about folding down book pages to mark the place. 'Bookmarks are for marking your place, not folded down corners,' he had bellowed upstairs to a young Matt one day, and Matt had instantly taken it on board, and searched through his own bookcase to make sure he hadn't committed the unforgivable sin with any other of his books his dad might come across.

Matt dragged the small stool on which he was sitting a little further on, and realised his father, possibly out of love for his wife and daughter, had a set of Shakespeare's plays as individual books, and a complete collection of the plays in one huge volume. Again, memories surfaced. His mother had been a loyal member of the local amateur dramatic group, and liked nothing better than when they were putting on a Shakespeare play. She was something of an expert on the Bard, and her children grew up appreciating his words, because they were used so frequently. He hadn't been at all surprised at Hermia's quote earlier that morning, and with a sigh he picked up *The Merchant of Venice*. It proved to be what it said on the cover, so he replaced it and moved on to *The Tempest*.

He quickly checked all the smaller books of individual plays, keen to get onto the next shelf. There were several encyclopaedia tomes, some larger books that contained pictures of each year in date order in the Second World War, and lots of other oversized books. He somehow felt that Dave would think along the lines of hiding where people wouldn't want to look – the factual books, as opposed to the fiction ones.

He reached across and lifted out the *Complete Works of William Shakespeare*, briefly wondering how the man had managed to find time to write so much without the aid of a computer.

He opened it to quickly glance inside and stopped. The entire centre of all the 1,023 pages had been carefully removed, and inside the hollowed-out portion lay a small black notebook measuring about four and a half inches by six inches. The spine of the book was easily one and a half inches, and when he levered it out and opened it, the paper felt flimsy. There were many filled-in pages, all bearing Dave's tiny handwriting. And Matt heard the voice of the nurse in his head saying, 'He only said one word, and I think it was Shakespeare.' Johnny had been telling them where the journal was hidden, not saying he was thinking about Hermia.

Each page was carefully numbered in pen, and he had a vision of his dad sitting one night and numbering them all.

And he knew his dad had been scared.

This journal was probably only a repetition of what was in his computer, but something in it was meant for his eyes only, and he had gone to extraordinary lengths to make sure it remained that way. Would this reveal the link to Hermia? Or was there no real link to Hermia? Had they just wanted her, in order to use her to get the information out of her father? Because he would. He would have given them anything to save his precious child.

He put the journal back inside the large book and called for Steve, who was currently balancing the mattress on his shoulders while searching underneath it.

After hearing the muffled grunt from his friend, Matt called out, 'I've got it. You can stop looking now.'

The mattress crashed back onto the bed, and Matt heard a stream of curses from Steve.

'You okay?'

'I will be when the bruising dies down,' was the sarcastic comment in return.

Matt grinned, then pulled his phone from his pocket as he heard the familiar ringtone.

'It's the hospital,' he said, as Steve appeared through the bedroom door. He lifted the phone to his ear and said, 'Matt Forrester.'

There was silence for a few seconds, and then Matt said, 'Thank you for telling me. Can I ask that you don't tell Hermia; I'd like to do that myself.'

He disconnected after saying a very quiet goodbye, and turned to Steve.

'He's gone. Johnny died twenty minutes ago. His heart just stopped.'

15

Hermia had cried on hearing of Johnny's passing, and Steve had immediately held her in his arms, taking care not to touch any part of her that would cause pain.

Suddenly it seemed obvious to Matt that his sister and his best friend's relationship had changed. Steve was no longer standing back.

'You two okay if I go and get us all coffees?' he asked, and Steve gave a quick nod of his head.

He took the stairs down to Huntsman level and joined the queue for the coffee shop, knowing he would need asbestos fingers to carry four takeaway cups back to the ward. Ray Ledger had just started his shift sitting outside Hermia's side ward and he had whispered to Matt that he needed to speak to him.

While waiting in line, he sent a quick message to Karen, saying he would have to take a rain check because he'd had to go to Hermia, and she responded instantly with a *No problem* message with three kisses attached.

With four lattes wedged carefully into a cardboard drinks' tray he had had to sell his soul to obtain, Matt reached Ray with a sigh of relief. Ray took his drink gratefully, and nodded as Matt said he'd be back out in a minute.

Steve and Hermia seemed to be even closer than when he had left them, so he placed the tray on the table, and explained he needed to speak to Ray. Steve held up a hand in acknowledgement.

Matt grabbed a plastic chair and sat opposite Ray. 'You okay?'

Ray nodded as he sipped his drink. 'I volunteered for this job, and I hope whoever did this to Hermia comes to visit her. He'll have more than a broken arm and a battered leg when he leaves. He'll be in a body bag.'

Matt grinned. 'That's what I like to hear; dedication to the job.'

'I've known your family for a long time, boss, been Team Forrester for many years. You've always been fair with me, and nothing is going to happen to that lass in there. Not on my shift, anyway.'

'She's hopefully coming home in a couple of days, and she's coming to mine. And I'm not boss. I'm Matt.'

'Okay, boss.'

Matt sighed. He was obviously always going to be boss, no matter what he said. 'Just make sure you check everybody. Simply wearing a white coat or blue scrubs doesn't qualify them to get into that room.'

Ray nodded. 'And I'm sorry to hear about Johnny. I know he meant a lot to you.'

'Dad's best mate for more years than I care to think about. It's like being orphaned twice over, both in the same week.'

Ray put his hand into his inside pocket and pulled out a piece of paper. 'This is that list of cars I gave you when I was on surveillance outside your dad's place. I did some checking myself, as I know you can't do it yourself now. This is the match-up of owners of the vehicles, all from around that locality except for one. And that one was a false number plate, attached to a silver Vauxhall Insignia. CCTV hasn't shown anything up except the car arriving; nobody got out of it, and then it went. It was there around ten minutes. Possibly just checking on police activity, could have been hoping to get into the premises, but they would have seen my squad car outside the building. I'm as sure as I can be – copper's intuition, boss – that this is connected. Yes, it could have been somebody rubber-necking a crime scene, but with false number plates?'

'And I think you're right, Ray.' Matt sipped at his coffee. 'It will surface again, that car. I can't ask you to let me know if it does, but make sure Karen is fully aware. Has she been to talk to Hermia yet?'

Ray shook his head. 'No, she's coming tomorrow morning. She knows your sister isn't going anywhere, so she's concentrating on your dad, and now Johnny.'

* * *

Matt leaned down to kiss Hermia. 'Take care, sis, and try to think about what he looked like. I understand DS Nelson is coming to take your statement tomorrow, so we'll be here to see you tomorrow afternoon. Hopefully you'll know more about your release date then.'

He walked to the door, and turned to see Steve kissing her – not in a brotherly way, and Hermia was returning the kiss, and not in a sisterly way.

He said nothing until they were in the car. 'You and Hermia...'

Steve grinned. 'Do I need your permission?'

'This is Hermia we're discussing here, mate. She'd take no notice if I said back off. She is definitely her own person, is my sister. Just don't hurt her.'

Steve laughed uproariously. 'Do you know how long I've

watched from afar? Turns out she's not too good for me, she's been waiting for me to make the first move. Pity she had to wait till she was lying in a shrubbery after being thrown from a balcony to tell me that. She said don't leave me, Steve, and I said never, and here we are now, sharing kisses.'

They drove home at Steve's speed, stopping off at Gleadless to collect Matt's car and fish and chips to save having to cook once they got in.

Matt took down two plates and sorted out their meal, while Steve got the salt and vinegar and poured a couple of beers.

'We're going to look like two beached whales if we have any more takeaways. Your job always like this?' Steve asked.

'More or less. It's why I have a gym membership.'

They sat at the kitchen table, and Matt liberally coated his meal in vinegar. He glanced up to see Steve watching him. 'I like vinegar.'

'You don't say.'

There was a clatter as the cat flap opened, and Oliver stalked in, heading for his own food. He miaowed as if to ask where they had been, and Steve promised him some vinegar-free fish. He put a small amount on a saucer, and Oliver became his instant friend.

'You looked at the journal yet?'

Matt shook his head. 'Not yet. It's in the inside pocket of my coat. I'll stick it in the safe overnight. Clever hiding place, wasn't it?'

'Smart cookie, your dad.'

'I'll make a start on it after we've eaten. Let's hope he's showed what a smart cookie he is, by leaving asterisks or something at the side of what he wants us to know about. Shit, I'm gonna miss him, Steve.'

'You think I don't know that? And the tears this afternoon from Herms were just as much for her dad as they were for Johnny. Did Johnny have a family?'

'As far as I'm aware, he only had a sister, and she died last year. I don't think they were all that close, because he seemed relieved he could leave his money to cancer research without any guilty feelings about not leaving it to her.'

Steve burst out laughing. 'God, they were a pair, weren't they, your dad and Johnny.'

They finished their meal reminiscing about the men who had been taken so dramatically from them, and then Matt moved into the dining room while Steve loaded the dishwasher, before returning to the work he had been doing on Dave Forrester's files.

The sombreness of Johnny's photograph being added to the murder board alongside Dave Forrester's almost took their breath away. They stood quietly side by side, staring at the pictures for a minute or so, then moved to opposite ends of the dining table, giving them space to work on whatever was needed.

They laboured in silence for a while, occasionally sipping at the beer they had brought through from the kitchen, until Steve spoke.

'Does the name Anthony Dawson mean anything to you?'

Matt gave a short bark of laughter. 'It means a lot to a lot of police officers. He's the one who always gets away. With everything, actually.'

'He's in your dad's files. Not a case as such, nothing like the other cases he's dealt with, but it looks as though he could be the other feller in an adultery case. The only reason it's jumped out at me is because his name is in red. There's nothing else in red anywhere in these files, nothing I've come across yet, anyway.'

'What's the date that file was opened?'

'Third of January this year. Opened by a Liam Marshall. Wife is

Diana Marshall. It seems as if Mr Marshall thought Mrs Marshall was having fun and games behind his back with Mr Dawson. There are charges against the job, initiated by Johnny. Seems he'd been doing a bit of following. Nothing conclusive over the two months it's been open, though, just that name in red. You come across anything in the journal?'

'Not yet, but he does seem to use the journal for his private thoughts on the cases they're connected with. Stuff he doesn't want to show on the actual files, personal thoughts about the people involved. Hang on...' Matt flicked through several pages until he reached the January notes made by his father.

'Well, guess what. Anthony Dawson gets a mention in here, also in red.'

'What's it say?'

'Bugger all. It says his name, then underneath it in his usual black pen, it says...' He hesitated, trying to decipher the spider crawl of his dad. 'I think it says *check with Hermia for any further info from prof*. For fuck's sake, Steve, what the hell has Herms got to do with anything? She prepares detailed reports for the council to help with decision making throughout the city; she's nothing to do with the underground activity that's going on. That was my job, not hers. We need her home, we need to find out exactly what she knows, or what she has squirrelled away in those papers she's taken over from her dead professor. And we need to give her the protection she needs just in case other people think she knows more than she does. Was that what her attack was all about, you reckon? Somebody wants her dead so she can't talk about stuff she knows that she doesn't know she knows?'

'Not sure you're making much sense, pal; there was a lot of talking about knowing stuff in that last little bit, but I'm with you on the protection side. Somebody wanted her out of the running, that's for sure. So where do we go from here?'

'I don't know. I need to think. If Dawson gets any sort of inkling we're on to him, he'll take us out first before he gets to Hermia.'

'He's that bad?'

'Not strictly speaking. He doesn't do the job himself, he orders it to be done. It's why he's never served so much as an hour inside. And if others end up inside, he looks after their families until they're back on the outside. What's bothering me is I know nothing about this Liam Marshall, or his wife Diana. Maybe this is Dad's first case I take on. Let's draw the bastard out, and see where it leads us.'

'Love the way you say *Dad's first case I take on*, then follow that up with *see where it leads us*. It's an I and then it's an us.'

'You my best mate, or what?'

'I am. Always have been.'

'Then that's the us bit. Actually, it's not quite as straightforward as that.' Matt tried to hide his grin. 'Dawson knows me, as you might guess. He doesn't know you. We could maybe use that to...'

'How did I guess that was coming?' Steve stood. 'I might need to move on to the whisky while I think this through.'

'It's for Hermia, to keep her safe.'

'Okay, it's thought through. You want a whisky as well?'

16

Thursday morning was overcast, and it briefly occurred to Matt that a week ago, he still had a dad, and his dad still had a best mate. He still had a job, and Hermia was happily making plans to sell her flat and buy a house. Steve was ensconced in his work where he dug up gardens and replanted them spectacularly, earning a lot of money into the bargain. Things had changed so much in that week.

He rubbed his eyes in an effort to make them focus a bit better, and swung his legs out of bed. Glancing at his bedside clock, he was surprised to see it was half past seven. That third whisky had clearly helped with a better night's sleep.

Ten minutes later, the smell of grilled bacon woke Steve, and he wandered into the kitchen, looking a little bleary-eyed. 'How much whisky did we have?'

Matt held up the almost empty bottle. 'That much.'

'I've got a headache.'

Matt opened the kitchen drawer, rummaged around inside it and threw a packet of paracetamol at his friend. 'Take three,' he advised. 'They'll work faster.'

'Would they work even faster with a bacon sandwich?'

Three more rashers were added to the grill pan, and ten minutes later, both men were nursing mugs of coffee and eating their breakfast. 'So,' Matt began, 'Anthony Dawson. He stopped me falling asleep at first; I was thinking about him, wondering where he is these days. We haven't had anything at work for some time, almost began to think he'd mended his ways. But if he was on Dad's radar for some reason, there was clearly something amiss.'

'But it does seem to be a case of possible adultery rather than something criminal,' Steve said, wiping a blob of brown sauce from his chin. 'Perhaps you need to talk to Karen. She can check up on stuff.'

'And put her job on the line. We can't do that. I'll ask her if he's crossed their path as part of the investigation, but beyond that is a no-no.' Matt picked up his phone and began to tap out a text message.

The response was immediate.

Calling for coffee. Hope you have the machine primed.

He smiled.

'She's calling round, isn't she?' Steve laughed at the smile that had settled on his friend's face.

'She wants a coffee.'

'I'll make myself scarce.'

'No! I asked her if Dawson had crossed their paths, and she said she's coming for a coffee. That's all.'

'Look, it's obvious she fancies you, and I know you've always had a bit of a thing for her, so stop messing about. Either go for it or don't go for it.'

'She's married, Steve.'

'Not happily, it seems.'

Matt sighed. 'I've been through a break-up. I can't do it to someone else, but you're right, we have always got on very well.'

'Look, pal, I'm a firm believer in the theory that there is one special person for everybody in this world, and it's not always easy to find them. Becky wasn't your special one, but what if Karen is? You could be missing out by not following your heart. What if her husband isn't her special one, but you are?'

'So by your theory, you think Dickhead Davis is Becky's special one?'

Steve laughed out loud. 'Nah, Becky will move on again soon when she realises what she lost and gained. She's not found her special one yet. But maybe you have. And maybe Karen has. How long has it been building?'

Matt felt his face go red. 'On and off for a few months. Bit of flirting, coffee breaks taken together, case discussions with just the two of us. But the kiss the other night was a first one. It's like my resignation gave her permission. I was supposed to be at hers last night, because her husband isn't home for a few days, but I had to call it off to be with Hermia when we told her about Johnny. Perhaps it's for the best.'

'Give yourself a break, man. You deserve some happiness.' Steve stood as the doorbell pealed. 'I'll let her in. Then I'm heading back to those files. I'm near the end, so now I've sobered up, I'll finish them. If I find anything else relating to Dawson, I'll interrupt, so be warned.'

Matt threw a tea towel at him. 'You let her in, I'll pour her a coffee.'

Steve took his drink with him, and seconds later, Karen walked into the kitchen. Her pale pink sweatshirt perfectly matched the hint of lipstick, and her jeans emphasised the slimness of her figure. He drew in a breath.

'I like Steve,' she said.

He smiled in response. 'You'd like him even better if you'd been party to what he's just been going on about. He's just about finished going through Dad's files now, so that will be something else ticked off our list.'

Karen walked towards him and gave him a gentle kiss. 'Good morning, boss.'

'Good morning, minion.'

Their normal work greeting suddenly became personal; no longer an everyday phrase that had evolved over time, but something between just the two of them. He put her coffee on the table, then pulled her into his arms. This time, the kiss wasn't gentle.

* * *

Karen began to slowly work her way through Dave Forrester's journal, initially struggling to read his spidery handwriting, but eventually settling into it and understanding it.

'So Anthony Dawson is the only name he wrote in red? What the hell was he trying to say? This was his private notebook, so he wouldn't expect anybody else to see it. Or was what happened last Saturday something he was afraid would happen? Did he leave this in red for you to find? Have you got the book it was hidden inside, or did you leave it back at your dad's place?'

'It's in the dining room. I'll get it.'

He returned moments later, holding the thick volume of plays. 'I'm impressed by this,' he said. 'I looked on YouTube to find out how to do it, and it takes a lot of patience to get it as neat as this has been cut. And a bloody sharp knife.'

She opened it, and stared inside. 'That's awesome.' She slid the journal into the hole, and it had a half-inch clearance at the top. She closed the book cover, and stared at it. 'You didn't guess it was in it? There's absolutely no way of knowing what it's like inside, is there?'

'Not at all. I did things the old-fashioned way. Took every book off the shelf and inspected it. And he'd a lot of books, believe me. We did have a clue, but not one we recognised. They called from the hospital to tell me Johnny had woken up, and that he'd said a word, Shakespeare. I'd been in with him earlier and talked to him because they said he might respond, so I told him Hermia was in the hospital, and I wanted him to wake up and tell us where Dad's journal was. He didn't respond in any way, so I eventually left him, but he woke later and said that one word. I assumed it was about Hermia. I didn't connect it to the hiding place for the journal, so checking each and every book proved to be a godsend. It was only after I'd found it that I realised Johnny was trying to tell us where it was. I'd also got some image in my mind that a journal would be a biggish book, possibly A4 size. It was a shock to realise it was very chunky but quite small. As you can see, he made notes in it most days, and some of the notes are little jokes he'd come across, or things he wanted to remember about what Johnny was working on. It's quite a fascinating insight into Dad's mind, but I wish he'd put more in it about Dawson.'

Karen stared into space, deep in thought. 'There's been nothing for such a long time. He's dipped well below the radar. When I get a moment, I'm going to check him out, plus this Diana and Liam Marshall. You have an address for them?'

'I'll get it from Steve; he's been going through the files, and he'll be able to pull it off for me. I'd never come across them.'

'Matt...' Karen suddenly looked serious. 'If this proves to be linked to the deaths of Dave and Johnny, you do realise I'll have to pass on all information to whoever our new DI is, don't you?'

'Of course. He's starting this weekend.'

She frowned. 'He is, but nobody seems to know who he is, or

where he's coming from. And I've no intention of asking Davis. Wouldn't ask him the time of day, because he probably wouldn't know it.'

She glanced at the kitchen clock and stood. 'I have to go, Matt. I'm heading off to the hospital to get Hermia's statement now she's been moved out of Critical Care; we need as much information as possible about this chap. Hermia's very lucky we aren't investigating another death attributable to him.'

He pulled her close. 'I don't know what's happening with us, but can I see you later? I'm going to see Herms this afternoon, but will be back home for four at the latest.'

'I'll bring us food. Will Steve be here?'

'I imagine so. He's going to the hospital with me. After me trying to get them together for a few years, suddenly it's happening.'

Karen laughed. 'Love is in the air... I'll see you later.' She picked up her bag and headed towards the front door as Matt placed their cups on the kitchen side.

Halfway down the hall, she stopped and turned around. 'And I'll bring a nightie as well.'

* * *

Ray Ledger was back on duty outside the side ward, and asked Matt and Steve for identification with a smile on his face.

'Any problems?' Matt asked.

'Not at all. Handover been smooth, and your sister seems to think she can go home tomorrow. I'll keep in touch, boss. Anything I know, you'll know.'

'Thanks, Ray, but you've a new DI starting soon, so don't get into any bother.'

'As if.'

Matt and Steve entered the side ward, and Hermia's eyes immediately settled on Steve. 'Hi, you two.'

They both kissed her, and sat either side of her bed. 'Rumour has it you're coming home tomorrow.'

'Not rumour. The doctor says I can go as soon as my medication arrives from the pharmacy in the morning. I need antibiotics because I fell into bushes, apparently. Oh, and painkillers because I hurt. And they said you two have to wait on me hand and foot, bring me chocolates and flowers, and do all the housework for six weeks.'

'If I check with the doctor, will he say the same things to me?' Matt asked.

'Probably not, but you get my drift?'

'We need you home anyway, and don't think you're going to laze away your days in recovery mode, because we need your help. We need to know what the hell your dead professor was working on. We can't get into your laptop to find out, so we need your magic finger to open it. I could use some sharp scissors to cut it off, then we could open it, but...'

'Er, no. I kinda need all my fingers. I could tell you the code to get into it, but I don't think you could work out what he was doing without me there, so you're going to have to hang fire till tomorrow. Just get here as soon as I ring to say I'm free, because I need a good night's sleep. They keep waking me up to do BP checks, and temperature checks, and any other check they can think of at two o'clock in the morning. So, you have anything to tell me?'

'No,' Matt said.

'Yes,' Steve said. 'Karen's coming this afternoon, and bringing her nightie.'

17

The sun shone directly onto Matt's face and gently woke him. His memory surfaced at the same time, and he moved slightly so he could look at the woman sleeping by his side.

She had indeed brought a nightie, a short white cotton one, but it was currently nowhere in evidence. He leaned across and kissed her shoulder, before getting out of bed and heading for the shower.

Karen was awake when he opened the en suite door, and he stared. 'My god, you're beautiful, Karen Nelson.' He dropped the towel from around his waist, and re-joined her in bed.

* * *

They were sitting at the kitchen table enjoying croissants and coffee when Steve came through the front door. 'This morning's papers,' he called, and Matt shouted that they were in the kitchen.

'Hermia's made the headlines,' he said.

Matt frowned. 'So whoever threw her over now knows she

didn't die. I'll be glad when we get her here, where we can watch her.'

'It's more about her neighbour who died, thank goodness, but her name is available to all and sundry now. What are you two eating?'

'Croissants. You want some?' Karen said.

'Thanks. Anybody else want coffee?'

'No, we're good, we've only just made ours.' Karen moved to put two croissants in the microwave, while Steve got his coffee. He joined them at the table. 'I had to go out early to a garden site to make a pergola safe, but it's beyond being made safe. I've demolished it, and I'll send the lads Monday to sort it out. The drunken husband crashed himself into it last night, and it collapsed around him. He was a sorry sight this morning. The wife isn't talking to him, he's got the hangover of all hangovers, and she's told him he's to sort out which plants are salvageable, so he's really pissed off.' He glanced at the clock. 'Hermia not rung yet?'

'No, wish she'd hurry up.' Matt sipped at his coffee.

'I'm going to head off home, Matt,' Karen said. 'I want to check some things, and hopefully you'll be going to the hospital soon anyway.'

'You'll ring later?'

'Of course.' She stood, gathered her small holdall, and bent to kiss him. 'Thank you for a perfect evening, Matt. No regrets?'

'None whatsoever. We'll speak later, and I'll text you when Herms is home.'

* * *

Hermia was ensconced on the sofa by mid-afternoon, and enjoying the sight of her brother and his best friend waiting on her. Her leg was painful but didn't prevent her walking; favouring it as she moved gave her a mobility she hadn't expected. She used a stick thoughtfully provided by Steve, and leaned heavily on it as she navigated her path both to the car to get from the hospital, and out of the car once she reached the cottage.

Her right arm was in a cast, and she had a follow-up appointment for three weeks, by which time she intended being fully recovered. She hoped.

Professor Hartner became the focal point of the evening when Hermia opened her laptop for Steve to look at the work of the man who had inconveniently died.

'Herms, what did he die of?'

'He was the guy who fell under the tram at the university stop. Killed him instantly. There was a big crowd and nobody saw anything. It was ruled an accidental death.'

Matt and Steve looked at each other. 'And do you still think it was accidental?'

Hermia's eyes grew rounder. 'My god! You think he was pushed?'

'I think,' Matt said slowly, 'something he discovered, or was told, in his research has led so far to four deaths, and you learning how to fly without wings. All we have to do is find out what it was.' He opened the small journal to the page that showed the name in red. 'Do you have any connection at all to the name of Anthony Dawson?'

She closed her eyes for a moment, deep in thought. 'Not that I'm aware of, but this research was dumped on me when I was halfway through a year-long project producing another report. I made it clear that would be finished before I took on Professor Hartner's project. As a result, I don't really know all that much about it. What am I not seeing here?'

'Somebody thinks you know more than you do. We need you to do as detailed a search as you can, because there's a name in that project, or even more than one name, that somebody would rather wasn't there.'

'And this Anthony Dawson could be connected?'

'We've no idea, but Dad wrote it in red, and I don't think it was because he couldn't find a black pen. He needed that name to stand out.'

'Okay,' Hermia said. 'I need a lap tray to hold my laptop, a notepad and pen, and a plentiful supply of gin.'

'You can have everything except the gin.' Matt grinned at her. 'You're on antibiotics and you can't have alcohol. I'll get the lap tray and a notepad.'

* * *

After an hour, during which time Hermia was fed painkillers, she fell asleep. She had found nothing significant up to that point, and Steve gently covered her with a blanket and left her to heal.

They moved into the dining room, and Steve began his search for the unhappily married couple, Diana and Liam Marshall. He soon discovered that Liam Marshall was joint owner of a small haulage company called Marshall's Transport Ltd, which he co-owned with his brother, Niall.

'You know anything about a company called Marshall's Transport, Matt?'

'Seen their lorries. Smart red trucks, artics and flatbeds. They run out of a yard down near Meadowhall. Do all sorts of different haulage jobs. Don't think they're mega big but they've a fair number of vehicles. Is this Liam Marshall's?'

'It is. Jointly owns it with his brother Niall. Not come across any issues or bad marks against them, but I'll keep looking.'

'Diana isn't involved with the business then?'

'Not as a partner or anything, but I suppose she could be a member of staff. Or even a driver. Now I've tracked down who he is, I'll put her name in and see what shows up.'

Nothing showed up by typing her name into Google, so he moved onto Facebook. There seemed to be a lot of Diana Marshalls, but only three who were definitely from Sheffield.

He tried to narrow it down, but found nothing to link any of them to a husband called Liam. 'I think we're going to have to give all of this to Karen. She has far wider access to information than we could possibly have, and even if we could access it, with her it would be legal.'

'Let's wait until Herms wakes up. She may be able to get at stuff we don't know about. She's pretty smart with computers, much better than me. And she has lots of access to council stuff, so we may be able to find addresses and suchlike that will give us a clue as to what's going on.'

'It was Liam Marshall that hired your dad to find out if Dawson and his wife were having an affair, but he used his company address for billing. Don't suppose he'd want his wife seeing an invoice arriving at their home address. But if this is only about a case of adultery, why are there four people dead? What's so special about Diana Marshall that it could lead to this? And are we targeting the wrong person by looking at Anthony Dawson?'

'You're turning into a detective, Steve. You want a job?'

'No, thanks. I've got one. I'm a landscape gardener, remember? Sort out collapsed pergolas, that sort of stuff. Employ quite a few people now, in my landscape gardening business. Remember?'

'I do. Is it too early for a beer?'

'It's morning. You can drink beer at any time in the morning. Of course, it could be a bit of a torment for Herms, who currently can't have any alcohol...'

'And we've got to show we're willing supporters of her cause by not having any as well?' The disgust was evident in Matt's voice. 'This is taking brotherly love too far. Cup of tea?'

* * *

Hermia woke to silence. She stayed where she was for a few minutes, knowing that to move would cause pain in her leg. It was only when she heard the kettle boil before switching off that she called out, 'Yes, please.'

Steve reached her first, and helped her to sit in a more comfortable position. 'Tea or coffee?'

'Either. Whatever you two are having. You taken things any further while I slept?'

'Found little bits about the Marshalls, but nothing to excite us and find a killer. We might need you to do that.'

'Legally or illegally?'

'Any way you can without getting locked up. I couldn't stand that.'

'Okay, I'll have a cuppa first, then carry on where I left off when I fell asleep. I'll be glad when I can cut down on the painkillers; they just knock me out.'

* * *

Karen arrived as they were discussing next steps in the investigation, and she listened to facts they had discovered already, promising to do a background check on the Marshalls, and also on Marshall's Transport. 'They've never caused us any issues that I'm aware of, so I don't hold much hope of discovering anything, but no stone unturned, as the saying goes.'

She helped Hermia get to the toilet, then helped her walk back again, Hermia clearly in pain but trying to hang on before taking further painkillers. 'They told me in the hospital that every morning when I wake up I'll feel a little better, because that's how healing works. I need to go to bed now and not wake up for three weeks.'

Steve helped her settle back into position on the sofa, raising the electric footrest to just the right angle for her. 'Okay,' she said, 'I'm comfortable now. I've had a sleep and a wee, followed by a cup of tea. What more could a girl want? Laptop, please, Steve, and I'll carry on trying to track down the elusive Anthony Dawson wherever I can find him.'

In the time it took Steve and Matt to make a Bolognese and Karen to nip to the corner shop for something for dessert, Hermia had put her slightly illegal head on and managed to get into newspaper files. She wanted photographs. She explained it all away in her head by saying to herself that the pictures would have been freely available at one time when they were in the papers, it was only now that she had to go a few feet under the radar to find them. She searched for some time, careful to cancel her search history as she went along. She went back four years, shutting off the sounds of laughter from the kitchen area, knowing how important it could be if she hit on anything at all.

And she found him. Anthony Dawson, one of the guests at a Young Entrepreneurs' Presentation Evening at the Cutler's Hall. There were nine people standing in a semi-circle to have the photograph taken, the central figure being a young boy of around sixteen. He was holding a trophy, so clearly was Young Entrepreneur of the Year.

Everyone in the picture was listed, and Anthony Dawson was

second from the left. The Lord Mayor was standing next to the winner. In between Anthony Dawson and the Lord Mayor was the man who had thrown her over the balcony.

18

Hermia saved the picture and article then pleaded with Matt's antiquated printer to print it out. After some thought and shunting backwards and forwards of printer cartridges, it obliged, and she shouted to Matt to collect the printout from the dining room.

He picked up the papers and carried them through to her. 'This is Dawson.'

'I know, but more importantly, this other man is the one who threw me over the balcony.' She tapped on the picture. 'He's apparently called Walter Vickers, but it doesn't say anything other than his name. You know him?'

Matt shook his head and turned to Karen. 'I don't. Karen?'

'No, but it won't take long to find out if we've ever had dealings with him. Walter Vickers? Walt Vickers? Wally Vickers? None of them are ringing bells, alarm or otherwise. You're absolutely sure he's the killer, Hermia?'

'No doubt in my mind at all. I was very close to him for the best part of an hour, don't forget.'

'Okay, I want him bringing in tomorrow. I'll go in early

tomorrow morning and start the trace on him. Matt... who would you ask to help you? Just one.'

Matt grinned. 'You.'

'No.' She grinned back at him. 'I'm you at the moment. So I need a me for me.'

Hermia looked at Steve. 'You understand what they're going on about?'

'Just don't listen, Herms. It'll fry your brain.'

'If you want my suggestion,' Matt said, suddenly serious, 'I'd talk to Ray Ledger.'

'Now why didn't I think of him?'

'Because he stays in the background, but he's pretty smart. He does things his own way. He was told to do surveillance on the shop, and any other beat bobby would have done just that. He wrote down every car that pulled up in the vicinity of the shop for the whole of the time he was there, and when he realised I couldn't follow up on the registrations now, he did it for me. And I honestly believe he would have given up his life for Herms in the hospital if there had been any threat to hers. I've always enjoyed chatting to him, get on with him really well, but I do think he's got our backs with this one. So if you want someone you can trust without having to think about it, I suggest him. And he knows his way around a computer; he's got a fifteen-year-old son.'

'The two facts go hand in hand?'

'They do in his case. His lad's taking IT up as a career.'

'Then I'll have a word. Be back in a minute,' and she disappeared into the kitchen. They could hear her muted voice, and she was smiling as she returned to them.

'He'll be in for seven in the morning, hopefully before the new DI is in. We can crack on and maybe find this murdering bastard who killed an old lady just because he needed to hide out in her flat.' Karen picked up the picture and stared at it. 'His face is familiar, but I can't for the life of me think why. He's not young, is he?'

'No, and it's why I believed he was Emily's brother. If he'd looked younger, I'd have been concerned, knowing how worried you two were for my safety, but I honestly felt comfortable in his presence, and he acted as if he was her brother. Spoke of her with a bit of affection, talked about watering her plants, that sort of thing. Then he threw me over the bloody balcony. I'm warning you, Karen, never trust a man who says he loves his sister.'

'Oy!' Matt lifted his fisted hand to her. 'One more wrong word from you and you'll be sleeping in the shed. Where are you sleeping, by the way?'

'Well, when I can climb stairs again, it will be in my own room, but for tonight, I think I'll sleep down here. It's a bit painful putting weight on this right leg at the moment.'

'So do you need the camp bed blowing up, Steve?'

He blushed. 'If that's okay with Herms.'

She laughed. 'This sofa opens out to a double bed. Why can't you sleep on the other half of it? Just don't move within a foot of me, because if anything touches any part of my body at the moment, it hurts.'

'Then I'll definitely sleep on the camp bed. I'll not risk rolling over in the middle of the night and having you screaming the place down. Matt would kill first and ask questions later.'

Matt checked his watch. 'Look, it's gone nine now, and I think in view of early starts and the fact that Herms needs pain meds at nine, we should be heading for bed anyway. I'll get the camp bed and bedding, Steve, and you can sort yourself out. Herms, you ready for your meds?'

She nodded. 'I was trying to hang on because they send me to sleep pretty quickly, but I'm really starting to need them now. Karen, can you help me to the toilet, please?'

'Of course. And if you need me during the night, just shout. I might as well stay over and go to work from here.'

Matt felt the smile stretch across his face, especially when he realised nobody was going to make any comment, that it had suddenly become a normal thing that Karen should stay over. A brief image of Finn flashed across his brain, and he knew they needed to talk, but not tonight. They could talk of serious things when Finn returned from his work trip, when Karen knew for definite what it was she wanted.

* * *

It wasn't an easy sleep for Hermia. The painkillers worked, and Steve had kissed her goodnight with tenderness, but without touching any part of her except her lips. She had reached up her left hand to stroke his face, and he had nodded. 'One day, I'll kiss you properly,' he whispered.

She could see him lying on the camp bed, and it appeared to be an uneasy sleep, but she was drifting in and out of sleep. Every time she moved, something hurt, but it was still better than being in the hospital.

And running around her head was the added worry of Matt and Karen. She had always known they were close as a working partnership, but she had never suspected for a minute there would ever be anything between them. It seemed Matt's resignation from the police had brought things to a head. It was a scary thought that Karen had a husband already, and they still shared a life. It might cause one or two issues when Finn found out.

And Steve... where would this lead? There had been boyfriends, but nothing serious enough for anything to go beyond the friends with perks stage, but she already knew her head had taken this beyond wanting just the perks. And she no longer thought of him as her second brother; she was now looking at him and thinking mmmmm. Nothing brotherly in those thoughts.

She closed her eyes and was almost drifting towards sleep five minutes later, when she felt the blankets move. 'Oliver, get off the bed,' she whispered.

'My name's Steve, not Oliver. You two-timing me already, hussy?'

Hermia giggled. 'You've seen sense then?'

'I have and it's nothing to do with an uncomfortable camp bed that's losing its air. It's to do with being in the same room as you and not sharing a bed. Now give me a kiss, and let's go to sleep.'

* * *

Karen's phone alarm sounded at six, and she felt Matt's arm slide around her as if to keep her by his side.

'I've got to get up, I've a date with Ray Ledger.'

'It's only six o'clock.'

'I've to be at work for seven, and I need a shower and some toast before I go. And at least one cup of coffee, or I can't function.'

He kissed the back of her neck and let her go. 'You do the shower bit, I'll see to the toast and coffee. Unless you need help with the shower bit...'

He shivered as he pushed back the covers. 'First thing is to put on some heating. Then I'll feed and water us.'

Fifteen minutes later, they were seated at the kitchen table, with Karen spreading marmalade on her toast.

'Happy?' he asked, looking at her face for the answer.

She sighed. 'I am. Very. Not sure what that means for us, but for me it means Finn and I are finished. No matter where we go from here, I can now see there's no future for my marriage. We don't talk, we hardly see each other, and I don't think for one minute he'll be surprised when I say I'm going. I'll go stay with Mum while I sort out my head. I'll take some stuff over to Mum's tonight, then have a chat with Finn when he gets home tomorrow night. If he gets home tomorrow night.'

'Any regrets for what's happened with us?'

She shook her head and smiled. 'The only regret is I didn't find the courage to do it sooner. Although it was a shock when you handed in your notice, it meant we no longer worked together. I took that as a sign. All I had to do then was find the right words to tell you how I feel. And those feelings are much stronger now.'

She wiped some marmalade off her chin. 'Nobody has ever made me toast before.'

Matt laughed. 'Toast I can do. Spag bol I can do. Curry I can do if I use a packet of curry mix. Can you make meat and potato pie?'

'I can. You want one tonight? I can make a big one for all four of us.'

'Have I ever told you what an amazing woman you are?'

'Frequently.'

She finished her toast, took a last sip of her coffee and stood. 'Should I just check if Hermia needs me for anything before I go?'

Matt shook his head. 'No, I'm sure she'll be fine. I popped my head around the door to see if they wanted a coffee as I was making a pot for us, and they were snuggled up together in the same bed, so I think one way or another, she'll manage.'

Karen bent to kiss him. 'I'll let you know if I find anything relevant. I can explain this away by saying I came to interview Hermia last night to follow up on her statement, as she was unsure about stuff. She did a bit of investigating of her own and spotted this Walter bloke on a photograph. I'll make sure nothing comes of her, or you, being involved. You got any plans for today, if I need to contact you?'

'I do. We're meeting Dad's solicitor at his shop. Today's the day when we find out if he left everything to Battersea Dogs' Home, or if he left us a couple of quid.'

She smiled. 'But you'd rather have him back.'

'Too right I would. It hurts so much to think about him, Karen, about the awful way he died, and now to lose Johnny as well...'

She put her arms around him and hugged him. 'We'll get them, whoever did it.'

'If I get to them first, it'll be a different outcome to the scenario if you get to them first. You know that, don't you?'

'I do. It's why I have to find them, and not you. I'm also going to ask Ray to look into the Marshalls today, because somewhere there is a connection. Their names are in the pot, and we have to look at why.'

She stood in the kitchen doorway and smiled at Matt. 'Take care. I don't want anything to happen to my personal PI.'

He smiled in return. 'If he's left everything to the dogs' home, I can't be anybody's personal PI; I could end up being one of Steve's garden gnomes.'

19

Anthony Dawson was a man who blended into the background until he was no longer in it. Then he was a formidable presence capable of striking fear with one hard stare. Saturday morning saw the hard stare from the sky-blue eyes directed at Dave Forrester's shop.

He needed a file, one he was certain would be in the shop. When Diana had told him Liam Marshall had asked the Forrester Agency to follow her, he had laughed. But now it seemed to be snowballing out of control, and Anthony Dawson liked to be in control, not out of it. And added to that had been the phone call from Dave Forrester asking him to drop into the office; that he had something important to tell him. He wouldn't say what over the phone, and now somebody had bumped the old man off, and he had to get into that office and find what it was Dave wanted to tell him, or show him.

Whoever had killed Dave Forrester had earned himself an enemy in Dawson. He didn't want police eyes on him, and he was starting to query whether Diana Marshall was worth all the hassle. The biggest problem was the possibility, probability, that the police had removed any computers containing Forrester's cases, but he reckoned there could be written files as well, and he needed his file. He guessed whatever Dave knew about him, it would be in a file somewhere.

And he needed to know how the fuck Liam Marshall had found out about his relationship with his wife.

Dawson exited his car and locked it, walking into a charity shop for the first time in his life. He headed for the window that looked directly across the road to the Forrester Agency premises, realising immediately he had a much better view of the place than from his car in the car park. Unfortunately, the area he was occupying was filled with ladieswear.

Thinking fast, he picked up a skirt in a size eighteen, then picked up and replaced several other items. His eyes remained glued to the window, as he took note of where cameras were placed with regard to the Forrester shop. He could see two; both were at awkward angles, definitely no longer covering the door, and he reckoned whoever had killed Dave Forrester had sorted out the cameras first.

'Do you require help, sir?' An elderly lady with glasses on top of her head was standing by his side, a smile on her face.

'No, I'm fine, thanks. I'm shopping for my mother, who asked me to call in to see if there was anything nice for her.'

'And what size are you looking for?'

'Eighteen, she said.' He waved the items draped across his left arm as if to confirm the size.

'Would you like me to put them behind the counter for you, so you can carry on looking without having to cart these everywhere?'

He wanted to say fuck off and leave me alone, but instead said, 'Yes, please.'

She walked away, carrying the four items he had fully intended dumping before leaving the shop, and then turned back to face him. 'Coats are over there,' she said, pointing to a spot away from the window.

He nodded, but remained near the window. His mother didn't need a fucking coat.

He continued to look out of the window, while picking up various items then returning them to the hanging rail. He wouldn't make that mistake again, of draping them over his arm as if he intended buying them.

He moved a little closer to the window when he saw the Land Rover pull onto the parking area in front of the agency. He recognised the tall figure who exited the driver's door. DI Matt Forrester. The other man and woman he didn't know, but guessed as the woman was walking with the aid of a stick that she was Forrester's sister. It seemed she'd fallen off a balcony or something daft like that.

Dawson decided it was time to make good his escape from this crazy woman and her shop, and he attempted to walk towards the door. Now Forrester's family had arrived at the shop, he'd no chance of getting in, so he might as well disappear for the time being.

The lady's glasses were now firmly on her nose, and she held out a loaded carrier bag. 'I packed everything for you, and you have some good-quality clothes for your mum there. You chose well, they're all designer labels. That will be thirty-two pounds, sir. Card or cash?'

'Cash...' He fumbled in his pocket for his wallet and removed three ten-pound notes and one fiver. He handed them over, and she placed them in the till, before passing him the bag. 'Did you want the change, sir?'

He had no idea of protocol in charity shops, or even if there was a protocol, so muttered, 'No, of course not,' and left with a flash of a smile on his face.

'I hope your mother likes your choices, sir,' she called after him. *Probably not*, he thought, *considering she's been dead for the best part of ten years.*

He crossed the road almost at a run, keen that Forrester didn't spot him, tossed the carrier bag in the boot and jumped in the driver's seat, pulling down the sunshade.

He sat for a moment, deep in thought. If Forrester was in that shop, he would already have access to the files, would no doubt have spotted the name Anthony Dawson, and would already be investigating him. The last time he had seen Forrester had been as he was being handed his belongings after a few hours in a cell, and Forrester's final words had been, 'I'll have you properly banged up one day, Dawson.' He would be fixated on him now, Dawson had no doubt of that.

The solicitor, Gloria Elland, arrived as Steve was pouring coffees for the three of them. She looked around Dave's downstairs lounge and sighed. 'I always treated this as a happy place to visit, and never minded seeing Dave here. Whatever legal things he needed doing, I was always willing to home visit. It saved him having to manoeuvre that damn wheelchair, and it got me out of the office. And he always made me laugh. Made a damn good coffee as well. And don't worry about having to cancel our appointment during the week, treatment after being thrown from a balcony always takes priority.' She smiled at Hermia. 'You're on the road to recovery, Hermia?'

'I am. Everything hurts, but they sent me home with pain relief, and I have these two running around after me, so I'm good.'

Gloria looked up as Steve handed her a coffee. 'Don't know if it's as good as Dave's was, but it's hot, and it's wet. I'll wait upstairs, Matt, until you've finished.'

'No, Steve. Stay down here. There's nothing that needs to be hidden from you. Is that okay, Gloria?'

'No problem, Steve. It's quite a strange will in view of how things have progressed since your father died, Matt and Hermia.' She opened up the document. 'Firstly, everything, and I mean everything, is divided equally to the penny between you two. However, the will stipulates that if he should pre-decease John Keane, the business is to pass to John until his death, when everything will revert to you two. Until then, you own the building, but Mr Keane has full and exclusive use of it until his death. Obviously, there was only a very short time between Dave's and John's deaths, so ultimately this means that everything is now split between you two. Your father did stipulate that he would like both John and you to keep the name the Forrester Agency until such time as the business closes.'

There was silence.

'Do you understand?' Gloria asked, looking at both of them.

They both nodded, and Hermia wiped the tears from her cheeks. 'He thought of everything,' Hermia said quietly.

'He did. There's a few donations he wants making, which we'll see to for you, they add up to £12,000. He has left £25,000 in a trust fund for Harry, which he would like you, Matt, to manage until Harry reaches eighteen. We will have a full breakdown sent over to you once probate is cleared of exactly how much you inherit. It is a significant amount; your father was good at what he did. He left a letter for me to read to you, but I have no idea what it says. He said to tell Hermia to get out the tissues.'

Hermia smiled. 'He knew me very well.'

Gloria removed the envelope from the file and opened it carefully.

Greetings, my wonderful kids. I am so sorry I've had to leave you, but always know how much I love you. If there is a heaven, I'll spend every day sitting on a cloud watching over you, blessing you, and sending you strength that will help you carry on without me. The business will eventually become yours, so pursue your own careers until that time comes, because I know Johnny will take care of things until the day arrives when he brings a bottle of whisky with him to join me on my cloud. Please tell Harry how much I loved him from the day he was born, and I don't think I need to tell you two how much I love you. You have both supported me through these last difficult few years, and I am truly grateful. I love you all from the bottom of my heart, and Matt, please tell Steve I include him in this love. He was as much a son to me as anyone could have been who wasn't genetically connected. Don't grieve for me, any of you, I had a wonderful life because of you two plus Harry and Steve, and I want no tears. Hermia, stop crying immediately! I love you all so much. Dad xxx

Hermia was sobbing. Steve was holding her tightly, passing her tissue after tissue, and Gloria delved into her handbag for a small packet of tissues to mop up her own tears.

'What a wonderful man,' Gloria said softly. 'Find who did this to him, Matt, and find him soon.'

* * *

Once Gloria had departed, the three of them sat back, unspeaking. Digesting everything they had heard. Hermia stroking the letter Dave had left for them. Steve wanting to hold her in his arms for ever, to take away the pain. Matt numb.

Eventually, Matt broke the silence. 'We have to talk.'

'You don't need me here,' Steve said. 'This is between the two of you, if you're talking about the will.'

'Stay.' It was almost a command from Hermia. 'Please.'

'Stay,' Matt echoed.

'I'd best stay then.' Steve grinned. 'Shall I make some tea, calm us all down a bit?'

And it did. Matt broke the peace by saying, 'So we have a business. And we have to start immediately, or we won't have a business.'

'Can I be a silent partner?' Hermia looked troubled. 'I'm doing a job I love, and I've kinda reached the top of that particular tree as head of department, which was my plan for the moment. I'd like to do that for at least three years. And could we really work together?'

Matt stared into space for a moment. 'I think I expected that,' he said finally. 'How would you feel about being a consultant to the business? You know so much that I don't know, even if it's only on the computing side – but it's not on the computing side, it's everything. Who else do you know who can quote Shakespeare at the drop of a hat?'

'I don't want paying. I earn enough at my proper job. And you know you can always call on me if you need me. Maybe in five years' time I could be ready for a change, and maybe the business will have moved on into areas that interest me, but at this moment in time, I'm not ready.'

Steve's head was going backwards and forwards between the two of them. 'She's talking sense,' he said.

'I know she is,' Matt joined in. 'And I think I knew this would be the outcome. I'm going to have to find someone to bring in, who can handle an immediate start.'

'I know somebody.'

'Who? Available immediately?'

Steve nodded. 'Me. Let me buy in, and I'll be your Johnny.'

20

Steve settled Hermia comfortably on the sofa and brought her laptop towards her on a lap tray.

She smiled at him. 'Thank you. I'll make a detailed start on Hartner's work now I've completed the initial run through of it, see what I can find that could possibly be so contentious it got me chucked over a balcony.'

'Don't make light of it, Herms. If it hadn't been a shrubbery, you'd be dead. What the hell can you possibly know that is so important to somebody? And he got nothing, because you'd already brought stuff over here, which I suspect puts you still in his firing line. We have to find what they want quickly, and I'm sure it is a they, because it was two men who attacked Dave and Johnny. I suspect one of them was this feller who attacked you, this Walter Vickers, but heaven only knows who the other one is. Anthony Dawson?'

'Maybe. Dad must have thought there was something that needed investigating, to have written his name in red. But can we just have a talk first?'

'About my offer to Matt?'

She nodded. 'Are you absolutely certain?'

'Well, it came into my head completely out of the blue, but to be honest, I had already decided to offer Matt a partnership in my business. I do very little of the actual work now, it's more an admin role, because it's grown. I've a fair number of employees, and once they arrive, they don't leave. I have six people who I set on in my first six months, and five years later, they're still with me, four of them in supervisory positions. The other two are happy not having the responsibility, they just like to get mucky and will happily dig away all day. The business is growing all the time, and when this happened with your dad, I kind of thought the agency would go to Johnny, as he was with Dave almost from the start. I never imagined they would die within a couple of days of each other, leaving you and Matt with a business that needs dealing with immediately before you lose any clients. My intention was to sit down with Matt, who, as you know, loves gardening anyway, show him my business plan for expanding the company, and ask him to come in with me. We've proved many times how well we work together, but then I realised I can have it both ways. I can buy into Forrester's, we can build a client base together, and I can promote one of my lads to do the work that I currently do.'

'And is all this truly what you want?'

'It is. And you.' Steve looked down at the floor, wishing he'd kept his mouth shut. This wasn't the time to discuss their relationship.

'And you?'

'You asked me if it's truly what I want, and I said yes, and you. I truly want you. Have done for years, but I can take it slowly. I'm not letting go, though, you should know that.'

Her giggle sounded like that of a five-year-old child. 'Me? You're not just feeling sorry for me?'

'Nope. Cards on the table, or the lap tray. I want you, and I'm going to make you want me. Okay?'

'Wow! Okay.'

He stared at her, wanting to hold her, to touch all the parts of her that were currently causing her pain. He wanted to take away that pain, make her whole again, and he wanted to kiss her. He liked kissing her.

'Kiss me,' she said. 'Kiss me properly, and don't treat me like some fragile little flower.'

So he did.

* * *

The meat and potato pie was an outstanding success. All four of them sat around the kitchen table and chatted about everyday things, until Matt stood to make them all a coffee.

'Herms, you comfortable enough in here, or should we go back in the lounge?'

'I'm fine here. If I start to hurt, I'll tell you.'

He poured out the drinks and handed them round, then looked at Karen. 'Do you want to start?'

'I don't have as much to tell you as I thought I might have, but Ray has been working on tracing Anthony Dawson and Walter Vickers all day. The strange thing is that there seems to be no connection with each other. I suspect they've only been in each other's company once, and that was for that presentation evening. I've a friend who works at the newspaper, and she's been through their files for me, can't find anything else that would help us. They both stay out of the limelight, don't even appear to live anywhere near each other. Dawson lives at Millhouses, Vickers lived at Thorpe Hesley. I went out to Millhouses with Ray this morning, to interview him. He wasn't there. Massive house, stinks of money. I spoke to a couple of ladies who were there, obviously cleaners because they'd arrived in a van with House Elves Cleaning Company on the side, and they said he wasn't usually in when they cleaned. They hadn't seen him at all, and they would be gone by the time he returned. It was frustrating, obviously, but there was nothing we could do so we returned to base, and Ray put Dawson to one side and concentrated on Walter Vickers.'

'And what did you find?' Matt was watching her face, her animated expressions as she spoke of working with Ray, getting on with the job, her frustration at finding out Dawson wasn't at home.

'Nothing. Bugger all. We have an old address for him at Thorpe Hesley, but the present owners have lived there for three years now, and they bought it after the old lady who had owned it died. So we've no idea if he ever lived there, or if it was just a made-up address. There isn't even a car registered to his name, so we can't track him down through that. Walter Vickers might not even be his real name, just one he uses every so often when he needs a name to hide behind. But if that's the case, then he's up to something, and it could be something Dave Forrester discovered.'

Matt frowned. 'Okay, tomorrow I'll be in that shop until I find something. I'm going through every file in every filing cabinet, I'm going to reread Dad's journal, and we need to see what Professor Hartner was working on that could have brought all this trouble down on our heads. And I want to see that accident report for Professor Hartner. Nobody just falls under a tram. A train maybe, but not a tram.'

Karen grinned. 'Is this DI Forrester talking, or Matt Forrester of Forrester Agency? Because it sounds pretty much like DI Forrester to me. And speaking of DIs, our new one arrived about eleven this morning. He didn't meet many people because I'd sent them all out doing assorted jobs like door-knocking, tracking down any further CCTV we might have missed, even talking to the staff in the charity shop because it's directly across from your dad's shop. I wanted him walking into an empty briefing room, and that's exactly what he did because Ray and I had taken ourselves off to talk to Anthony Dawson. Anyway, it turns out he's only temporary, your successor. It's DI Daniel Armitage, transferred temporarily from Central, friend of Superintendent Davis, I believe.'

'And no friend of mine,' Matt said, his voice a growl. 'Nasty piece of work. Don't trust him with as much as a paperclip, Karen.'

'I've got his measure, don't worry. Horrible little weasel. Ray and I walked back in, and he must have been looking out for us, because within about thirty seconds, he followed us through the door. He wanted a full briefing of where everybody was, what I'd been doing, wanted to know if you'd been in touch, nightmare afternoon. Anyway, at four o'clock I went to his office, said good-night and walked away. He called me back, asked where I thought I was going, and I said home. I'd started at seven, and I was going home to write up my reports in comfort.'

Matt turned to Steve and Hermia, concerned that she looked a bit pale. 'You okay, Herms?'

'I'm fine. Tried to keep off the meds today, but I think I'm reaching the point where I might need some. It's because I've stopped working, so no need to panic. When I'm concentrating on something, I don't notice the pain so much, but now I've stopped to eat this delicious pie, it's bothering me again. I'll take some now, and I'll be good again in about ten minutes. However, I've been working my way through Hartner's stuff. That man certainly believed in doing a thorough job. He interviewed a lot of people, some just ordinary people on the streets, others out and out villains. And that's where it gets interesting because we're touching on names now.'

'What names?'

'I'll list every name I come across, but certainly Anthony

Dawson is mentioned as being high up in the chain, and someone called Wally is talked about – Walter Vickers? At the moment, there's no confirmation of that, though.' She smiled up at Steve as he handed her two painkillers, then swallowed them before carrying on. 'I don't think Hartner set out to get names, I think he was trying to build a picture of how strong the criminal side of Sheffield is, and what the council, combined with the police, of course, can do about it. That was the idea behind the report, and it was meant to take a year at least, but so far there's only about three months of work according to the dates on his notes. Drugs come under a separate heading, because it's not all about drugs. There's protection for a start, and that's the section he's listed Anthony Dawson in, and he's starred his name, which I suspect means he's top of the pile, or very near it.'

'Well, certainly his house at Millhouses would lead me towards that conclusion,' Karen laughed. 'Let's hope that one day a judge will be in a position where he can order the seizure of all his assets, and send him away for many years. We've tried to get him before, many times, but he's a proper worm, can wriggle his way out of anything.'

Matt sipped at his coffee, a thoughtful expression on his face. 'I'm more concerned about tracking down Walter Vickers. It seems odd that he doesn't appear to live anywhere, doesn't even own a car, and yet he's active enough on the crime scene to want these notes from the professor. What's the thing that's worrying him so much? What's he hiding that we can't see yet?'

Hermia gave a brief nod of her head. 'That was my thought. The picture that I found of him at that presentation evening is strange. I can't find him anywhere before that. I must admit I had to stop looking, but I will go back to it, because that seems to be the first time he's heard of, so where was he prior to four years ago? Was he making his way onto the Sheffield scene, establishing himself? It would be good to get Anthony Dawson into an interview room yet again, and find out what he knows about the man who was in the photograph line-up with him.'

'Don't worry, once we track him down, the question will be asked.' Karen glanced at her phone as it began to ring. 'It's Ray.' She hesitated. 'No, I'm going to take it. He wouldn't ring without good reason.'

She listened, then smiled. 'Send for two cars as back-up, and I'll be there in ten minutes or so. We'll take them both in.'

She looked at the others around the kitchen table. 'I have to go. Ray has been doing surveillance off his own bat outside Dawson's home, and the man himself has just turned up with a woman who looks suspiciously like Diana Marshall. I'll ring later to let you know what's happening.'

Matt stood and hugged her. 'Take care. You know he's a bastard. And thank you for the pie.'

21

Anger had burst out of Anthony Dawson. 'You can't fucking arrest me for nothing! And you can't arrest her just because she's with me. I want my solicitor, and I want him now.'

'We'll make sure he's with you before we question you, sir. I'm sure when he knows it's you, he'll be there for nine o'clock tomorrow morning.' Karen smiled at the man she considered to be a weasel of the lowest order. 'You'll both be held overnight and interviewed tomorrow morning.'

Diana Marshall's face lost all colour. 'But my husband thinks I'm at an Ann Summers party. He can't know I've been with Ants.'

'Think he might find out, Mrs Marshall.'

Her head dropped. 'He'll kill me. Or Ants.'

'Shut up, Diana,' Dawson snarled. 'Not another fucking word, or I'll kill you.'

'That your answer to everything, Mr Dawson? Killing people?'

He glared at Karen, and she nodded at the officers who had arrived to transport Dawson and Marshall. 'Take them in, and get them booked in.'

Karen was back with Matt by ten, and smiling happily. 'He's locked up, I'm interviewing him in the morning. Wants his solicitor, of course, but I think he thought it would happen tonight. She's bricking it, because she's now got to tell her husband she wasn't at an Ann Summers party, she was out with the new man in her life. I suspect she's about to lose everything, because her husband is now likely to dump her from a great height, and I don't think Dawson is bothered about her anyway, he was really off with her. Is Hermia okay?'

'She's fine. Steve's helped her go to bed, but she's walking without the stick now. Still a slight limp, but a definite improvement. We've had more of a talk about Steve coming in as partner, and we're going to ring Dad's solicitor, have her sort out any papers we need to sign. Hermia will be a consultant, because she wants to go back to the uni, carry on with her work there. She made that very clear tonight. Steve's not giving up any part of his business, he's going to delegate, he says.'

'Big changes coming then.'

'Big changes forced on me.'

* * *

It had been an uncomfortable night for Dawson. His guess was that his name had been in Forrester's files, but just how much had Dave Forrester known? Surely they couldn't arrest him for screwing around with somebody else's wife? He thanked the lord Diana hadn't known anything of his business, so could tell them nothing; he'd deal with the fallout that would be on his way via Liam Marshall when he got out of this shit-hole. He had no idea of the time, but he figured Everett must be here by now, prepared to go into battle for his client and get him released within the hour.

He paced the cell floor, feeling more unnerved with every minute that passed. He was almost at boiling point when the cell door finally opened, and he was escorted to the interview room.

* * *

Karen verbally logged everyone in. She took Ray in with her, as her DI didn't appear to have arrived at work, opened her file and said good morning. There was no response other than a glare from Dawson.

'Mr Dawson, I apologise for the lateness of the hour, we interviewed Diana first. You'll be pleased to know she is now on her way home.'

He groaned. More shit to deal with when he got out of this place.

'I don't give a fuck what she's doing. I want out of here right now.'

Karen smiled at him. 'Good luck with that, Anthony. You are here because you're being questioned with regard to the murders of David Forrester and John Keane. Can you tell me where you were on Saturday, 12 March, please?'

She watched as his face lost any bluster, any colour. 'Hang on, bitch, that's nowt to do with me.'

'Prove it,' she said.

'Not for me to prove it,' he responded, 'that's for you to do.'

'You're right, it is. And that's what I'm doing right now. If you don't have an alibi for Saturday, then it's quite possible you'll be taken back to your cell for the foreseeable future, while we carry on with our investigations. Now do you want to tell me where you were on Saturday, 12 March?'

Dawson turned to look at his solicitor. 'Is she for real?'

James Everett gave a slight nod of his head, and made a note on his legal pad.

Dawson stared at Karen and slowly a smile crept across his face. 'Saturday, 12 March you say? You're gonna love this, DS Nelson. From about half eleven until about quarter to three, I was in a pub called the Old Crown on Penistone Road, along with a cartload of Wednesday fans. I was with half a dozen or so of my mates, and the only time I wasn't with them was when I went for a piss. We left there just after half past two to walk up to the ground, and I got to my seat about ten minutes or so before kick-off. We won. Six-nil.'

'Names.'

'What?'

'Of these mates you were with.'

'Bill and Jack, they're brothers, Craig, Adam, Frank and Arnie. Can't tell you their surnames 'cos I don't know them, but they all have season tickets round about where I sit.'

'And where do you sit?' She could get full names and addresses from the club if necessary, but her heart was sinking at the thought that he had nothing to do directly with Dave and Johnny's deaths.

'Three rows behind your mate, DI Forrester.' He smirked, and her heart sank even further.

She looked across at Ray and he raised an eyebrow in query, before saying, 'PC Ray Ledger leaving the room.'

'We'll have those names in a few minutes if Sheffield Wednesday cooperate. If we have to get a warrant to get the names and addresses, you'll wait here until we get the information we need.' She stood. 'DS Nelson leaving the room.'

She picked up her file and walked out, aware that his eyes never left her.

* * *

Anthony Dawson was on his way home by four that afternoon. Sheffield Wednesday had cooperated, but they had to wait for somebody senior enough to give permission for the information to be handed over.

He got out of the taxi, trying to ignore the figure of Diana Marshall, waiting patiently on his front doorstep, complete with two suitcases. 'Don't go yet, mate,' he said. 'I have another customer for you.'

He walked towards her, and she remained sitting on the steps. Although he'd never said it, she was confident he loved her, and they could plan a future together. Unfortunately for her, he hadn't told her he loved her purely because he didn't. He wasn't that sure he even liked her.

'Diana?'

'He threw me out.'

'So what are you going to do?'

'I thought I could stay here with you. I've brought a few clothes, but he wouldn't let me take anything else.'

'Well, I hope you're okay for money, because you're going to need to find a hotel room. The taxi's waiting for you.'

She stared at him. 'I can't stay here with you?'

'Nope. I'll carry your suitcases for you.'

She stood. 'Don't fucking bother, Ants. They're on wheels, I'll manage.'

She dragged the cases to the bottom of the steps, and stalked across to the waiting cab. 'The Hilton,' she snapped, and the driver got out to load the suitcases in his boot. She climbed in without looking back at Dawson, and within two minutes had disappeared. He smiled, took out his key and unlocked the door.

He needed a shit, shower and a shave in any order, and then he was going to bed, hopefully to catch up on sleep he hadn't had the previous night.

* * *

Karen waited until she was in the car before contacting Matt. She didn't want anybody at the station, other than Ray Ledger, to know that she was in touch with him; she hated not being able to simply ring his number and he be there.

They spoke for some time while she filled him in on the actions of the day, confirming that Dawson hadn't appeared to know Walter Vickers in any way; he had merely confirmed he was somebody in the line-up for the photograph, he hadn't even known the Lord Mayor's name, never mind some strange geezer he'd never seen before. It was hard for both of them to say good night. Finn was home, and she had to return there.

Matt suddenly felt bereft as he disconnected their call. He smiled to himself; if he had known his resignation would have escalated what had been growing for months, if only he hadn't been so blind, then he would have walked away much sooner.

He hated the thought she was going home to him, to Finn. But there had been no discussion of them ending their marriage, no commitment to what they appeared to be discovering about each other, and he knew the time would come when they would have to make decisions.

And they also needed to discuss finding the man who had attempted to kill Hermia, to find what name he was using, where he lived when he wasn't inhabiting people's homes like some sort of cuckoo.

They needed time together, more time than a quick meal and a passion-filled night. They needed to talk, to get to know each other outside of a work environment, and Matt in particular felt he wanted to know how serious she was before he let himself get more emotionally involved. Fall in love with her.

He checked in with Hermia and Steve, and was pleased that Hermia had cut her pain meds down and intended moving into her bedroom the following day; she felt she would be able to handle the stairs, and could they please organise some large plastic bags that she could put over the cast on her arm, so that she could have the supreme luxury of a shower?

Oliver was by her side constantly, as if aware that she needed the healing qualities that animals tended to exude when something was wrong. She explained to the cat that if she were to trip over his body as he constantly entwined himself around her legs, she would be in a bit of a pickle, but he chose to ignore her words, and stayed by her side.

As did Steve.

22

There was a knock on the door, and Matt looked at Steve, who was busy making bacon butties. 'Nothing to do with me, pal,' Steve said, 'I only work here, don't live here,' and he waved the spatula at his friend.

Matt stood and walked down the hall and looked through the spy hole. He saw the top of a head and quickly removed the dead lock and safety chain. 'Harry! Where's your mum?'

'Can I come in?' Harry's voice was low, and Matt pulled him inside, holding him tightly for a few seconds before ushering him through into the kitchen.

'Might need more bacon on the grill, Steve.'

Steve looked at Harry and grinned. 'You okay, pal?'

And Harry burst into tears.

* * *

With a bacon sandwich and a can of Coke inside him, Harry's normal attitude returned, until Matt deepened it again. 'So, you're not at home.' He glanced at his watch. 'And I imagine your mum is going to be panicking very shortly and ringing me to see if I have you. Here's the trade-off. I'll ring her and say you're with me and you'll be back tomorrow. I'll tell her you've turned up here, a bit down in the dumps. After I've covered your arse, we'll talk. That sound okay?'

Harry nodded without speaking, so Matt immediately spoke to Becky. Becky wasn't so easy to fool – her son had shown no outward signs of being fed up with his life.

'How the hell has he got to yours?'

'He's apparently walked. Leave it with me, I'll sort it and deliver him back to yours tonight. Has something happened to upset him?'

'Not that I'm aware of. He went to his room after tea and played on his computer, until he shouted down to say he was going to bed.'

'You didn't get up with him this morning?'

'Oh, take off your detective head, Matt. No, I felt ill earlier, so I stayed in bed. I assumed Brian had sorted him with some breakfast.'

'Okay, I'll keep him with me today, bring him back to you tomorrow. That good with you?'

'It's fine, but he's in big trouble for doing this. We can't encourage this sort of behaviour, Matt.'

'The lad's unhappy, Becky. What sort of behaviour would you like to encourage? That he bottles it all up and goes on the streets, or even worse, when he reaches fourteen and discovers how he can really get into trouble?'

He disconnected, feeling too angry to continue the conversation. Something had triggered Harry's actions and he wasn't taking him back until he knew what it was.

Matt returned to the kitchen deep in thought. Was it his grandfather's death, compounded by the death of Uncle Johnny, that had brought this on?

Steve and Harry had been joined by Hermia and all were deep in conversation about goalkeepers. Harry had slipped effortlessly into the role in his under-twelves side, and they were discussing the merits of different goalies in the Premier League.

Matt poured himself a cup of coffee and handed Harry a glass of orange juice. 'Come on, we need to talk.'

Harry looked at Hermia and Steve, hoping they would come to his rescue, but all they gave him was a smile. He followed his dad into the dining room and they sat side by side at the table. Harry looked up at the pictures attached to the board and frowned. 'Thought you'd left the police.'

'I have. Now it seems I have an investigation agency all of my own. Your granddad left it to me and Hermia, but she doesn't want it at this point in time. One day hopefully it will pass to you. But that's only if you want it. If you want to move forward in football, that's fine. If you want to work on a bin lorry, that's fine as well. As long as you're happy, you can do what you want. But it's clear you're not happy today. Want to talk about it?'

There was a brief shake of Harry's head and he stood, moving to stare intently at the murder board. 'I always thought I'd follow you into the police.' He hesitated. 'But not all policemen are like you, are they?'

Matt felt his heart plummet into his boots. 'What's wrong, Harry? Something at home?' He stood to join Harry at the murder board, and put his arm around his son's shoulders. 'If it is that, it can be sorted.'

He felt Harry's body give a convulsive jerk, and then the tears started again. 'I came downstairs last night to get some water. They were talking in the lounge. She doesn't want me any more.'

'What?' Matt's first inclination was to laugh loudly, but his son's face told him that would be the wrong reaction. 'Look, Harry, you are the most important thing in the world to your mother. Never doubt that for a minute. Much more important than Brian, and definitely more important than me. She's loved you from the day we found out she was pregnant, and nothing will ever change that. So what's happened? Something between her and Davis? He got somebody else new?'

'No, I heard them talking. She's having a baby.' And the tears changed to deep, heartfelt sobs.

Matt pulled his son closer and led him over to the sofa, where they sat side by side. He waited until the tears subsided, and Harry was quieter. 'Time for a talk, Harry. Just because your mum is going to have another baby, doesn't mean she'll love you any less. Women have this wonderful capacity to mete out their love equally between their children, and there's no finite end to it. You don't, won't, have to share that love. What she feels for you right now will be exactly the same when the new baby is here, and it will be exactly the same amount of love she gives to the new baby. Don't ask me how this works, I don't know, but it does. Never ever doubt how much she loves you. Hermia and I shared our mum, who loved us equally. I need you to be a big lad about this, wait for this new little one to arrive, and you'll see for yourself. And I can tell you it's good to be a big brother, because not only will your mum love you, but the new baby will as well. It's a win-win situation, Harry. When I take you home tomorrow, we'll talk to your mum about how upset you've been, and from now on, I'm sure she'll tell you everything. She simply doesn't realise what you heard last night, because it was a private conversation between her and D... Brian. I promise you we'll sort it tomorrow, then, like your mum and Brian, you'll be able to enjoy this special journey with them.'

Harry's head dropped as he digested his father's words. Matt prayed he'd done enough to settle Harry's mind, and help him get through a difficult few months. He had no doubt that once the baby arrived, Harry would welcome it, but until that time, he had to be helped through the trauma of seeing his mother's stomach grow as the baby grew inside her.

'So shall we forget this stuff until we can talk to your mum tomorrow, or do you want to go home now and talk to her without Brian being there?'

Harry frowned. 'Can I stay with you for today? I don't call him Dad, you know. You're my dad.'

'What do you call him?'

'I called him Dickhead because I heard you say it to Aunty Herms, and Mum sent me to my room, so now I call him Brian. He is, though. A dickhead, I mean.'

'Okay, that's enough. You can only use that word once you've turned eighteen. Deal?'

'Deal. I can use it in my head, though...'

It briefly occurred to Matt how alike they were, father and son – no, correction. Grandfather, father and son.

* * *

Hermia was busy on her phone replying to various messages from friends and colleagues checking in on the state of her health when they returned to the kitchen. Steve glanced up.

'Everything okay?'

'It's fine. Crossed wires. We'll sort it when I take him home tomorrow. He's staying with us for now, so we can either get him digging gardens with you, Steve, or he can go into the office with me. I need to get myself sorted there, set it up how I want it. And Gloria is popping in after lunch with some paperwork for us to sign, Steve. Hermia, you're absolutely certain you want no part of the agency?'

'Certainly not,' she said with a degree of asperity. 'I don't want throwing off any more balconies, thank you.'

'I've to nip over to Crosspool just to give the okay to some work the owner wants doing, and to discuss prices, then I'll head back to Gleadless,' said Steve. 'I should be there for around half ten, then we can delve into what Dave has been working on, or not working on. Herms, you coming with me? I don't want to leave you here on your own.'

'Oh, lordy me. Am I going to have babysitters for the rest of my life?'

'No, only until we find the feller who threw you over, because he wanted you dead, Hermia,' said Matt. 'Not injured. He may still want you dead, because whatever he was looking for, he didn't get. I'm guessing he thought it would be in your flat; he didn't realise you would have already started moving stuff out. Stuff like your work papers, your laptop, your iPad… and while he's still out there, your babysitters will be by your side.'

'Okay, I give in. I'll take some of the professor's findings with me, and work from Dad's flat while you two… three… are downstairs getting things organised. Do the lunchtime sandwiches come out of petty cash?'

'Have we got petty cash?'

'Bottom drawer of Dad's desk,' said Hermia. 'Key is on Dad's key ring.'

'He's bought you sandwiches before?'

'Certainly has. Best dad anybody could wish for.'

Matt frowned. 'He never bought me a sandwich. I had to buy them for him and Johnny, if I happened to call in around lunchtime.'

'More fool you,' Hermia laughed. 'It's memories like these we need to hold on to, isn't it?'

* * *

Matt and Steve stared around the large working space they had. It was clear that Dave had been the boss. Johnny had a desk, but it was positioned off to one side, occupying the same work area as Dave's desk.

'If we're going to take this on properly and progress it, we need separate spaces. Clients want privacy when they're talking to whichever one of us they get, so I think we should have a wall dividing it up. I think Dad and Johnny worked more together so didn't need different workspaces, but if we're committed to this venture, we have to start as we mean to go on. Dad's space at the back can be left as our kitchen area, but this front part needs a dividing wall, individual offices for the two of us. I also think we should convert one of the bedrooms upstairs into a huge filing cabinet, make it a secure place where nobody but us can access anything. If we keep the lift, it will make it easy to take things up there, because if there's one thing what has happened has taught me, it's that we need to be security conscious.'

Steve grinned. 'Yep. No more keeping handwritten journals in a hollowed-out book.'

'We were lucky with that one. We had the time to find it, the time to work out his quirky case numbering leading to a journal, but we'll be more straightforward and will need added security. And nobody gets in here without an appointment, and without us knowing them. I'm not convinced Dad and Johnny died because they were working on something, I think it's because they wouldn't give Hermia up. And she's no idea yet what she knows. We have to start work today, get the beginnings organised. These filing cabinets, old-fashioned though they may be, can be transported upstairs. We need as much out of here as possible to give us room to get the alterations done. Do you know any decent builders, Steve?'

'Us.'

Matt sat down with a thud. 'You're kidding. I know we did my house, but there was no rush with that. I was quite happy in your back bedroom while I waited for the house to be fit for habitation, but this we need doing yesterday.'

'Look, I don't know what it is, but there's something wrong in Harry's life,' said Steve. 'If we do this, can't he help? And learn some skills along the way. Let's crack on with finding who's after Hermia and why, because there's no rush to sort this. Harry could stay at yours for the school Easter holidays, and help out here. Bit of father, son and Uncle Steve bonding. Get him away from Dickhead at the same time. Talk to Becky when you take him home tonight, and we'll discuss it further then. Or we can pay mega bucks out and get somebody in to do it. Your decision, pal.'

23

"'Though she be but little, she is fierce!'" Hermia muttered her favourite quote from *A Midsummer Night's Dream*, thinking she would have got on with Helena if she was smart enough to see that about her friend Hermia.

Eric Hartner's notes were detailed, and although it was clear some had been transcribed onto his computer, then printed out and collated into a physical file, a lot of it was in his own handwriting, a spiderish scrawl that was difficult to follow. She suspected he had a secretary who took on the job of working through his notes, and was probably used to the foibles of his penmanship, but Hermia was struggling.

He had interviewed many people in the course of gathering information to be put into the report that would ultimately be presented to the council, and she felt a tingle run through her at the thought that somewhere in here was something that Walter Vickers, or whatever his name really was, wanted.

Many names had been mentioned during Eric's research, and Hermia was listing every one of them. Once everything was collated, Hermia would hand the document over to her brother and bow out gracefully. She hoped.

For a small moment in time, she had toyed with the idea of working alongside him, building up the business their father had started, but when the thought of leaving the university hurt so much, she knew where she wanted to be. And it made her more determined than ever to continue with Hartner's work, especially as Matt had thrown suspicion on the manner of Eric's dying. Nobody had queried the accidental death verdict, but the CCTV at the tram stop hadn't been working, and there had been nothing to show that he didn't simply fall, overbalance, in front of the tram as it coasted into the platform.

There had been an immediate meeting at the university once the fatality had been confirmed, and within hours of his death, she had taken possession of all his notes. A promise had been given that she would move straight onto his project once her current one was completed, and now that she was working more thoroughly through his notes and thoughts, she regretted not having started it sooner.

It was becoming very clear that the comments from people in the lower echelons of their department who had constantly made remarks about his 'skiving off' proclivities had been incredibly uninformed. He had tackled the requested report head on, each trip out listed, every person interviewed collated. She suspected that the audio files he had added would make interesting bedtime stories, albeit of the nightmarish variety. And the final document to be sent to the council would have been an eye-opener with reference to a return to the gangland side of Sheffield. Several names had been mentioned by different people, and she wondered what Hartner had said to these informants to convince them to speak out. He couldn't guarantee them any sort of immunity other than saying he wouldn't release their names to anyone.

She felt sick. Now she had their names. She suspected it wasn't any one particular name that was the problem, it was the multiplicity of names, and the fact that Eric had recorded the interviews.

She pushed everything to one side and began to move around the flat. Her dad had been happy living here, he had made life as easy as he could by installing the lift, by having his beloved books gathered together all in one place, and by sharing his life with a friend who would have died for him. Who had died with him. She brushed away tears, the feelings of anger and love still so raw.

She knew she had to find somewhere secure to hide Hartner's notes; whoever was behind all of this needed these findings destroying, along with the memory stick containing the recordings. And she needed Matt and Steve to carefully go through everything she had collated for them. This was a bundle of dynamite, and she wanted nothing to explode before they had seen and evaluated everything.

She packed everything carefully away in her briefcase, then pushed it under her dad's bed. That little action made her smile. Why on earth she would think that was a safe place she couldn't imagine, but it was certainly safer than leaving it on the kitchen table.

She made drinks for everyone then headed downstairs, using the lift. She figured there was less chance of dropping the tray that she was carrying carefully balanced on her cast-covered arm using the small box-like structure than walking down the stairs.

'Two cups of tea, two cans of Coke,' she said. She looked around. 'Good grief, you three have been busy.'

'We have to do some reworking of the space,' Matt said. 'We actually need two separate offices, so we've decided to turn Johnny's room into a filing space, and just have desks down here. We're keeping the lift. We've moved the desks to get some idea of where we need the new walls. We're lucky it's an ex-newsagency, because the central doors have windows either side. We don't need to fit new windows, although I'd like to see added security on them. What's happened has shown it's all too easy to take out CCTV cameras, so it's a priority we get concealed ones installed as well as obvious ones. You have anything to tell us?'

'I've been working away like a little beaver while you three have been doing boy things down here. So let's stop for a drink and a chat. Harry, if you want to do your usual thing and go on Grand-dad's PlayStation upstairs, it's set up to go.'

Harry didn't need telling twice. He grabbed his can of Coke, jumped in the lift and disappeared.

'There's something you didn't want him to hear?' Matt said quietly.

'He's struggling with enough at the moment without hearing us discussing anything connected to his granddad's murder. He's not old enough to listen to us hypothesising about why Eric Hartner died and why two men he loved dearly both died. I've spent the last hour and a half going through Eric's notes, and while I can't hazard any guesses at this stage, I think it's pretty clear that somebody has spoken out of turn. There are many interviews, some with the villains themselves, some with people who know them and are scared of them.' She paused for a moment, gathering her thoughts.

'I've listed every name mentioned and I need you to go through it, Matt. Maybe cross-reference it with that list of cars that were near the shop on the day Dad died, the list Ray Ledger did for you.'

'You trying to teach me to suck eggs?' Matt asked with a smile. 'Did you recognise any of the names?'

'No, but I didn't really expect to. He's been very thorough. Every name is linked to where he heard it, and if he heard a name from more than one person, all of them are listed. If they are mentioned for a specific reason, be it drugs, burglary, GBH, he's noted that as well. I also have a memory stick with interviews on it where they gave him permission to record, so I need somewhere where I can put this little lot securely.'

'Where is it now? Harry can't see it, can he?'

'No, it's under Dad's bed in my briefcase, but this is obviously what they are looking for, whoever they are. It must have been very clear that there was nothing in my flat when Vickers came to look around. He asked about a safe, because he wanted to keep some documents secure, and I said I didn't have one. My office was almost empty because I'd taken my laptop, and my briefcase with all this stuff from Hartner in it, and they were at yours. I suspect I became superfluous to requirements, so he killed me, or thought he had. Matt, these people are killing for this information. When Eric died, his research notes were in a secure room at the university, so they couldn't get at it there, but according to the accident report, they never found his briefcase. I think they've dismissed his death a bit too quickly, and I think it should be looked at again.'

'I'll talk to Karen.' Matt's tone was grim. He'd followed Hermia's well thought out logic with ease, as had Steve.

'What bothers me,' Steve interrupted, 'is are they going to come for Herms again, because they must have realised by now that she isn't dead? I don't think they'll stop until they've got this paperwork, and it's destroyed. So where do we put it?'

'I've had a think about that.' Hermia tried not to laugh. 'I think we hide it in plain sight. I think we stick all of it in a large McDonald's paper bag that they send out with delivered orders, and dump it in Steve's blue recycling bin. We just don't put his bin out for collection this time. It won't stand out in all the other paper rubbish, and I think it'll be pretty safe there. Or we could hand it all in to the investigation but I don't think somehow you'll want that, Matt.'

'And the plus side of that is we get to order a McDonald's takeaway tonight. I also think we should duplicate everything, and put the duplicates in the safe, with all the names redacted. Let's see them work their way through that lot. Or we could confuse them altogether by hiding a couple of sheets here, a couple of sheets there, almost like an Easter egg hunt, then it definitely won't be a quick in and out for them, and we might stand half a chance of catching them.' Steve smiled as he spoke, thinking about the promise of a McDonald's meal.

A disembodied voice reached them from halfway down the stairs. 'Or you could let me take whatever it is home with me. Nobody will risk looking there for it; don't I live with Dickhead?'

'Oy,' his dad said. 'You're not eighteen yet!'

Hermia looked at Steve and shrugged. 'Not sure what the relevance of being eighteen is, but there's not a cat in hell's chance I'll put Harry into any sort of danger. But he can join us for a McDonald's delivery tonight.'

'Will that be helping you?' Harry asked.

'Too damn right it will. And we can have McFlurrys as well.'

Harry gave it some thought, then nodded. 'Okay, I'll settle for that. And I'm not going to say anything about any of this to either my mum or him. Brian.'

'Good lad. Have you closed down the PlayStation?'

He laughed. 'Not been on it, I was sitting here listening to you three, because I guessed I wasn't supposed to hear what you were talking about.'

Matt sighed. 'This kid is so like me, it's scary. You coming to stay for a few days in the Easter school break? We could do with a hand in here, sorting out the offices.'

'Will you pay me?'

They all turned their heads as the front door opened and Gloria smiled at everyone. 'You're all becoming partners then?'

'No,' Hermia said. 'I'm resigning after giving it further thought,

Matt and Steve are plotting to take over the world, and Harry here is going to be CEO. Come on, Harry, let's go upstairs while Gloria sorts out a bit of paperwork.'

Harry pulled a face, clearly not wanting to miss anything, but he followed behind his aunt as they headed upstairs.

24

Harry enjoyed the McDonald's meal – all of them did, but as adults they weren't allowed to say they had – and watched as Hermia wrapped the physical notes written by Hartner into a plastic bag. She screwed up the large McDonald's paper bag to make it look tatty, added the plastic bag and its contents, then took it out, heading towards Steve's house, where she buried it in his blue paper recycling bin. It would stay there until she felt she could recover it. The small memory stick disappeared inside a cut in the lining of her shoulder bag. It had hurt her to cut open the lining of the Louis Vuitton bag, but it was as secure as it could be in there.

Harry was taken home to face the music that evening instead of waiting until the following day, and promised to behave. Hermia had convinced him it was better to face his worries and get the telling-off over with, and get on with his life. Matt arranged for Harry to return to his for a few days during the Easter break, explaining to Becky about the changes they needed to make to the office, and Becky agreed to the plans provided her son didn't pull the stunt of leaving home again.

It was only after the boy's departure to his bedroom that Matt brought up the issue of why Harry was so upset, and his ex-wife looked shocked. 'I didn't want to tell him until I got to twelve weeks, but I guess I'd better sort that as soon as possible. He thinks I don't love him? He's barmy. I'll talk to him tomorrow, Matt, I promise.'

* * *

Karen turned towards Matt as she climbed into bed. 'I persuaded Finn to go to work tonight, instead of in the morning. He said he needed an early start, so I gently steered him out of the door and towards a hotel for the night. I needed to see you, Matt. As soon as I said something, he was taking his suitcase out to the car and he was gone. I think there's definitely another woman in the mix, but I don't feel anything. No anger, no jealousy, purely relief and acceptance.'

'Do you feel like this because of us?' He gently stroked her cheek.

Shaking her head, she touched his hand. 'Not at all. I've been feeling like it for ages, knew the signs, but haven't even questioned him about there being somebody else. We live separate lives, and he'd only been gone five minutes when I rang to see if your hotel was open for visitors.'

He smiled. 'It will always be open for you. I've a lot to tell you, but we'll talk over breakfast. I hope you don't mind but I've discussed you a little bit – okay, maybe a lot – with Harry, who approves of my finding a new lady, as he put it. Anyway, forget all of that, I can think of other things to do right now.'

She gave a small tinkle of laughter that could almost have been a giggle if she'd been twenty years younger. 'I've been thinking of those other things all day today.' Her phone's ringtone of the *Dixon of Dock Green* theme tune pealed out, and she groaned.

She checked the screen and answered immediately. 'Nelson.' There was a pause while she listened. 'Have you notified DI Armitage?'

There was another pause. 'Then keep trying him until he does bloody answer. Get a forensics team there, and I'll be about fifteen minutes before I'm on scene.'

She disconnected and turned to Matt. 'If this case isn't sorted soon, I'm going to end up a sexually frustrated old hag.'

'Daft as it sounds, I miss this.'

'Being called out?'

'Yeah. Not knowing what you're going to find, starting a new case, that sort of thing.'

'Well,' she said, shrugging into her jeans, 'this isn't a new case. In fact, without knowing anything beyond somebody's dead, I'd say at some point it's going to cross over into an existing case. Your dad's.'

'What?'

'The dead person... apparently it's Anthony Dawson.' She leaned across to kiss him. 'I'll see you later perhaps, but either way, I'll fill you in on all the details as quickly as I can.'

* * *

Karen arrived at Dawson's home to find the forensics team already in place. Outside was a young man, sitting half in and half out of his car, with a PC kneeling down so they were on the same level, talking to him. As Karen approached, the PC stood.

'DS Nelson, this is Richard Hogan. He's a pizza delivery driver. He found the deceased when he came to deliver the pizza.'

'Thank you. Can I ask you to cover the gates? Make sure nobody else comes in unless they're part of my team. I'm expecting

DCs Kevin Potter and Phil Newton, and PC Jaime Hanover. Also, there's a chance DI Armitage might arrive.'

The PC walked across the parking area and stationed himself at the gates. Karen turned to the young man with a smile. 'Okay, tomorrow we'll need a statement from you, but for tonight, can you tell me what happened?'

Richard gulped. This was way beyond his job description. 'I arrived about half an hour ago, elevenish or so, maybe a bit longer, and the front door was slightly open. Mr Dawson is a regular customer. I deliver here at least once every week; he likes barbecue chicken pizzas.' Richard looked down to the floor, aware he was waffling. 'I pushed open the door but before I could shout his name, I saw the blood. It was all around his head...'

'Did you touch him?'

He shook his head. 'I went closer to see if I needed to help him, but it was obvious he was beyond helping. So I came outside and dialled 999. That PC and his mate were here pretty fast, and they asked me to wait to talk to whoever was in charge. That you?'

She chose her words carefully. 'I am the senior officer here at the moment. When you arrived with the pizza, did you see any other vehicles nearby? Pass a car leaving in a hurry, anything like that?'

He thought for a moment. 'There was a bike, a motorbike. I can't tell you anything about it, the make or anything, but it was leaving the end of the road as I turned on to it to come here. And, of course, I couldn't tell if it was a man or a woman. It could have come from anywhere along this road, I didn't see it pull out of this driveway.' The enormity of what he was saying suddenly seemed to hit him. 'For fuck's sake, I could have been shot if I'd been seconds earlier.'

'How old are you, Richard?'

'Nineteen.'

'Then you'll live a long and happy life. It's clearly not your time to go yet.' She smiled at him. 'Have you contacted your employers?'

'Yes, I told them what had happened and I didn't know when I could get back to the shop. They said just to go home, and they'd see me tomorrow night.'

'Then do that. I'll take all the details of who you work for and stuff tomorrow. Have you left your name and address with the constable?'

'Yes, he's got it all; phone number, date of birth and stuff.'

'You think you'll be okay to drive home?'

'I'll be fine. Mum's waiting up for me.'

'Then I'll ring you in the morning and we'll make arrangements to take your statement.'

He swung himself round into his seat, and she closed his door. He put down his window. 'Thank you,' he said. 'All that blood...' He put the car into gear and drove away, stopping at the gate to thank the PC.

She turned to enter the house, not looking forward to it. She could cope with a cut finger, but Richard had mentioned the amount of the blood a couple of times, and she knew it was going to be bad.

It was considerably more than bad. Rosie Masters was standing to the side, waiting for the photographer to finish his work, and she turned as Karen reached her.

'Do we have a definite ID?' Karen asked.

'We do, although not from his face. There's not much left of that. He had his wallet in his hand when he was shot, and his name according to his driving licence is Anthony Dawson.'

'He was expecting the pizza delivery lad, he would have been taking money out to pay him. Only it wasn't the pizza delivery. It must have been over in seconds. I'm assuming it was the bullet that killed him?'

'Well, I'll know for definite once I get him in the autopsy suite, but off the record, I would say so. I can't see anything else, and the shot took away most of his face, as I said. He must have upset somebody pretty bad for them to do this.'

'He has.' Karen frowned. 'But like you, I can't say too much until I have more facts.'

As soon as the phone call specified it was probably Anthony Dawson, her thoughts had spiralled rapidly towards Liam and Diana Marshall, but it was a pretty harsh penalty to pay for committing adultery. Especially as it now appeared to be all over, according to what Dawson had said as they released him after interview.

What the hell was connecting all these people that had suddenly triggered off such a murderous rampage? Dave Forrester, Johnny Keane, the attempted murder of Hermia Forrester, Emily George and now Anthony Dawson. Had the same person instigated all the attacks?

Walter Vickers had certainly been responsible for the attack on Hermia, and therefore logic said he was the person behind the murders. But why? What on earth had all these people done to merit dying?

And where the fuck was he?

* * *

Karen watched as Anthony Dawson's body was driven away, and once again wondered what had prompted Dave Forrester to highlight his name in red, in a journal where everything else was written in black. Even his computerised list of current cases had shown his name in red. Something had hit a note with Dave that set off alarms, and she wasn't convinced it was purely the case of adultery with Diana Marshall.

She'd have Liam and Diana brought in at some inconvenient hour and find out exactly where both of them had been from around 10.30, because Anthony Dawson had definitely been alive at that point, ringing for a pizza. And could the motorbike be relevant? There had to have been three shots, because the CCTV cameras trained on the doorstep and the entrance gates had been blown apart, prior to the knock on the door, which he would have assumed was his pizza being delivered. A silenced gun? He would have heard the first two shots if it wasn't silenced, and would have had the sense to ignore the door, but that hadn't happened. There had been no reports of gunfire, but neighbours would be questioned as soon as they started to surface for their breakfasts. Being questioned about gunshots would certainly put them off their full English. Gunshots in this classy neighbourhood? Out of the question. But there had definitely been three.

Just as she was about to head for her car, DI Armitage rang her. He apologised, said he had been asleep and he hadn't heard his phone, but did she need him to be on scene now? She answered with a very curt no, she was just leaving to go home to get some sleep, because unlike him, she had heard her phone.

'Forensics will be here for a while, and we'll come back in tomorrow and search the house. I can't do anything until daylight, and I'm bringing two suspects in for questioning tomorrow morning, but they're not really suspects, so don't build up your hopes.' She could hear the anger in her own voice, and knew Armitage would sense it as well. 'If you want to be part of the interview, I'll be starting at eight. Sir.'

The last word was said almost as an afterthought, and when he said he was meeting Superintendent Davis at his home for breakfast before having a meeting, she wanted to withdraw the word.

'Very well. I'll take PC Ledger in with me, I know he'll be there.

I'm going home to bed now to get a couple of hours' sleep, so I'll see you tomorrow, maybe.'

'Yes. Good night, Karen.'

He disconnected and she wanted to hurl her phone into the bushes, and hear it shatter. In fact, really she wanted to hurl it at Armitage's head and hear it shatter. She rang Matt and said she was on her way. He had answered within two seconds. What a difference in DIs, she thought. One obviously had much better hearing than the other.

* * *

Matt opened the door to her as she pulled onto his driveway. 'I've made hot chocolate. Drink it, then straight to bed.'

'"To sleep – perchance to dream..."'

'"Aye, there's the rub..." This Shakespeare malarkey has infected us all,' Matt said with a laugh. 'My mother has a lot to answer for; she lived and breathed Shakespeare. Come on, tell me a little of what's happened, then we're off to bed, because I don't doubt you'll be up in a couple of hours and heading off to the station.'

She slumped onto the kitchen chair, and sipped at the hot chocolate. 'This is delicious. Can I just drop my head onto the table and sleep?'

'Not while I've got a bed we can share.' He laughed. 'And that's nothing to do with Shakespeare.'

25

It was a gloomy, overcast Monday, and Diana and Liam Marshall had been placed in separate interview rooms, with both of them professing to have no idea why they were there. Diana had clearly been roused from her bed – no make-up, hair barely brushed, and a jogging suit that did nothing for her. However, they had found her still in residence, so Liam hadn't turfed her out. Yet.

It was almost ten o'clock before Ray and Karen entered Diana's room, and Karen quickly logged them in. Diana had refused a solicitor, saying why the hell should she need a solicitor when she'd done nothing illegal?

It soon transpired that neither of them had done anything illegal; they had been in A&E between nine in the evening and two in the morning, as she had accidentally slipped down the stairs and broken her ankle. She displayed her leg so that they could see the large boot affair that she had tried to conceal inside joggers. She confirmed that Liam had been with her for the whole time she was there, and had accompanied her for every step of the way at the hospital.

'How did you fall downstairs?'

'I just slipped.'

'Not pushed?'

'No, not pushed.' Diana dropped her head.

'If somebody had pushed you, we could help you, you know that, don't you?'

'Of course. I slipped.'

Karen sighed. If the price Diana had to pay for sleeping with Anthony Dawson was a broken ankle, then so be it. Liam Marshall would be sweating in the other room, wondering what his wife was saying, and if he would end up arrested at the end of it.

Karen took details of arrival and departure times from the hospital, and told her they would be checking up on everything. She was free to go.

'So what was this all about?' she asked.

Karen stopped as she was leaving. 'Oh, sorry, I forgot to mention. Anthony Dawson was murdered last night. We knew we had to rule you and your husband in or out as soon as possible. Go home, Diana, and rest that ankle.'

Diana's face drained of all colour. 'Anthony's dead?' she whispered. 'Murdered?'

'Yes. I'm going to talk to your husband now, and I'll make sure that he knows the next time you look as though you're about to slip on the stairs, we'll be coming for him. Take care, Diana, because we're about to tell him about Dawson as well, and he seems pretty volatile to me. Don't let him see that you're upset by the news; you really can't run with an ankle boot on.'

* * *

'What the fuck? Dawson's dead?' Liam's face hadn't drained of colour, it had changed into something resembling a beetroot. 'Is this why I'm here? You think I did it?'

'Why did you think you were here, Liam? Perhaps because your wife fell down the stairs? Can you tell me your movements last night from nine o'clock?'

'Well, as you know already about the broken ankle, you'll also know I was at the hospital with my wife, having it x-rayed and such. Five fucking hours we were there, that A&E was heaving with drunks and yobs. I don't know how those poor nurses cope, but I know I couldn't do it.'

'We have the details from your wife, so we'll be checking up on them at the hospital. We'll also be checking you're looking after her, make no mistake about that. You're free to go, Mr Marshall, for now, but we know where you live. Don't make us come and get you again.'

She walked out of the room, accompanied by a stern-faced Ray Ledger. It was clear that neither Liam nor Diana had had anything to do with Dawson's death in the physical sense, but he knew Karen wouldn't stop until she'd ruled them out of organising the killing by somebody else. Just because they had an alibi didn't mean they hadn't paid for the gunshot.

They both headed back to the briefing room, and Ray went to get them a coffee each – and with instructions to track down some half-decent sandwiches if he could.

She began to type up her report.

'Everything okay?'

She looked up to see Armitage in front of her. 'Subject to confirmation of alibis, everything's fine.'

'So what are you doing next?'

'Completing my reports for the action so far, then I'm heading out to Dawson's house. Forensics will have done all they need to do by now. I can meet you there.'

He waved a hand in dismissal of her suggestion. 'Can't, sorry. I'm off out with Superintendent Davis in about an hour.'

She nodded, and returned to typing her report, effectively dismissing him. As he left her desk, she muttered under her breath. 'Enjoy your game of golf, DI Armitage. Hope it pisses down with rain. Sir.'

* * *

Matt, Steve and Hermia had taken up residence in separate rooms at the office. Gloria had assured them that everything concerning the change in ownership would go through very quickly once probate had happened, and they could get on with making any changes necessary. Hermia was listening to the memory stick recording, this time taking notes of anything that was said. Professor Hartner had had a very gentle, probing kind of way of speaking, and it suddenly hit her just how much she missed him. They had spoken most days, not necessarily about work, and she had found him to be a knowledgeable, interesting man, with no family other than a cousin who lived somewhere in Derbyshire, and who he visited most weekends. She let his voice wash over her, and felt tears prickle her eyes. She had no doubt, in view of developments since his death, that he had been deliberately pushed under the tram, and she knew she wouldn't rest until they proved it.

She was at the point in the interviews where he was speaking to somebody called Cookie, a true Sheffielder by his accent. He initially tried to deny there were gangs, but then spoke of gang leaders who it didn't pay anyone to cross, and then he named a name, Derek Parker. She felt sure that it was the simple gentle nature of Eric that had drawn the name out of Cookie, and caused Cookie to immediately back off, saying he shouldn't have said anything, he'd be in bother if it ever got out he'd spoken of him.

Hartner's tone of voice never changed. He reassured the scared man, told him he wouldn't be mentioned by name and not to worry about it. And how big was the gang this Derek Parker controlled?

Cookie then said he had to go, he couldn't talk numbers, had nothing else to tell him, and for fuck's sake, don't reveal his name because everybody knew Cookie.

Hermia paused the recording and went to the kitchen area to make drinks. Steve seemed to be very quiet, but he was downstairs on his own, drawing up plans, taking measurements, and occasionally making the odd phone call to suppliers. Matt was in Johnny's room, continuing to work through the handwritten journal, still wondering why Anthony Dawson was written in red. What had his dad come across that had raised a red flag against the man, and why hadn't he asked if Matt knew anything about him? That would have been an obvious starting point.

He looked up and smiled as Hermia brought in a coffee and a couple of biscuits.

'Found anything?'

He shook his head. 'No, was just wondering why Dad didn't ask me if I had any dealings with Dawson. Whatever had raised Dad's hackles on this, it was more than Dawson screwing Marshall's wife. That wasn't even his case, it was Johnny's. Whatever he flagged him for, it was something much more serious.'

'I've reached the part on this interview recording where I reached before, but now I've made notes. If anything crops up with his name in the next section, I'll let you know.' She walked across to the lift shaft and called down to Steve. 'Coffee ready. You want it down there or up here?'

'I'll come up,' he called back. 'I want to see if Matt likes what I've done so far.'

'I do,' Matt called out. 'Just do it.'

The lift whirred into motion and Steve joined them in Dave's lounge. He carried a large rolled-up piece of paper, which he promptly spread out on the coffee table. 'It's amazing what you can do with left over wallpaper,' he said, anchoring the four corners down with jar candles.

The drawing divided the downstairs area into a small reception point, and two large offices. All measurements had been recorded, and there were some pricing annotations on the reverse of the paper.

'We need a reception?' Matt asked.

'Maybe not initially, but if we want this business to grow, we can hardly be chatting to a client, then have to go and deal with somebody who's walked in off the street asking for advice on not paying parking tickets. And once we've done this construction, it's constructed. We can't be changing things because we've suddenly realised we need somebody to manage us, because we will.'

Matt leaned back on the sofa, feeling overwhelmed. What had his dad left him? And, of course, Steve was right. They couldn't do this on their own, and the time was coming when they would have to approach the stand-by employees Dave had used for surveillance jobs and other such tedious work, and tell them of the changes, get them to commit to the new owners in the way they had committed to his dad.

'This is brilliant,' he said, pulling the plan towards him. 'And you'd make a good landscape gardener if ever you thought you might try that next.'

Steve grinned. 'Piss off, mate, just piss off.'

* * *

Hermia found it a little difficult washing the cups with only one hand, but she managed, leaving them to dry on the drainer. She wasn't going to risk drying them as well. She returned to the recordings, with both men having disappeared downstairs to pace out the measurements and see if they needed to change anything before getting quotes for the items they would need.

She put on her headphones, laid her head back and got her arm into as comfortable a position as she could, resting it on a cushion. Her leg was almost back to normal, although bruised and scratched, but the arm was another matter altogether, and combined with the weight of the cast, she felt discomfort most of the time.

Then she started to listen. She was three interviews in when she heard it.

'Brothers come in very handy, don't they?'

26

She listened twice more to the voice, but more importantly, to the words. It was him, the so-called Vincent Walker, and yet Eric Hartner had said he went by the street name of Quinnie.

She immediately checked back through all the earlier notes and found him. Someone called Dickie Bird – why the hell did all street names seemingly end in ie, she wondered for a brief moment – had accepted a coffee from Hartner and had spoken about the various characters he knew, and some he only knew of, but included in the ones he knew was Quinnie. 'Top bloke,' he had said. 'Looks after me. And I help him if he needs me.'

Alongside her notes on Dickie Bird, she had written the comment, 'Well spoken, sounds quite young.'

She did briefly wonder why they had spoken to the professor, all these underworld people. Flattering of egos, maybe? Or maybe, like her, they had simply liked him. But somebody hadn't liked him. Somebody realised they had said too much, and had assumed his notes would be in the vanishing briefcase, but they hadn't been, they had been locked away at the university. And now they were with her, and she had a bloody broken arm to prove they still wanted the notes.

One of the people he had interviewed was prepared to kill to get them. And yet she had heard nothing incriminating, nobody had spoken out of turn, it was more a confirmation of the existence of the problem in Sheffield of a growing gangland culture.

She started a second list of people that needed further investigation, and headed it with Dickie Bird and Quinnie, AKA Walter Vickers, AKA Vincent Walker. Hermia continued to listen to the words of Quinnie, and she knew it was him, the man who had thrown her over her balcony. 'My god,' she said softly, 'you were really pissed off with me, weren't you? You tried to kill me just because; you didn't need to do it, you could see I hadn't got these notes in my flat.'

'You talking to me, sis?' Matt called from the other room.

'Nope, talking to myself. I think I may have found the beginnings of something for us, or at least for Karen to get her teeth into.'

Matt appeared in the doorway. 'Tell me,' he said, and sat down beside her.

* * *

The range of sex toys in Anthony Dawson's sumptuous bedroom would give her something to dine out on for years, Karen thought, with a grin etched onto her face. The man certainly knew what to buy to treat his ladies. The room itself was mainly black and red satin with discreet lighting helping with the romantic ambience. Such a pity he appeared to have been a complete plonker.

She took a last glance around the room before closing the door behind her, thankful she would never have to go in it again. She wondered how an estate agent would market this particular property, and how any prospective clients would view it.

The office had been thoroughly checked by the forensics team, and they had removed all tech equipment for forensic examination back at the labs. She knew eventually she would get the report, so just popped briefly into the room.

It was normal. She did a 360-degree turn in the middle, and it was normal! The walls were cream, the desk was possibly antique but gave a feeling of completeness to the room. The leather desk chair showed signs of wear, and fitted in perfectly. The room exuded wealth and class, completely at odds with the Anthony Dawson she knew from earlier encounters in various interview rooms. She opened the filing cabinets but there was very little in them. She guessed it would all have been removed for a detailed examination, and she slid the four drawers back in.

She stood in the doorway and looked around the room. If there was anything to be had from this office, it would already be in the relevant department of the forensics unit.

She briefly looked through the two remaining bedrooms, both obviously normal, both guest rooms. Sex was only for the master bedroom, it seemed.

The bathroom revealed medication in the wall-mounted cabinet – paracetamol, Omeprazole, Simvastatin, Metformin and Viagra – and she smiled. So Anthony Dawson hadn't been particularly healthy, but obviously the multitude of high-end sex toys needed a medical aid as well, to get him through the night.

Alongside the electric toothbrush, there was a pink one, possibly with DNA on it from Diana Marshall. There was nothing else to show that she had been a frequent visitor to the house. The whole bathroom was very masculine; black and white tiles in an eye-catching design, a large square-head power shower, expensive toiletries and grey towels. Anthony Dawson clearly hadn't met a woman he wanted to spend the rest of his life with.

Karen moved downstairs, carefully avoiding the bloodstains on the hall carpet, and went through to the kitchen. Again, it felt very masculine. Nothing was out of place except for the pizza that had been delivered, which was still in its box, the lid covered in blood from where young Richard Hogan had dropped it, probably overwhelmed by fear.

Thinking of the young lad who had tried to show he wasn't scared but had given away his fear with the tremble in his hands, she realised she had promised to ring him, to arrange for him to visit the station to complete a statement.

She hoped he'd managed to get a good night's sleep, but she doubted it. And she hoped the mother who had waited up for him would help to console him, soothe his frazzled nerves. So much blood, so much blood. She had an odd moment when she felt something was slightly off-kilter in the kitchen, but shrugged and dismissed the thought. A kitchen with blood stains that had spread from the hall, the shooting point, was probably the off-kilter bit.

The lounge was neat, but without flowers or other things that would indicate a woman's touch around the place. The cushions were tidy, perfectly matched the shade of the wallpaper on the feature wall, and with a navy suite that was the perfect colour for the rest of the room.

He obviously had a cleaner who did the job properly, who took pride in her work, because the whole house was slightly fragranced with furniture polish, and it was dust free. Karen thought of her own home that had a quick flick with a duster every other week; work life came before housework.

She looked into every cupboard, every drawer, in the beautiful units Dawson had bought for the lounge, but found nothing. No address books, note pads, nothing to indicate he needed to keep a check on his life. Maybe she would find out more once his phone had been investigated.

She tried again in the dining room, but still found nothing to help with any sort of follow-through on his life. It did make her feel that he was a lonely man, but thieves and rogues who reached the top of their tree tended to be forced into loneliness.

And Dawson was a man at the peak of his... even in her thoughts, she hesitated to use the word career. At the peak of his lifestyle choices.

And that really only left her with the downstairs toilet and cloakroom, and the hall. Sterile, both places, although the hallway carpet was somewhat discoloured by an ugly blood-stain. It briefly flashed across her mind that this super-efficient cleaner would have a hell of a job getting out the discolouration.

Karen did a second walk round, unable to accept that there was nothing out of the ordinary in this sterile house. She recorded her thoughts into her mobile phone as she did a quick video for each room, then finally locked the door behind her before heading back to her car.

She sent a text to Ray Ledger saying she would be back in an hour, and could he check on the post-mortem status, then drove to Gleadless to see if Matt was there.

* * *

Karen found Steve busy working on the plans, and just ending a phone call when she walked through the door. 'You should keep this locked,' she said. 'Aren't you the team who have been attacked?'

He grinned at her. 'One of us is, and she's working upstairs, so presumably I am the one who will repel all boarders. Matt is up there as well; they're listening to some recordings that Hartner made.'

'Really?' She moved to get in the elevator. 'I'm not here for long, got to take a statement from the young lad who found Dawson last night, and he was pretty shook up, so I need a gentle calm head on when I talk to him. You need a drink sending down or anything?'

Steve waved a can of Coke and a Mars bar at her. 'No, I'm good, thanks.'

The elevator moved, and she joined Matt and Hermia in a very short space of time, although neither of them noticed it was her and not Steve; they were deeply engrossed in listening to the recordings.

'Hi.'

Matt jumped up and swiftly crossed the room, kissing her on the cheek. 'You okay?'

She nodded. 'Just been in the sterile environment that Anthony Dawson called home. Sterile everywhere except his bedroom. Now that was a work of art, and I dread to think what's gone off in there over the years.'

'Diana Marshall appreciated it.' Matt laughed. 'Is it that bad?'

'Makes the Sexy Superstore look like amateurs,' Karen confirmed. 'So what are you two enjoying?'

'Another link to the bastard who threw Herms over the balcony. It seems the professor interviewed him for this report he was collating. And it's not so much his accent that stands out, because that's pretty bland, it's what he says. Listen.'

Hermia took the recording back to the few words she had recognised and played them.

'He said that to you?'

Hermia nodded. 'He did. It was part of a conversation about him watering his sister's plants while she was away, and keeping an eye on her flat. In reality, he had killed her. And she wasn't even his sister! Just a clever ruse to get into my flat, and keep an eye on my comings and goings. Luckily, every time I popped in to remove further things, either Steve or Matt was with me. The first time they weren't was when he tried to kill me.'

'So what name is he going by on the recording?'

'Quinnie appears to be his street name, and the first time we hear of it is from somebody called Dickie Bird. He seems to think Quinnie is a good bloke.'

'A man of many names then,' Karen said thoughtfully. 'I wonder what his real name is underneath all these twists and turns.'

'I don't doubt we can find out if we can ever get his fingerprints,' Matt said. 'You think he had any connection to Dawson's murder?'

'If he did, he left no sign of it. That pizza delivery driver said he saw a motorbike leaving the end of the road as he turned onto it, but that's all we have unless something shows up at the autopsy. And I don't think it can have, because Ray would have contacted me by now.'

Matt stared through the window, deep in thought. 'Whoever he is, he's kept well under our radar. Or he's new to Sheffield. Put his name in HOLMES when you get back, and see if it throws anything up.'

She smiled at him, blew him a kiss, and said, 'Yes, boss.'

27

Karen returned to an almost empty office. She made herself a coffee, and was sitting down at her desk when Ray Ledger came through the door.

He glanced around then walked over to her. 'Everything okay, boss?'

'As okay as it can be without Matt here, and with...' She let the words trail away, recognising it wouldn't look good if she said what she really thought about Armitage.

Ray laughed. 'Not another word. I can guess what you so very nearly said.'

'So you'll not dob me in?'

'Nope. You'd only tell them I agreed with you.'

'You manage to get in touch with that young lad? Richard...' She hesitated, clearly allowing her brain cells to work. 'Hogan!'

'Tried twice this morning, but it went straight through to voicemail. I figured maybe he didn't sleep too well last night after coming across that scene, so I'd leave it till this afternoon. Was just heading back to my desk to try again.'

'Tell you what, grab a coffee, take ten minutes, and we'll go and talk to him. It's only a statement we need. He saw a motorbike that may or may not be connected because it was coming out of the road end, not Dawson's drive, and he pushed open the already open door to call Dawson's name and saw he was dead. He'll not even have to appear as a witness, they'll just read his statement out, so there's no big deal out of seeing him. We can have a talk with him, make sure he's okay, then take his statement. Another job crossed off the list. What's of bigger importance is somebody who could have a street name of Quinnie, but who also goes by Vincent Walker, and Walter Vickers. Bit of a mix and match with his Ws and his Vs, methinks. But Hermia has listened to his voice on a recording Professor Hartner made and she's 100 per cent certain it's the bloke who threw her over that balcony. You heard of a Quinnie?'

Ray shook his head, pouring out his coffee. 'No, can't say I have. There's a Queenie who runs some street girls, but she's a woman and far too fat to chuck anybody over a matchstick, let alone a balcony. When we get back from taking this statement, I'll start a new file and see what I can find.'

He walked back to her desk and pulled up a chair. 'Want a Mars bar?'

'I'd kill for a Mars bar.'

'No, don't do that.' He walked over to his desk and unlocked his top drawer, then relocked it after removing two chocolate bars.

'You keep it locked?'

'Have to. Some proper thieves and rogues work here, never mind sending them out to look for others for us to prosecute.'

They sat happily eating chocolate and finishing their coffee, then stood and made their way down to the car park.

Karen put the address given by the upset Richard into her satnav, and within fifteen minutes, they pulled up outside a large house that had been converted into small flats. Ray heard Karen mutter, 'Strange.'

'What is?'

'He said he lived with his mum, and she was waiting up for him. I kind of imagined he lived in a house of some description if he still lived at home, not in a block of what I presume are student flats in this area. We're very near to the university.'

They locked the car and walked up the flight of steps leading to the large front door.

'Did you say 28a?' Ray asked.

'I did.'

He rang the bell, and waited. After about thirty seconds, a female voice said 'Hello?'

'Hiya, DS Karen Nelson and PC Ray Ledger. We're here to speak with Richard Hogan. He's expecting us.'

'Who?'

'DS Karen...'

'No, I mean who do you want?'

'Richard Hogan.'

'Never heard of him, and I'm sure he doesn't live in any of the other flats. Sorry, can't help.'

'Can you open the door, please? We'd just like two minutes of your time.'

There was a buzz, followed by a click, and they walked in. Flat 28a was on the ground floor, and the door opened as they approached it.

They showed their warrant cards, and the girl held her flat door wider. 'Come in if you want, but I don't really think I can help.'

They followed her through to the tiny open-plan lounge/kitchen area, and she moved some papers from the sofa and dumped them on the coffee table.

'Revision and research,' she said. 'Exams looming and I've just realised I've a lot to revise before I even buy a new pen. Sara Reuben, by the way, in case you need my name. What's he done, this feller you're after?'

'You're sure you don't know him?'

'Don't recognise the name. You have a picture?'

Karen shook her head. 'No, the first and last time I saw him was around eleven last night. He's a pizza delivery driver, drives a silver Ford Focus. Very well spoken, nice looking, bit young in his features really.'

Sara screwed up her face as she tried to visualise from Karen's slightly unhelpful description, but shrugged. 'No, I can't bring him to mind. Maybe if you ever get a picture, come and show it to me. He gave my address?'

'He did, but something tells me it was an address picked at random, not one he knew, because he actually said he lived at home with his mum, and she was waiting up for him. He also said he couldn't remember the postcode, he couldn't think properly but he'd find out what it was for when he came to the station to give the statement. We thought this meant it was a house, not student bedsits.'

'Can I offer you a drink?'

'No, we're good, thanks, Sara. We'll leave you to your studies. Good luck with the exams. I'll leave you with my card, just in case anything comes to mind and you realise you do know him, just not from this environment. He could work at the Student Union for example, could be anything at all. Just keep an open mind. Thank you for your time – we'll see ourselves out.'

* * *

'Nice lass,' Ray said. 'But it was obvious she didn't know him; she wasn't just flannelling. Now we've got a bit of a conundrum, haven't we?'

'Certainly have. It changes my thoughts completely. I knew there was something slightly wrong about the kitchen when I went to see it, but I put it down to lack of sleep. It was the pizza. It didn't fit the box; it was much too small. And it was burnt around the edges. Like the sort you get from a supermarket and cook in your own oven. Never turns out quite the same as from a pizza shop. That lad was no delivery driver. Yes, he was very scared, very out of sorts, but I think he was exactly what he portrayed himself to be. A young lad who was into something way over his head. We just need to find out why, and you can bet it will lead us to the who.'

'Couldn't agree more. It's looking more and more as if this Richard Hogan, or whatever his real name is, went there to kill Dawson. But how did he know Dawson had ordered a pizza?'

Ray frowned. 'Did he say who he was delivering for?'

'No. He was so dithery and shaky, I didn't think I'd get much out of him anyway. I, in what I thought was my wisdom and turned out to be my stupidity, thought he'd have calmed down by today and he would be able to give a coherent statement. He stayed there to misdirect us with the motorbike, I reckon. And if we found his fingerprints where they shouldn't be, he had a good reason – he had delivered the pizza. I just don't know how Richard Hogan knew Dawson had ordered a pizza. And what happened to the real pizza he had ordered? Has Dawson's mobile been checked yet? I'd like to know the name of the pizza shop he rang, to place his order, then at least we can start to track down this Hogan feller and work out what the hell is going on.'

* * *

And it was spelled out basically in words of one syllable. Dawson hadn't rung for a pizza, but he had received a phone call an hour before he died from a withheld number. 'Just supposing,' Ray said, his brain cells running at around fifty miles an hour inside his head, 'just supposing somebody rang and said they were whatever his normal pizza shop is, and they were having a special promotion for their regular customers of pizzas for half price for one night only. You'd fall for it, wouldn't you? If Hogan was a regular at the pizza shop, he'd know the staff's names, and he could have used any of them to make it even more authentic. Hello, Mr Dawson, it's Antonio from Pizza Milano, and I'm contacting our regular customers to show them how much we value them. Pizzas, any size, are on at half price, but it's only for tonight. Will you be wanting one, Mr Dawson?'

Karen sighed. 'Unfortunately, I think you're probably right. It would be so easy to do, and he did receive that phone call, he did get a pizza, and he didn't ring for one. And he was approaching the front door, wallet in hand, fully expecting to pay money out at the door. To a pizza delivery driver. Instead, he got Richard Hogan with a gun in his hand. And a silenced gun at that, because nobody seems to have heard any of the shots that took out the cameras, or the killer shot that took out Dawson. This Hogan is no novice with a gun, I'll wager. Let's get one of the uniforms visiting every rifle range in Sheffield. I'll sit with the police artist – is this new one really called Van Gogh by all and sundry? – and describe the lad as I remember him. I was with him for the longest time, I think.'

Ray laughed. 'They all call him that because he's so good at his job. Let's just be thankful they've not had to call him Picasso.'

'We can do multiple copies of whatever he can produce for me in half an hour, and get the uniform to see if he or she can get a result on it. He has to be a good shot, to take cameras out with one attempt.' She picked up her phone, spoke briefly with who Ray assumed was Van Gogh, and replaced the receiver. 'He can give me an hour now, he says, but when I get there, I'll tell him I need it quicker than that.'

'Okay, don't hassle him, he usually has a couple of days to do an expert job, and you're giving him half an hour.'

'I need this putting to bed. This young lad has really pissed me off, and my prime focus should be on who killed Dave and Johnny, not some jumped-up little squirt who's taken out one of the big bad boys of the Sheffield underworld. And on top of everything else, we need him off the streets before some of Dawson's minions work out who did it. His life won't be worth tuppence then, and I'll have another killing to investigate. And I need to see the connection between Dave Forrester's murder and this one – it's there somewhere, I just can't see it yet.'

'You're sure we've read this right?'

Karen nodded, her face grim. 'Oh, I'm sure, all right. Let's get him locked up for his own safety, and he'll start to confirm everything we believe happened. And once he's in Strangeways for life, it's out of our hands what happens to him.'

'You're all heart, boss, all heart.'

28

Ray was just packing up to go home as Karen returned to the office. 'Been a long Monday,' he said. 'I'm heading home so the wife doesn't forget who I am, then going out later to talk to folks.'

'What folks? You need back-up?'

'Nah, just folks who'll be in the city centre pubs, and who I know will talk to me. I'll ask questions without them knowing they're being questioned, don't worry. You got the picture?'

She held out Van Gogh's impressive portrait of how Karen remembered Richard Hogan looking, and Ray looked at it. He whistled. 'Christ, this is good.'

'It's as close to reality as we're going to get. I'm going to print off a few copies, so don't go out tonight without one. I know we're concentrating on the Forrester case for you tonight, because you've moved on to Quinnie, but just maybe somebody will recognise this face and solve everything in one swoop.'

'Love your optimism, boss.' He took the picture to the photo-copier and ran off twenty copies. 'We too late to get it on *Calendar* tonight?'

'We are, but I've booked a tentative slot for tomorrow night, in case we still haven't found him.'

'You going home now?'

'I am once I've got these copies to Ian Jameson. He volunteered his services in an odd sort of way.'

'You bullied him?'

'Not at all. I asked him if he could do it, and he said no, he was taking Jaime to the cinema. I didn't even know those two were an item... anyway, I said the film would be on tomorrow night as well, so he agreed the two of them would go visit rifle ranges instead of Cinecentre.'

'And what did the lovely Jaime say to that?'

'She doesn't know yet. I scarpered and left the explanation to him.'

* * *

It was at the sixth range, with only one left on their list actually listed as a Sheffield range, that they struck lucky. They were seriously beginning to think that the following night was going to be taken up by visiting ranges in Chesterfield and Barnsley when the man's eyes lit up. They showed their warrant cards, then the picture. The man on reception duty glanced at it, then looked more closely.

'I do know him, yes. Comes here with his dad, but the lad is a far better shot. More accurate, stands perfectly. Don't tell me he's in trouble...'

'No, not at all. He was a witness to something, and we need to contact him for a bit more information, that's all. His name?'

'Simon Marshall. His dad is Liam Marshall.'

'Address?'

There was a hesitation. 'You want his home address? The

address that is on their gun licences? Only... with data protection laws being what they are...'

Jaime moved to the counter. 'Give us the address, sir.' She smiled sweetly. 'You don't really want us to come back tomorrow with a warrant to force you to produce the address, but also all addresses on your books, do you?'

He looked at her, and she smiled once more. His fingers ran smoothly across his keyboard and he sent a document to print. Silently he walked over to the printer to retrieve it, and then just as silently carried it back to the reception desk.

Jaime looked at it, tucked it into her bag, and said, 'Thank you. I'm sure we won't need to trouble you again. Unless, of course, it turns out to be inaccurate. That might be frowned upon by the licensing authorities.'

Ian kept his face straight until they were back in his car, then collapsed into laughter. 'He was scared of you!'

'Quite right too, I'm a scary person.'

'Jaime, you're the least scary person I know. A proper pushover. Think we should notify the boss right now, or wait until the morning?'

Jaime glanced at the dashboard clock. 'I think she'll want to know now, especially in view of who it is. I know it's nine o'clock, but it seems a copper's never off duty.'

* * *

Karen was on the sofa with Matt's arms around her, munching popcorn, when her phone rang. She said, 'Hi, Jaime,' then listened to what the young PC had to say. 'He's sure?' She listened again, then thanked Jaime, promising her she could go to the cinema the following day.

She turned to Matt. 'Okay, guess who our young man is.'

He thought for a moment. 'Okay, and this is only a guess because it feels logical, but I think it's somebody connected to the Marshall family, or business.'

'Smart arse,' Karen said. 'According to the chap at the rifle range, Liam and his son Simon use the range a couple of times a week, and Simon is an expert shooter. He's identified the drawing as Simon Marshall, the son.'

'Well, he may be an expert shooter, but he's not very bright. You've tracked him down within a day and even worked out how he did it. However, can you please bear in mind he'll have guns at home, so weigh up the pros and cons of having armed protection when you go to arrest him.'

'Well, actually, it was Ray that did most of the working things out, getting into the killer's mindset, that sort of thing. He might like the privilege of the arrest, and I'll certainly have him in interview with me.'

Matt laughed. 'He's also very good at arresting people. Very quiet, cool, calm and collected as they say.'

'He's out in the city centre tonight meeting contacts. He's trying to find something out about the mysterious Quinnie. You any closer to finding anything about Dawson? Why your dad thought he needed to be highlighted?'

'Nothing at all.' He reached across and grabbed a handful of popcorn, scattering it across Karen as he pulled back his arm.

She picked out the popcorn from her cleavage. 'Could it have been something simple like he thought Dawson might be in danger? He was investigating him with the Diana Marshall affair, and now it seems possible, if not probable, that it's their son who has killed him. Had your dad realised there was danger, and that was why it was in red? Had he warned Dawson? Or had he got somebody else lined up to warn him as he was being paid by

Marshall? It's quite possible we'll never know the truth of what your dad was thinking.'

'I know. I've always been more concerned with the bastard who tried to kill Herms. Something's niggling away at me... I don't think Dawson has any connection to Dad's murder. As a DI, I would have done exactly what you've done and worked everything, to see if there was a connection, but as a private citizen, soon to be a private eye, I can bring a little more of the what if into it. So, what if this Quinnie teamed up with Dickie Bird to pay a visit to Dad and Johnny, and it got out of hand? They took nothing, because what they wanted was Hermia. It would have made more sense for them to get Dad to contact Herms, tell her the situation, and she'd have been over there with all the files they wanted. Except, of course, Dad would never in a million years have put her into that danger. It gets more complicated the more I think about it. Could this Quinnie bloke have thought somebody had said too much about him? Hermia's still working through the interview recordings, so maybe there will be more, but what we've got so far is really only identification that Quinnie is the bloke who's hell bent on killing my family. Let's hope Ray gets some help from his acquaintances. Might cost him a bob or two, but there's always somebody happy to talk for the price of drugs. Has he taken somebody with him?'

'I asked him to, but he said he works better on his own. He'd be too busy worrying about somebody else, if he went what he called "mob-handed". He'll just mingle and chat, he said.'

Matt gave a slight nod. 'He has quite a few informants that he's gathered into the fold over the years.'

The door opened and Hermia entered, followed by Steve bearing a tray with tea and biscuits. 'Late-night snack,' she said. 'Then Steve's going to help me have a shower so that I don't get the cast wet.'

He placed the tray on the coffee table, then smiled. 'I get all the rubbish jobs. Fancy having to help the most beautiful girl I've ever seen have a shower. What is this world coming to!'

* * *

The music was loud, the chatter of the customers almost drowned out by it. Ray walked towards the bar, his eyes roaming to see who was in the room. He'd already seen a couple of his informants in other bars, but they'd nothing to tell him. He was starting to worry that it might all be a waste of time. He'd lost count of the number of times over the years he'd done this kind of covert work, but it had usually paid off.

He reached the bar with some difficulty and ordered a pint of lemonade. It could potentially be a long night, so drinking alcohol might not be a smart move. He paid for the drink and then moved towards the end of the bar where he could lean against it and not be in the way of paying customers.

He spotted one of his narks he only knew as Threesome, and gave a slight raise of his glass in acknowledgement that they had seen each other. He'd never felt inclined to ask why Threesome had such a name, not really wanting to hear the answer.

It took Threesome almost fifteen minutes to reach him, moving a few feet at a time.

'Pint, Threesome?' Ray finally asked, when the man was by his side.

'That'll do nicely, Mr Ledger. Not seen you for a while. You good?'

'Very good, could do with a chat. Let's stand here and act like we don't really know each other. Yes?'

'No problem, Mr Ledger.'

'It might look better to a casual observer if you called me Ray and not Mr Ledger.'

'Okay, Mr Ledger.'

Ray signalled down the bar to the barman, and he produced a pint of lager. Threesome swallowed half of it, then smacked his lips. 'What do you want to know, Mr Ledger?'

'Ray. The name's Ray.'

'Oh, yeah.'

'You know someone with the street name Quinnie?'

Threesome didn't answer immediately. In fact, he appeared to freeze, and Ray felt slightly panicked that the use of the name could cause so much fear in a man known for being quite handy with his fists.

'Threesome? You okay?'

The man relaxed a little, and nodded. 'Yeah, it's just... it's best not to tangle with him. He's been here about a year, but he makes the others look like amateurs. I keep well clear. I heard...' and he paused, unsure whether to continue or not.

'You heard? Is what you heard worth twenty?'

Still Threesome hesitated. Ray waited.

'I liked Dave Forrester and Johnny Keane,' he said slowly. 'I met up with Birdie a couple of nights ago in the Plover, and he was well-cut when I met him. Big mouth. Bit of bragging about you lot not knowing who'd done Forrester and Keane, and saying as how the wheelchair had tipped over and he'd cracked his head on the floor. Sickening. Fuckin' sickening to listen to him. And then he was going on about Quinnie taking care of him, that he'd see to them not getting caught.'

Ray took out his wallet and palmed two twenty-pound notes. He said goodnight to Threesome, asked him to keep in touch if he heard any other news, and they shook hands. Ray Ledger's hand was empty after the handshake.

29

Ray walked down to the multi-storey car park that served Theatreland, and fished around in his pocket for the parking ticket. He paid the extortionate parking charges with a grimace, and popped his credit card back in his wallet after retrieving his parking ticket from the slot. He was looking at it as he reached his car, unaware of the man following him.

His mind was on Threesome's words that Dickie Bird and Quinnie had been the ones who had attacked Dave and Johnny, and although he could report that to Karen and Matt, they would never get Threesome in a court to confirm the words that Dickie Bird had used. It was more than his life was worth, and his use as an informant would be compromised for ever. He reached into his pocket for his keys, and was suddenly aware of movement behind him. He half spun around, a movement that probably saved his life, as the cosh landed awkwardly on his head, knocking him out before he even hit the floor.

A car pulled up behind Ray's car, and his assailant jumped into the passenger seat. With a screech of tyres, it vanished down the ramp, and disappeared into the night.

* * *

Matt and Karen reached the hospital just before eleven, to find Ray was under sedation. Angela, his wife, was already in the visitor's room, and they joined her; Matt disappeared to get coffees for them all, leaving Karen to take the older woman into her arms to offer what comfort she could. Angela explained that two people returning from a night at the Crucible had returned to their car parked next to Ray's car, and had immediately phoned for help.

Matt felt sick. He'd known Ray Ledger for a number of years, had tried many times to persuade him to move on within the police to higher rankings, but Ray had been adamant that he had joined to be a police constable, and he was happy at that level, happy to work in whatever area was required of him, had built up a regular network of informants – and now he had paid the price. He had been seen talking to somebody, and until he came out of the coma he was currently in, they didn't know who had been chatting to him. Which meant not only Ray was in danger, so was his informant.

They stayed for some time, then after saying goodnight to the PC on protection duty, they left the hospital, with both Karen and Angela feeling a little more optimistic that all would be good, after a long discussion with the doctor. Matt stood to one side, listening, but couldn't help feeling he'd been here before with Johnny.

* * *

Karen and Matt headed back to his home, talking about the imminent return of Finn. Karen knew she had decisions to make, decisions that didn't depend on any actions of Matt's. Irrespective of how she felt about her ex-boss, she had zero feelings for her husband. She needed to move out, to get away from what had become a home with an atmosphere. Not toxic, she knew Finn wasn't a violent man, but a saddening, loveless atmosphere, nevertheless. It was time to move out, to take stock of her life and become her own person instead of Karen Nelson, Finn Nelson's wife.

They managed a meagre three hours of sleep before Karen's alarm woke them, and while she showered, Matt went downstairs to make coffee. He pressed the toaster as he heard her coming downstairs, and she appreciated the fact that he was making her breakfast. Early morning breakfasts would always be the rule, whether it was copper or ex-copper.

'I could get used to this.' She smiled at him.

'Good. That's the plan.' He returned the smile.

Matt needed thinking time, quiet time, and he wanted to go through everything he could find – his dad's desk, his filing cabinet, if necessary every damn book on his bookshelves, just in case he'd carved up another book to store something inside. He watched Karen drive away, then picked up his jacket, checked he had his car keys, and let himself quietly out of the house. It was only six o'clock and he didn't want to wake Steve and Hermia, who seemed to have taken to sleeping together on the bed settee remarkably well. He grinned as he thought of all the years he had spent trying to get Hermia to see what she could have in Steve, and it took throwing her off a balcony to make her wake up and see the world in a different light. See Steve in a different light.

It was still not fully dawn when he reached Gleadless, and he entered the office, calling for the lights and heating to come on. He left the blinds closed – he didn't want any clients calling – and he was glad Hermia had suggested putting a note on the door saying

'Temporarily closed due to bereavement'. He listened to the answer machine; there were many messages of condolence, and requests to be kept informed if the business would be continuing, so Matt added the names and numbers to his growing list of people to contact. If the business was to pay for him and Steve, they needed to keep as many of Dave's clients as they could.

It was only as he got to the last message that he felt sick. He recognised the voice from Hartner's recordings.

'Listen to this, Forrester. Your mate spoke to Threesome last night, and this is what happens to narks.'

There was a horrific scream and the voice cut in once more.

'That was his second eye going.'

He could hear moans, and then a further scream that made him want to be sick.

'Both kneecaps. He'll never walk again. Never grass to a copper again either, 'cos his tongue's coming out as well.'

There was a moment of silence, then the voice came back.

'That's finished him off. He's gone. They can have a pint together in heaven now, can't they, Ledger and Threesome. Don't fuck with me, Forrester.'

The recording stopped and Matt sat on the worn leather desk chair at his father's desk with a thud.

* * *

Karen listened to Matt's voice, hearing the anguish in it.

'Okay, I'm doubling up security on Ray, because this Quinnie bloke obviously thinks he's dead either by his hand or somebody he ordered to do it, and I don't want him finding out he's still alive and coming for him. That's the first thing. Secondly, I'm heading over to your office to download that message. I've sent Kevin Potter and Phil Newton to bring Simon Marshall in; they're heading back now with him, but they'll book him in. I want to be interviewing him by about half past nine, give him time to get proper wound up by the time I walk through the door. I'll cover myself by leaving a message for Davis and Armitage to tell them what I'm doing, but I'm not bothered what they think.'

'You don't need to be bothered,' said Matt. 'You can tell what you're dealing with here by just listening to them killing Threesome. Let them hear the recording. I don't think this is a put-up job to fool us, Karen; this is genuine torture.'

'I'll be there as soon as I can, certainly within the next hour. I need to arrange extra protection for Ray before I do anything.'

He finished speaking with Karen, and headed upstairs to begin the search of the books, starting where he had left off with Shakespeare. He was looking for anything at all – he didn't really think his dad would have hollowed out a second book, but he did think he might have hidden something that would explain what he had against Anthony Dawson that would cause his name to be written in red. And he also felt deep inside that Dave had been on the verge of talking about what was bothering him about Anthony Dawson. Could Dawson have approached his dad for help? Was this the reason for the red pen? One person involved in two cases? One case to be recorded in red to keep it separate from the other case, which would be recorded as usual, in black.

He stopped the search for a moment when he received the text from Karen to say she had arrived, and he went down in the lift to let her in. He held her in his arms for a moment then moved behind her to take out the mail from the wire basket hanging on the back of the door. 'I suppose all of this is my responsibility now,' he said, waving it around. 'If it's bills, I'm not sure that's something I want to know about.'

Karen laughed. 'Oh, I think he'll have left you enough to cover them. Are we listening to this recording first?'

'We are. You sit in Dad's chair.'

She did, and wriggled her bum as she sat. 'Wow, this is comfortable.'

'Yep. I apparently inherited that as well.' He reached across the desk and looked at her. 'Are you ready? Prepare yourself; this isn't good to hear.'

Karen gave a slight nod, and he pressed the play button of the somewhat old-fashioned answering machine.

She listened, unmoving. Her face had lost all of its colour by the end, and she looked up at Matt. 'I need to record this and get it back into work. Somewhere, there is a dead body that can potentially lead us to this Quinnie, because you can tell it's him, and he'll have left some sort of DNA evidence on it. Unless he's been smart and chucked it in a river somewhere. And there's another voice in the background, not as loud as Quinnie's voice so must be further away from the mobile phone. There were definitely two of them. And it makes it worse just hearing it as an audio message, and not seeing the video. He doesn't want anyone knowing what he looks like, does he? I think I feel sick...'

Matt ran into the kitchen and grabbed a glass of water for her. 'Drink it slowly,' he said, 'and try to put it to the back of your mind for a bit.'

Slowly her skin became less grey, and she stood. 'Would your dad have an Apple charger somewhere so I can download this directly from the machine?'

He opened the top drawer of the desk, handed her a bright pink cable and grinned. 'I'm guessing his old one broke, and Hermia supplied him with this one.'

She plugged in the cable, downloaded the message, and disconnected the machine. 'I'll have to take this and get it locked away securely, so you might want to get a new one. We don't want this one going astray; it's as good as a written confession, is this.'

'So you felt it was genuine as well?'

'Without a doubt. You can't scream like that without horrific pain being inflicted, and having eyes removed and kneecaps smashed is about as bad as it gets.'

'I feel at a bit of a loss with all of this. I don't have access to any of the police stuff...'

'No, but I do. You come up with anything at all, Matt, and I can use all of everything back at the station. It will only be for this one case, your dad's murder, because in future you maybe won't be dealing with such criminal stuff, but this one's special, and I'll do all I can to help. The only thing is your name is not to be mentioned. Davis made that very clear.'

He pulled Johnny's chair over to the side of his dad's chair, and put a hand on the post. 'I'll open this down here, then move back upstairs to continue going through the books.'

The first was a letter of thanks from a client, and the second was a photocopy of a decree absolute, so Matt guessed that was two satisfied customers. The next was a brown padded envelope, and he hesitated. It had no stamp on, and was addressed to him.

Karen took it from him. 'I outrank you. Let me do this.'

'No.' He took it back. 'I don't think you should. Maybe if you hadn't just listened to that recording...' He picked up his dad's letter opener, and slit along the sealed flap. He tipped it up, and out fell a small sealed IKEA bag.

Inside was a tongue.

30

They found the body dumped in an industrial wheelie bin near the Wicker Arches. The unfortunate cleaner at the offices belonging to a small company specialising in making pen knives went to empty the firm's rubbish in the bin. She saw the face first, and her screams drew one of the bosses outside, fearing something awful had happened to her. It had.

Karen had a small note delivered to her within seconds of recording who was in the interview room with Simon Marshall, who was showing definite signs of stress, and she apologised, saying she would have to delay the interview as something had cropped up. She and Phil left immediately to meet up with Kevin Potter and Jaime Hanover, who were already on scene. A forensics team was despatched at the same time, and the white tent was being erected as she arrived.

'It's bad, boss,' Kevin said, stepping naturally into the protective role he always adopted around women.

'I know. I heard it happen. Is his tongue missing?'

Kevin looked at Rosie Masters and she nodded. 'It is. How did you know?'

Karen told her of the evidence bag now admitted for examination, and containing a tongue. 'It was delivered by hand to Dave Forrester's old office, and I happened to be there when the package was opened. I was there to download a message off the answering machine that I am assuming is this young man being murdered. Are both his eyes missing?'

'They are. I'll know more when he's in the autopsy suite.'

'There's more,' Karen said, 'but I'll leave you to find it. I don't want you to miss anything because I've told you too much. How quick can we get an ID on him?'

'Well, unless he's stolen it, his Covid vaccine card is in his wallet, and it says his name is Terence Taylor.'

Karen sighed. 'His street name is Threesome. He met up with Ray Ledger last night, and now Ray is in hospital after being attacked, and Threesome is dead. Ray has been lucky to escape with his life. It seems he was quickly found, but if he hadn't been...'

'Right, I'm going to make a start so you can do your job, Karen, and find the little runt who did this, and hurt our Ray. He's a favourite of mine, is Ray.'

With the tent now properly concealing the bin, she entered through the flap, leaving the police officers on the outside.

'What do you want us to do, boss?' Phil asked.

'CCTV. Somebody must have recorded what went on here. He definitely didn't climb into the bin on his own. I want more officers down here—' She looked up as a car pulled up. 'Just not that officer,' she said under her breath. 'DI Armitage!'

'I just heard about this.'

'Oh, I heard about forty-five minutes ago.'

'Sir.'

'Sir. I stand corrected.'

'Yes, you do,' said Armitage. 'You seem to have a bit of an attitude, DS Nelson.'

'I don't think it mentions anything like that in any of my reviews, sir, but I'll take your word for it. My attitude today could be down to the fact that we've lost DI Forrester, and I have PC Ledger in hospital, all due to this case. And there's also the fact that we've lost two ex-coppers of the highest calibre to it as well, so I feel entitled to have a bit of an attitude at the moment. I'm sure I'll feel better tomorrow.'

He stared at her with his mouth open. 'Erm, good. I'm sure you will,' and he walked over to the tent. Karen was tempted to warn him what he would see, but didn't give in to the temptation. He very quickly came out of the tent, and went back to his car. He used his asthma spray, put the car into gear and drove away.

Simon Marshall suddenly looked much older than his nineteen years. He listened as Karen spelled out exactly how she thought he had committed the murder, using Ray Ledger's words as he had read the crime. She could tell by the flush that was growing in Simon's cheeks that she was spot on, but he stuck to 'no comment' as his responses.

'Simon, you seem to be forgetting that I can identify you as the lad who was there at the scene, who had told me the cock and bull story of delivering a pizza and finding Anthony Dawson dead. But the pizza you delivered didn't come from any pizza shop, did it? I put it to you that the pizza, approximately eight inches in size and in a box for a twelve-inch pizza, was cooked at home, that you saved an empty pizza box from a previous delivery to your home, and you used it as a prop to commit murder. Did you contact

Anthony Dawson and tell him his local pizza delivery had a special offer on for that one night, and did he want to take advantage of it?'

He dropped his head, and his solicitor lightly touched his knee. 'I forgot to bring the pizza back out with me,' he whispered.

Karen heard the solicitor say, 'Oh, no,' and Simon looked at him.

'They know,' he said. 'They know what I did.'

'Tell us about your gun skills, Simon.'

'I'm a good shot.' The words were mumbled.

'That was how we identified you,' Karen said. 'I described you to our police artist, who came up with a first-rate likeness of you, and we realised whoever had taken out the cameras had to be pretty handy with a gun, so we went round the gun clubs. And guess what? We heard all about how good you were, how accurate your shooting is... but I do have to tell you that by the time you're released, all those skills will be long forgotten by you. Are you ready to tell us why you killed Anthony Dawson, Simon?'

'I'd like to speak to my client, DS Nelson,' the solicitor said.

'I don't want to speak to him,' said Simon. 'In fact, piss off. Can you make him go?'

The solicitor stood and left the room; suddenly the atmosphere lightened. 'I killed him because he caused all that trouble at home, screwing my mother, my dad in a foul mood because he knew about it, and I didn't know what else to do. I thought if he was dead, it would all go away, so I came up with everything you said. I had to wait till the police arrived, because I couldn't stop shaking, I couldn't drive. So I said I was just the delivery lad.'

'Richard Hogan. False address, false phone number, but did you really think so little of South Yorkshire Police that we wouldn't track you down?'

She turned to Phil Newton. 'DC Newton, can you take Mr Marshall's statement, have him sign it, and then can you take him to the desk and have him charged with the murder of Anthony Dawson, please?'

'Yes, ma'am. Come on, son, let's get you sorted out.' Simon Marshall now looked so much younger than his years as his shoulders dropped, and he was escorted out of the interview room. Karen sat for a moment, gathering her thoughts. Liam and Diana Marshall would regret the arrival of Anthony Dawson into their lives till the day they died.

* * *

The briefing room was full. Everybody was back in, awaiting instructions for what to do next with the Terence Taylor investigation. It seemed that cameras trained on a bin bay had never merited the expense, and with the call detailing the murder being timed at a couple of minutes after midnight, and the cleaner finding him at seven in the morning, it was only a short period of time that had to be viewed on any CCTV in the area. Nothing had been seen.

Karen went over once again the detail from Hermia's attempted murder, committed by the man they now believed was going by the street name of Quinnie, and the fact that they believed he had been in Dave Forrester's office during the time of the two murders, possibly with a second man going by the name of Dickie Bird. They had still found nothing to suggest why anybody had to die, but further investigation was progressing. She made it sound as though she was the one doing the further investigation; Matt Forrester's name wasn't mentioned at all.

'We believe there is some connection to work that was being done for the university by a Professor Hartner, who died in a tram accident a few months ago. His work has been passed on to his second in command, Hermia Forrester. This now leads towards a separate investigation into whether his death was an accident, or if he was pushed as the tram arrived at the station. Jaime, can I ask you to take that section of the investigation on, please?'

Jaime nodded, her cheeks reddening because she had been singled out. 'And choose one of our new intake to help you. As I'm sure everyone has noticed, we have six new foot soldiers who have been allocated to help us in view of the investigation stepping up a notch.'

Jaime had been chatting to one of the women already, and discovered they had a shared interest in reading crime fiction, so Jaime moved around the back of the room until she was by her side. 'Tanya,' she whispered, 'you up for this?'

'Too right I am,' Tanya said with a smile that stretched from ear to ear. 'I thought I'd just be walking around doing door-to-door stuff. When do I get my sergeant's stripes, then?'

Jaime grinned. 'About five years, give or take a year. But it's a start.'

Karen saw them talking and felt relieved. Jaime was the quiet one in her team, and she hoped teaming up with Tanya would not only put her in a more senior role, but it would build her confidence.

'Okay, now we have the murder of Terence Taylor to deal with. I actually have a recording of it happening, of the voice of the previously mentioned Quinnie giving out graphic details of what he is doing to this man, and it is very difficult to listen to. I do want to remind everyone that any mention of any of the work going on in this office to anyone – family, friends, media – could result in you losing your job, so what happens in here stays in here. Okay?'

There were several shouts of 'yes, boss', and she had to trust that they meant it. 'Okay, I'm going to play this recording, which was a phone call to an answering machine in the office of the late Dave Forrester, but it was intended for the ears of his son, ex-DI

Matt Forrester. Mr Forrester also had a small package hand delivered, containing the cut-out tongue of Terence Taylor. This is being confirmed by DNA as we speak. Now, everybody settle down, and listen to this. I warn you, it's not pleasant listening.'

The room went quiet, and she switched on the recording.

31

Matt finally finished going through all the books on the shelves. He had discovered five bookmarks, but nothing to make him shout out, 'Yes!'

He was sitting deep in thought when his phone rang, and Karen told him of the happenings of the morning.

'Where are you?' he asked, concerned that somebody would hear her words.

'It's okay, I'm in my car. I'm heading to the autopsy suite; Rosie is about to start Taylor's PM.'

'So Dawson's murder is cleared up?'

'Well and truly. Marshall just caved when I spoke of Ray's thought processes as to what had happened, and it really was just a shot in the dark on my part. I thought he would argue back, and it would go on for hours, but he admitted it, said it was because Dawson had destroyed his family. He's been charged, and he'll be in front of the magistrates tomorrow before being remanded into custody. Part of me feels sorry for him, he's still just a kid, but he's been brought up around guns, so he knew exactly what he was doing. I'm starting to think Dawson's name being in red was to keep it in front of your dad's mind, to warn Dawson he thought he was in danger. We'll never know for sure, but knowing Dave Forrester, I'm sure he would have passed on concerns, even if he didn't like the person he was warning.'

Matt sighed. 'I guess you're right. Let's put this to bed. We need to concentrate on finding this Quinnie bloke, and we can all breathe easier.'

'Matt, I have to go. Finn's ringing. Finn never rings, so I'm a bit concerned there might be a problem.'

'Okay, take care, Karen. Is Finn home tonight?'

'Possibly. Speak in a bit,' and she disconnected.

Karen sat outside the autopsy suite with her engine running. She had simply not thought about turning it off. Finn had gone. Left. Taken all his stuff, and gone. As she would have known, he pointed out, if she had been at home herself. She could have the house if she could afford the mortgage payments; if not, she could sell it and buy a smaller one, he didn't care. He'd found somebody else who made him feel as though he came first in their life, not second to a bloody corpse. It had been a long text.

There was a tap on her car window and Josh, Rosie's assistant, was peering in at her. 'You okay, Karen?'

'I'm fine, just taking a minute.' She switched off her engine, gathered up her notebook and her bag, and walked in alongside Josh, who felt as though he wanted to put his arm around her and give her a cuddle. There was something wrong with her, something upsetting, but she obviously didn't want to talk about it, so he squeezed her elbow as she entered in front of him, and he whispered to her that he would get her a water.

She sat down and gave a half wave to Rosie, who responded with a thumbs up as she wielded her scalpel.

Karen watched but didn't see. Although there had been very little between her and Finn for a long time, it had still come as a shock that they were no longer a couple, married or otherwise. Now they were separated. A whole new ball game. And her finances would have to be carefully calculated as the house was large, bought with the intentions of having at least two children, until they had realised they didn't really see each other often enough to make babies. Maybe she should sell it and buy a tent.

'Karen?'

She heard Rosie's voice as if from a distance, and shook herself. 'Sorry, Rosie, my mind was elsewhere.'

'That's okay. I said we've sent his T-shirt for testing, because we need to be certain it was all his blood on it. They used something very sharp to take out his eyes, and scissors, I believe, to cut out his tongue. It's possible some of the blood may have come from whoever did this to this poor lad.'

'Then fingers crossed,' Karen said, dragging herself back into the world of death. She tried to keep her mind on what it was supposed to be on, but escaped half an hour later, asking Rosie to forward the report as soon as it was available. Rosie had confirmed the smashed kneecaps, and she had calculated it had been done with a large head hammer. His hands and feet hadn't been touched and Karen had watched as Rosie took samples from under his finger- and toenails. She suspected that they would have started working on them if he hadn't died first, as his feet were bare when he was found in the bin.

She left the autopsy suite and headed back to her car, not knowing what to do. She should return to the station, she should listen to reports from her team out chasing leads, she should fire up her computer and complete her report following the morning's interview with Simon Marshall. She should do all of those things, but what she really wanted to do was fold herself into Matt's arms, and let him take the strain from her.

She drove back, but instead of going over the Manor Top, she followed the ring road round and headed towards Gleadless. Matt's car was still outside the office, and she pulled hers in beside it. She messaged him to say she was outside, and the door was opened with some speed. She stepped inside, and opened her arms. He folded her into his own, and held her.

'It was a bad one?'

'Not as bad in the flesh as hearing it over your answering machine,' she said, 'but bad enough. It's been a shit day, and I needed to come via Gleadless to see if you were still here. I also had a text from Finn. I wasn't quick enough to take his phone call, so I thought I would return it later. I didn't get the chance. He sent a text. I've been dumped via text, Matt.'

'He knows about us? Oh, God, Karen, I thought we'd been careful...'

'No, he knows nothing, although he did make a sarky point about me not being home to see that he'd left. I think he only suspects there's somebody else, he doesn't know for certain, but it's all irrelevant because he's found somebody else anyway.'

The top of Karen's head fit neatly under his chin when he bent his head, and she stayed there, enjoying the moment, knowing that everything was happening for the best, but it was still hard to say goodbye to a dream that had started many years earlier while she and Finn were still at school.

'He's walked away from the house as well, collected his stuff, so he says, and I can have the house. I can't make any decisions yet about it, but in time I'll have to. I feel rubbish, Matt, and yet I'd moved on from him anyway. I moved on a long time ago, I just had to wait to tell you.'

He stepped back, placed his hands on her shoulders and held her away from him. 'Are you happy with me?'

'You don't need to ask. I came to you because I knew you were what's known as an honourable man.' She smiled. 'I had to make the first move because we'd still have been skirting around each other if I hadn't, but to answer your question, I am truly happy. And I feel even better now I can slide into bed beside you and not feel just a little bit guilty about it. Let's face it, lying to Finn was always going to be a stumbling block with us, and now we'll probably never see him again if he means what he says about not returning to the house.'

'We should tell Steve and Hermia. I don't think it bothers Hermia that you're a married woman, but Steve's a bit old-fashioned about such things.' He gave a gentle laugh. 'And this whole new situation sits a hell of a lot better with me. We're no longer having an affair, we're having a love affair. There's a difference.'

'I knew you'd make me feel a lot better. I haven't a clue what went on in that autopsy because I'd just read the text from Finn, and I couldn't think straight. I kept feeling tears pricking at my eyes, then Josh brought me a glass of water because he sensed something was wrong with me, and I kept switching off from what Rosie was doing. It was a complete waste of time, I should have called somebody else in to take over from me, but I couldn't take the hassle of having to explain why I couldn't do it. One thing I remember Rosie saying that only now is sinking in is that she's sent Threesome's T-shirt for testing, because it was covered in blood, and she's hopeful it's not all his. We may get a significant lead from that if she's right. She said a sharp knife was used to gouge out his eyes, and scissors were used to cut out the tongue. Let's hope they cut themselves while they were killing him.'

Her phone rang, and she glanced at the screen, then up at Matt. 'It's Ray.'

It was only as she clicked to answer it that she realised it could be his wife using his phone, so she said a very tentative, 'Hello.'

'Karen? It's me.' Ray's voice was weak, but it was him.

'Oh, Ray... you're okay?'

'I don't know, but I need to tell you what Threesome told me. The people who killed Dave and Johnny are Quinnie and Dickie Bird for definite. He didn't know why, but he knew it was them. Look after Threesome; if Quinnie finds out...'

'Ray—'

There was a sudden silence, then Ray's voice became even more feeble. 'They've already got to him, haven't they? Do you know who hit me? They meant it, Karen, they meant to kill me. I was bloody lucky to not take the full force, but I didn't know who it was. He had a balaclava over his face.'

Karen's voice was gentle. 'Ray, we don't know yet who went after you, but we do know who went after Threesome. We'll get them. Now you get better, do what the doctors tell you to do, and don't you dare come back to work until you're fully fit. Oh, and Rosie sends her love.'

Ray's laugh was faint. 'Don't tell my Angela that.'

He disconnected and Karen stared at her screen. 'He's alive,' she said. And then the tears really came. 'I honestly thought he wouldn't make it,' she sobbed. 'He looked so pale. Thank God for our NHS, they've saved one of the best for us.'

Matt held her until her tears stopped, then made her sit down while he made her a hot drink. 'You need a soothing drink. Tea?' She nodded her thanks, and fished around in her bag for another tissue. Today was a day when she should be considering buying shares in Kleenex.

32

Hermia woke on that Wednesday morning, aware for the first time in several days that nothing was hurting. Steve handed her two painkillers, and she placed them on the coffee table. 'I don't think I need them,' she said. 'Nothing seems to be hurting at the moment, so I'll leave them there until, or if, something does hurt. Can you do me a favour and get me the files back out of the blue bin, please? I don't have much more to read through, and it's something crossed off the to-do list if I can complete that. It's taken far too long to do it, I know, but I'm feeling so much better.'

Steve smiled at her, loving her renewed enthusiasm. He still had sleepless hours when all he could see was her body lying on top of the flattened shrubs of the shrubbery, and he had felt scared to death that she hadn't survived the fall. 'I'll go now. If I'm not back in fifteen minutes, come and find me.'

'Don't make jokes about it. It's scary enough at the moment. Maybe I'd better go with you. I could do it myself, but it's hard getting something from the bottom of a wheelie bin when you've a cast on your arm.'

He looked at her, a frown on his face. 'I hope I didn't hear the words "I could do it myself", Hermia Forrester. Remember what happened the last time you said you could do it yourself? Somebody threw you over a balcony. So let's have no nonsense about doing things, because you can't. Wait there till I get back, then I'll make us some breakfast.' He grinned. 'Then I'll help you shower.'

She grinned back. 'I don't think you quite get the idea behind helping me to shower. You're supposed to hold the carrier bags over my cast while I wash myself, but we seem to be doing it the other way round, with me holding the carrier bags.'

'That's okay, I'm happy to do it the way we've been doing it. I'm very adaptable and versatile. I'll nip next door to the blue bin, get those files, while you're coming alive.'

'Okay, and maybe we should talk about Matt and Karen, and Karen's news about Finn.'

'Why?' He crossed the room, picking up his jacket as he went. 'Have you seen the way they are with each other? She would have left Finn before much longer anyway. She's fancied Matt for ages, so this situation is an absolute no-brainer.'

'But he's my brother! Aren't I supposed to offer words of wisdom and protection to him?'

'Nope. He wouldn't thank you. Now be good, will you, just for ten minutes or so. I'll run, because it's pissing it down with rain.'

He left the room and she heard the front door open and close.

* * *

Steve returned with the bundle of papers hidden inside his jacket, protecting them from the rain. 'Good for us gardeners,' he grumbled, tipping the paperwork inside its McDonald's bag on to the bed settee. 'We're going to have to have another McDonald's now, because this bag is wet through.'

'Oh, no!' Hermia tried very hard not to laugh. 'Such hardship, having to force chicken McNuggets and a cheeseburger down me.'

'But that's exactly my point. You have two Happy Meals just so you get the toys, but that means you get two lots of fries.'

'Who's having a McDonald's breakfast?' Matt asked, popping his head around the door.

'Nobody, Steve said the McDonald's bag holding the professor's files is wet through now because of the rain and we'd have to have another McD meal tonight, but I hadn't actually thought we could have a breakfast instead. You're a smart brother at times, Matt. Go on then, who wants what?' and she leaned back, pen poised, prepared to write down their orders.

* * *

With food cleared away, along with the wet paper bag, Hermia went into work mode, and sorted through the pages she had already read. She had been initially surprised that Hartner had made so many handwritten notes, but quickly came to realise that the penned pages were not only the interviewees' thoughts, they were also his. The files transferred to her laptop were more clinical, factual. His written words told a story of gangland behaviour mainly in the East End of Sheffield, with a considerable amount spilling over the Rotherham border. It was getting worse; people were afraid, and there were several individuals that were leaders inspiring fear. Almost everyone he had interviewed had used the words, 'Well, keep this to yourself,' or a similar phrasing.

She had used a yellow highlighter pen to pick out any names that were mentioned, and the name Quinnie had only been highlighted once, so she went back until she found it, in words spoken by Dickie Bird. She used that word as the starting point for continuing to carefully read the professor's thoughts and observations.

She found it mentioned a second time by somebody who would only say that his name was Nat. She remembered Nat from the recorded interviews. There had been several who had insisted the professor switch off the recorder, and Nat had been one of them. The professor only had his words noted in writing. Nat had spoken of Quinnie, how he hadn't been on the Sheffield scene long, but had arrived with a well-established drugs route already in place, and how that had upset some people. Hartner had asked him for more details, stressing nothing he said would be linked to him, and he had said, 'Well, when your brother's in it big time, it's already a done deal.' Questions about who the brother was were ignored. He said he didn't know, just knew there had been a brother.

Hermia scribbled heavily with the highlighter to make sure the section stood out. Brother. That word again coming from the lips of this killer.

She carried on, still highlighting any names that were revealed from the mouths of others. She became engrossed in some of the stories – how the bigger names had helped out the interviewees when they had been struggling, when they needed money, when their families had problems, and she recognised the scale of the problem for the council, who were looking to clean up one of the biggest cities in the country.

Steve had left her to work, and moved out into the conservatory to tidy up the plants initially, but then to read his newspaper. He was surprised to see her standing in the doorway, and put down the crossword immediately. 'You need something, Herms?'

'A ten-minute break. I've just read about a baby dying a week after birth, and one of these thugs paid for the funeral. It's just at odds with other stuff I've been reading – the drugs, the places where you can get a gun with no questions asked – I'm beginning to see what Eric meant when we had a chat about it one day. He said it was disheartening from top to bottom, but occasionally there was a tiny glimmer of light. He also said it was the most difficult report he'd ever been asked to produce, and he would be glad when it was done and he could become normal again. It's kind of why I've put off working on it, deciding to finish my own work first before taking on his. I think he was a brave man to go out and interview people, he put himself in danger doing it, and I'm more convinced than ever he was pushed under that tram. They wanted him out of the way, and to stop asking questions.'

'You won't be expected to do interviews with any of Sheffield's finest, will you?'

'No, he'd actually completed that part of the planned programme. He'd done about two-thirds of the work involved for this report, and was onto the collation stage, getting all his information into some sort of logical order, and ready for it to be typed up for presentation to the council. He still had a couple of months' work left to do, but the foot-slogging side was complete. If we can't find something from his notes, then we're never going to find it.'

'So how does this link to your dad?'

'The only link that I can see is they intended torturing him for my whereabouts. Apart from that, there is no link. Dad didn't know Hartner, and I know Hartner knew of Dad, but only because I spoke of him. Constantly. I couldn't have had a better father.' She gave a slight laugh. 'As if either Dad or Johnny would have given me up.' She felt tears begin to well in her eyes, and roughly wiped her sleeve across them. 'So I'm taking a break and having a think about what I've read, what I've heard. There's a considerable amount of fear out there, and that leads me to think that the problem is much bigger than anybody has imagined, but it's not for me to say that, they'll have to reach that conclusion for themselves. I think they will.'

Matt wandered through into the conservatory, a partly peeled onion in one hand and a knife in the other. 'You okay, Herms?'

She sighed. 'As if. But I will be. I know Karen will have him under lock and key one day, this Quinnie whoever-he-is, and that gives me comfort.'

Matt hesitated. 'We have further information – Ray is doing okay, and rang Karen last night to tell her what Threesome had told him. It was Quinnie and Dickie Bird who attacked Dad and Johnny. She went in early this morning to get feet on streets in the East End looking for either of them. It will be on this evening's local news programmes along with their pictures, one of which is the picture Steve took of him on your balcony. Unfortunately they have enough connections for them to be in hiding now until all the fuss dies down, but they don't know Karen's determination on this one. They really shouldn't have recorded themselves killing Threesome. That seems to be the one thing that's tipped her over the edge, and now she's gone completely unprofessional and she's blazing mad. She'll not rest until she's got them in that interview room, and she's charging them.'

'Good for Karen. I'll look forward to getting in the witness box.' Hermia's face showed anger, and it occurred to Matt just how alike the two women in his life were, strong women who would succeed at whatever they set themselves to do.

'And is Karen okay? With the Finn thing?' Steve sipped at his water.

'I think she's relieved, although they've been together since they were about thirteen, so it's a strange situation at the moment for her. But time will heal that, and I'm going nowhere. We talked for a long time last night, mopped up a few tears – hers, not mine – and she's making no quick decisions about the house. He's told her she can have it, but she's a bit worried that she won't be able to afford the mortgage, and it's far too big for one person anyway, so I think in time that will go on the market. But it's early days, we're still getting to know each other, and she is thinking the next time she hears from Finn, it will be to be served with divorce papers, as he's got this new person in his life now.'

'Lots of change for all of us.' Hermia's mouth trembled slightly. 'I wonder what Dad would have said to all of this. It's only ten days or so since Matt and I were kind of discussing going on holiday together, both happily single, and now look at us.'

'And Wednesday won six-nil, on the worst day of our lives. We'll make Dad proud, we'll find these men who think it's okay to kill indiscriminately, and we'll watch them in the dock.'

33

Karen felt tired. She had joined her colleagues as they had made their presence felt in a huge area, showing the two pictures that would be viewed on television that evening, but getting no response whatsoever.

Most people simply closed their doors and said they didn't know either of them, or merely shook their heads and said, 'Sorry.'

At two o'clock, she called it a day, and headed back to the office via the hospital.

Ray looked battered with the huge dressing around his head; his wife was by his side, holding his hand. He looked up with a smile when he recognised his boss.

'Karen! I'll be back at work tomorrow.'

She laughed. 'Ray Ledger, I don't want you back at work for at least a month. Is that understood?'

Angela Ledger shook her head. 'They've not even said he's moving from ICU to a normal ward yet, so he's in hospital for some time, thank goodness. He's safe in here, he's not safe out there. He's proved that. Am I safe, Karen?'

'You haven't been home yet?'

Angela shook her head. 'No, I feel better here, but once he leaves ICU, I won't be able to stay.'

Karen felt slightly sick that she hadn't considered the safety of Ray's wife and his property. His children had left home; his son was somewhere in Africa, and their daughter had married an American and was in New York, so she guessed they were safe enough, but who knew what this crazy man would do? Angela needed to stay somewhere a bit more protected until they had Quinnie under lock and key.

'When you're ready, Angela, I'll have someone escort you home to pick up some clothes and anything else you might need, and we'll install you in a safe house for a few days, just until this killer is caught. He's completely unpredictable, so I'd feel happier with some protection around both of you.'

Angela nodded her acceptance, worry lines across her brow. 'It won't be until tomorrow. They're keeping Ray on ICU until tomorrow at the earliest, because it was such a bad head injury. They want to monitor him for another night, then make the decision in the morning, so I can stay by his side until he has to move.'

'And how's our wounded soldier feeling today?'

'Fine,' Ray said. 'Unless I want to move, or breathe, or think. Apart from all of that, life's good.'

'Well, you'll be pleased to know we've got half the force out on the streets with photos of Dickie Bird and this Quinnie, talking to everybody, but there's precious few want to talk to us. There's a feeling of fear across the entire area, and nobody's saying very much. It seems to me these two have never been seen before, they're completely unknown... you know the situation.'

'Well, Matt's sister knows him. She needs to be guarded, boss. If he gets to her again, he'll make sure he kills her this time.'

'Stop worrying, Ray. Just get better. Do you need anything?'

'Only to hear you've caught them. And I'd like to be the one in the interview room with you.'

She laughed. 'Not going to happen, Ray. I'd end up having to lock you up. I'll try to get in to see you tomorrow; just rest and you'll be out of here in no time.'

She had a quick word with the PC on guard duty outside ICU, showed him both pictures and told him if anyone even vaguely resembled either man, he was to get help immediately.

'Don't worry, ma'am. Ray's a mate. I'll not let him get hurt again.'

She nodded and walked away, praying that was the truth.

The rain was starting to come down heavily again, and Karen pulled her hood up, giving it a tug around her face. 'Thought it was supposed to be March winds and April showers,' she was grumbling to herself, when she spotted the man at the side of her car. She stopped her intended journey back to her vehicle, moved to the side of a large white van so that it concealed her and peered around the side. The man was now leaning against the back of the car, trying to light a cigarette despite the heavy rain.

She was some distance from him, but she was sure he wasn't either of the two men they were actively seeking. He was rotund, about five feet six inches, and almost bald. Eventually the cigarette was lit, and he continued to lean against her car boot while he smoked it. She slowly took out her phone and called for assistance.

She watched as the car in the bay next to hers pulled away, and she knew the cigarette had been a delaying tactic until the other car moved. He threw the cigarette onto the floor, then stubbed it out with his foot. He looked around, then bent down by the side of her car so that she could no longer see him.

Karen's phone rang and she answered it immediately, guessing it was someone coming to assist her.

'We're just entering the Barnsley Road entrance, ma'am. Is he still there?'

'He is, although I don't have visual of him at the moment. He's bent down by the driver side of the car. I am in the top car park, first aisle in, and parked next to the pay machine. It's a red Sportage on a 2018 plate.'

'Please stay where you are, DS Nelson. Then we don't have to worry about you, just your vehicle.'

He disconnected and she watched as the squad car turned into the car park at some speed, then drove up the first aisle. It stopped at her car, and the two officers got out immediately, with the small man slowly rising to his feet, and holding up his arms in surrender as he realised he would never outrun the fit bobbies standing in front of him.

His hands were secured behind him, and then the first officer rang Karen again.

'You want to come to your car now, ma'am? You won't be able to take it anywhere; I think he's cut the brake pipe, but we're arresting him for malicious damage. You may want to add attempted murder to those charges.'

She heard the man splutter and say, 'Ey, 'ang on, I've not attempted to kill anybody.' She wiped the smile from her face as she reached the trio.

'Who are you?' she asked, and he dropped his head. The rain splattered onto his baldness. 'And just what did you think might happen to me once you cut my brake pipe? Did it not occur to you

I might not be able to stop this rather large car without brakes to help me?'

His head now lifted, and he shook it to wipe away the rain that he could no longer remove with his hands. 'I can't say owt.' His voice was guttural, hoarse.

'Really?' Karen raised her eyebrows, expressing surprise at his comment. 'Then we have a problem, don't we? You see, I believe you've been told to do this by someone called Quinnie.' He visibly stiffened. 'And I'm going to make sure that when Quinnie's face goes live on *Calendar* tonight, someone will be saying that we have arrested you, and I will have your name by then, and that you've given us information involving Quinnie in this attempt to kill me.'

And now the stiffening of his spine became more apparent. 'Yer can't do that!'

'Oh, I can. And I will. And when you're sent on remand, somebody in there will already have been given the word to make sure you can't say anything ever again. Get what I'm saying?'

She pulled her hood a little tighter around her face, aware of the sudden extra heavy squall of rain. 'So start to talk while we're waiting for help to move my car.' The second officer had just disconnected his phone after organising a breakdown vehicle to come for Karen's Sportage.

'It'll be ten minutes or so, ma'am,' he confirmed. 'It's only on Herries Road, won't take him long. We'll stay with you until he gets here with the truck, then we'll remove the prisoner and take him to Moss Way. You want me to send another car for you?'

'No, that's fine,' she said. 'I'll organise my own lift home. Book him in for an overnight stay; I'll interview him in the morning, and give him the bill for the repairs.'

Suddenly the man came to life. 'Oy! I've no money to pay for car repairs. And I need a fag.'

Karen stared at him, her face like thunder, her eyes like steel.

'Then I suggest you tell us everything, sir, starting with your name. The judge will want to know how regular a thing this car damage spree is, and how many years to give you. And you can't have a cigarette with your hands in cuffs, can you?'

'Sammy Sutherland,' he muttered, his reluctance to say it aloud showing in the tone of his voice.

'Well, Sammy Sutherland, you've an interesting couple of days in front of you.' She turned to the taller of the two officers. 'Thank you for your help. I'll be fine now. Put him in the back of the car, and I'll wait for the repair truck.'

'We'll wait another couple of minutes, ma'am.' His tone was firm, and she shook her head. He didn't want any trouble falling down on his head because he'd left her in a car park with no back-up. She stared at him and took out her phone, turning away from the men to keep her conversation with Matt private.

'I need rescuing.'

'What's wrong? Where are you?' Matt sounded panicked.

'Northern General top car park. My brake pipe's been cut. Everything's under control and we've arrested the little scrote who did it, but it's pissing it down with rain, I'm wet through and in a bad mood, and I could use a lift home from a tall, dark and handsome man.'

'I'll see if I can find one somewhere for you,' he said with a laugh, realising she wasn't hurt, just inconvenienced. 'Fifteen minutes. Can you wait in reception out of the rain?'

'It'll make no difference at all, I'm like a drowned rat. No, I'm waiting here until the car is loaded onto the truck, then I'll park my bum on the steps and wait for you. First aisle in the car park, you'll see me.'

'Who's there now?'

'My two Sir Galahads who turned up just a little too late to stop him cutting the pipe, but well in time to catch him in the act. He's called Sammy Sutherland, and wouldn't you know it, he's the only one not in the rain. He's already in the back of the car waiting for transport to Moss Way, moaning 'cos he can't have a fag. But I'm done. I'm heading home, getting into my PJs, and drinking several cups of tea. I'm really cold and really wet. And I won't have a car in the morning, so I'm going to have to ask for a lift to work at some ungodly hour.'

'That's no problem. I'll be your third Sir Galahad. I'm so sorry this has happened, Karen, but it can be sorted. And at least you're not hurt. I couldn't have handled that...'

'The truck's just coming up the hill. I'd better go. See you in a bit, I'll just get this idiot bloke off to Moss Way so the truck has room to manoeuvre, and by the time they've got it loaded, you'll probably be here. It's been a rubbish day, Matt, but I'm calling a personal halt to it because I need time out.' She pushed her hood back a fraction as the rain was dripping directly from the edge of it into her eyes. 'And see if you can find the switch to turn off this bloody rain!'

He laughed. 'I'll have a look. Take care, Karen. Is the truck with you now?'

'It's hovering at the bottom end of the car park, waiting for the squad car to move. I'd better go.' She didn't want to go, she wanted to carry on talking to him.

'Okay, sweetheart, love you.'

'Love you too.'

And suddenly the rain and the lack of brake fluid didn't matter any more.

34

Matt pulled into the car park and saw her immediately. He didn't think he'd ever seen somebody look so bedraggled before, and that, combined with the relentless rain and the ever-darkening skies that were closing in on the evening, made him realise she needed some warmth in her.

She climbed in beside him in the Land Rover, and leaned back with a sigh. 'I'm being followed, aren't I?'

He nodded. 'You are. And cutting your brake pipes means they want you dead. The weather helped them, because under normal circumstances, and even as little as ten minutes later, you'd have dashed down there, keen to get out of the rain, and jumped straight in your car. Can I suggest we go straight to your house from here, pick up whatever you need in the way of clothes and stuff, and you move into mine along with the other refugees I've acquired?'

She laughed. 'You'll soon be overflowing with bodies.'

'Yours will always be welcome. And I suggest we get a hot drink at yours, get some warmth into you. You're shivering.' He turned the car heater up a notch, and started the car. 'Do we need to get some milk?'

'No, my coffees come out of a Tassimo.'

'Well, make sure that's part of the divorce settlement. Custody of the Tassimo. That'll be a first in court.'

He drove down the steep hill out of the hospital grounds, then up and onto Barnsley Road. Fifteen minutes later, he pulled up outside her home, and felt relieved she didn't look quite so frozen and grey. He had kept a close eye on any following vehicles, but with Sheffield's workers heading home, the traffic had been heavy, and he wouldn't have known if any had actually been following him.

'Wait here a moment,' he said, 'and give me your keys.'

She handed them over, too comfortable in the big car to argue. She heard the car doors lock as he left her, and watched as he entered her home. She giggled as she knew he would recognise his own date of birth as he entered the code she had just told him on her alarm, but what the hell. She'd freely admit she'd fancied him for a long time, knew his birthday, and Finn had told her to put in a code when they'd had the system installed.

He came back out two minutes later, and the car doors unlocked. 'It's fine. I've no idea how to work that coffee thing, so come on, wench, warm us up.'

* * *

Karen made their coffees, then went upstairs to shower and change. She bundled everything she took off into a large carrier bag, with the intention of sorting it all out at Matt's place; everything was soaked.

Matt was in the lounge when she arrived downstairs, carrying a suitcase and the bag of wet clothes. 'You want another coffee?' she asked before planting a kiss firmly on his lips.

'No, thanks. I want to get you home; I feel safe with you tucked away with everybody else. This is a bloody strange case, Karen. We know who is doing the killing, and I imagine you being followed has been ordered by this Quinnie as well, but we've no clue as to his whereabouts.'

'Well, let's see how long he can survive after *Calendar* has been on tonight.' She glanced at her watch. 'It'll be on in ten minutes. I think they're doing it as an interview with DI Armitage, but it's the only contribution he's made to the entire investigation. I'm not bothered about what's said, I want those pictures out there. Dickie Bird's picture is our mugshot of him from when he did a short sentence a couple of years ago, but we've used Steve's picture of Quinnie – it's the only one we have.'

'Shall we watch it?'

She looked around. 'Well, I'd say yes, but I no longer appear to have a television. I'll text Herms and get her to record it for us.' The text was sent, followed by receipt of a thumbs up. 'We can watch it when we get back to yours.'

'Finn's taken the television?'

She nodded. 'The awful thing is I hadn't even noticed. I rarely watch it, and he'll have taken 95 per cent of the DVDs, I'm sure. Plus anything else vaguely smart technology. He bought them, in all fairness, so he's quite entitled to them. At least he didn't take the Tassimo.'

'Let me guess. You bought that.'

'I did. I had to call at Jaime's one day to pick her up, and we had a coffee at hers before we left. That was from her machine, and within two days, I'd treated myself to one. In our job, and especially with Finn being away so much, I threw away so much soured milk it was unreal. Now I don't need it for a drink. This smart machine even makes my hot chocolate.'

He pulled her close to him. 'You feeling better now?'

'Much better. I'm warm again. This is the thickest sweatshirt I've got, so I want no cracks about it having Hogwarts on the front; I'm a fan, get used to it, pal.'

'Never read them,' Matt admitted. 'And I think it's because I didn't have Harry entirely in my life, only intermittently. He loves the books, and if he'd been with me, I don't doubt we would have read them together, but somehow I've missed out. It's starting to look as though I might have to remedy that.'

'Good. It's time you were educated in the finer things in life.' She stood to take their cups into the kitchen to wash them, and he walked into the hall. There was a torn piece of paper on the mat that most certainly hadn't been there when they had entered the house. He picked it up and the words jumped out at him.

We followed you here.

Karen joined him, and he showed her the note without saying anything. He waited.

'For fuck's sake,' she said. 'This means whoever has very quietly pushed this through my letter box was still sitting in the car park when I got in your car. They had to be. They probably took that little toad who cut my brake pads to the car park anyway.'

'Who knew you were going to the hospital?'

She thought back to earlier in the day. It felt like a lifetime ago. 'Nobody. I'd had enough of talking to people, and I messaged Kevin to say I was going back to base. It was only as I set off that I realised I was only five minutes away from the hospital, so I stopped off there to see Ray. Does this mean I've had somebody watching me all day and I didn't click on? This is spooky, Matt. I don't like it.'

'Neither do I. We need the name of every officer who was on walking duty in that area today.'

She smiled. 'That's my DI thinking on his feet. One day, I'll be able to do that. You mean one of ours is passing information on?'

'I mean I've no idea, but it's a starting point for ruling them out. This Dickie Bird, or even Quinnie himself, may be simply adept at hiding in plain sight, blending into the background so that you don't really see them, but equally it could be some bent bastard in the pay of Quinnie. And they're obviously worried about you. They think you're a smart cookie who would be better off out of the way. And I bet they now know exactly what's happening between us, which adds a further problem.'

'No, it doesn't. I'll talk to Davis, tell him everything, that we require protection at yours. He can't refuse it, surely. I know he doesn't like you, but he certainly has to protect me, and I'll be at yours.'

'There'll be patrol cars driving past ours at irregular intervals all night, so I'll get that organised when we get home. I may not work there any longer, but I still have friends.'

Home. She liked the sound of that. Already the house that belonged to Matt felt a lot more like home than the house she had shared with Finn for so many years. And Matt's house had a television.

'Okay, but at the very least, I'm having it out with Armitage tomorrow. He's going to look like the golden boy after tonight's broadcast, but so far, he's done naff all.'

Matt picked up her suitcase, and she tucked the bag of wet clothing under her arm. 'Come on,' he said, 'put my birthdate into your alarm system, and let's get out of here.'

She smiled at the thought he had realised it was his birthdate, and set the keypad with the code. She checked the door was locked, and walked down the path towards the car. 'I feel as though we're being watched,' she said carefully.

'So do I, but I think that note was meant to make us feel like that. Traffic has calmed down a bit now, and it will be more obvious if we're being followed. I think they are expecting us to stay at yours overnight, not go gallivanting off out again. You were such a drowned rat, they probably think we're now tucked up in bed getting warm. Which we should be, by the way.' A smile briefly flashed across his face, and she squeezed his hand.

'Later, babe, later.'

'Babe? Do I look like a babe?' He sounded outraged.

'Not in the least.'

'Good, now buckle up and let's get going. If you pull down the visor and angle it, there's a mirror that will reflect the road behind us. Use it, we need to make sure we're not being followed. If we spot anything, get back-up called in. We can weather the storm of you being with me later.'

She fastened her seat belt, then spent some time adjusting the sun visor. 'Okay, all set. Let's go.'

Matt nodded, put the car into gear and drove away from Karen's house.

* * *

It took some time to explain to Steve and Hermia exactly what had happened, and Hermia immediately got on to her insurance company to add Karen as a named driver.

Karen breathed out slowly as Hermia announced she was now covered. 'I really get to drive a Porsche? What the hell will they say when I park this in the police car park?'

Hermia laughed. 'They'll all want you to take them somewhere in it, guaranteed. I went through it at the uni, when I first got it. They all thought I was earning a small fortune, but it was actually Mum's inheritance that paid for it. Nice car to drive, though. Use it till you get your own back; we can't have you without a car.'

'Hopefully mine will be done tomorrow, so I'll only need it for one day.'

'Use it as long as you want, I can't drive with this damn cast bending my arm at the elbow, so enjoy it. I'll just keep your name on the insurance; it might make life a little less fraught if you know you have a back-up vehicle. It's why Matt got the Land Rover; it's a tough one to disable.'

'Thank you, Hermia, you're a star. It means Matt won't have to get up to take me in the morning, with all the comments that might ensue from that little jaunt.'

'I'll be following you,' Matt said.

'Why?'

'To see who else is.'

She thought about it for a moment then nodded. 'Okay. That makes sense, except we didn't see anybody follow us to this out of the way place earlier, so they won't know where I am, and they certainly won't connect me to this super swish car.'

'I'll be following you,' Matt repeated, and she shut up. Argument over.

35

It felt quite strange to Matt to be pulling into the car park at Moss Way police station. Just two weeks, and already it seemed as if it was part of another life. And yet there was a strange sense of relief. No matter what happened, the following day would be spent in his father's office, contacting all the clients and telling them that he would be continuing his father's business, and he would be making appointments to speak with all existing clients over the following two or three weeks.

He watched as Karen parked the Porsche and smiled. She would have loved driving it, of that he was certain, because he had enjoyed it the only time he was allowed to drive it. She gave a swift wave to him, followed by a thumbs up to say she was okay, and she headed through the back door of the station, before disappearing from his sight.

Matt turned the Land Rover until it faced the exit and slowly pulled out. His unease hadn't lessened, and his eyes felt like swivel sticks as he tried to look everywhere at once. It all seemed normal, and he headed up towards Gleadless.

He took his time, and felt as though he was looking through

the rear-view mirror more than he was looking through the windscreen. He reached the bottom of Birley Lane, where he would normally have turned left to head towards White Lane, but at the last second, he put on his right indicator, followed almost immediately by his left one to indicate he was going left at the staggered crossroads. It took him onto Base Green estate, and he drove along various odd little roads as he wove his way through the estate, each road taking him towards Seagrave Avenue, where a quick left turn at the top of the steep road would see him outside the office.

He spotted no following cars and breathed a sigh of relief, while all the time admitting to himself that he would be going through this ridiculous behaviour until Quinnie was locked away in a cell. The previous day's actions showed a skill at following cars, and there would be no rest until the danger was squashed.

He eventually pulled onto the parking area in front of the office, and sat for a moment. No car followed him, and he watched until quite a few vehicles had driven past him on White Lane. None slowed down or even looked at him, so he gathered up his laptop and his briefcase and climbed out of the car. He hesitated, still unsure it was safe, then walked towards the office door, calling himself a wuss.

He unlocked the door, headed for the alarm and gave a huge sigh of relief. Then he sent a quick text to Karen to confirm his safe arrival, and she responded with an equally fast response.

Waiting outside Davis office. He wants to see me.

* * *

Karen was raging. 'How dare he?' she spluttered, and Matt laughed.

'Calm down, he can't tell you to do anything you don't want to do. And unless you're dating a criminal, he certainly can't interfere in your personal life. How did he know?'

'About you? God knows, I didn't ask, I was so blazing mad. He didn't even ask about the way the case was going, just wanted you out of my life. Hypocritical bastard after what he did to you. He really doesn't like you, Matt.'

'Tell me about it. He puts up with me because I'm Harry's dad, and there's not a lot he can do about that, but don't forget I told everybody I could I'd seen his bare arse performing gymnastics with my wife, once I'd got over the initial shock. And don't worry about him and his warped ideas of what's right and what's wrong, he's only there temporarily. I'm in the office all day, so if you're out and about in this area, pop in and I'll give you a hug. Take care, and keep looking in that rear mirror. You heard anything about your own car?'

'It'll be done by two this afternoon, and after driving Hermia's car this morning, I'm seriously thinking of trading mine in for a Porsche.'

'Wouldn't recommend it; Davis will think you're on the take from Quinnie.'

'As soon as I get the word from the garage, I'll bring Herm's car up to your office. Would you mind running me over to Hillsborough to get mine, please? Then we'll sort out getting Hermia's back to her later.'

'That's fine. I'm trying to sort out Dad's current clients and his ex-clients. I need to contact them all, explain the situation in case they don't know what's happened, and hope we can manage to keep them all. He seems to be on a retainer with some of them, no active cases, but he was available when they needed him. Smart, wasn't he?'

'Oh, he was. Lovely man all round. I'm going to crack on now, and just so you know, I think I left Davis under no illusions about my feelings for you.'

'Good. Do you know how happy you make me?'

'Thank heavens for that. I told Davis we were very happy, you, me and Harry.'

He groaned. 'Stirrer. See you later, and try not to drop yourself into any other problems today.'

'I've kind of had one issue put on the back burner. I sent Jaime and Tanya out to try to get some further information on the tram accident, but they've reported back that there's nothing. No CCTV of what happened from any buildings in the area, the CCTV on the tram showed nothing, and they apparently spent most of last night going through all the statements that were taken at the time. Nothing. Unless we get a confession from bloody Quinnie, I think we're going to have to shelve investigating his death. That makes me feel angry.'

'Don't write it off yet; something could come to light ten years down the line and you will be able to tick it off. He can't stay one step in front forever.'

* * *

Sutherland was next on Karen's agenda, and she took Phil Newton into the interview room with her.

Sutherland looked drawn; he clearly hadn't enjoyed his night in a cell, and he glared as the two officers entered the room. Karen logged them in and sat down, staring at the man in front of her.

'Okay, no messing about, Sammy, we've got a busy day in front of us, even if you haven't.'

He said nothing, returning her stare.

She laid her hand on the file in front of her. 'Right, Sammy, who paid you?'

'To do what?' His voice was deep and guttural, and his words unclear as a result.

'Cut my brake pipes.'

'Wasn't me. I saw fluid on the ground, so I bent down to see what it was. Then the coppers arrived.'

'Then I think you should know I watched you do it. I called for the back-up, and I arrested you, or don't you remember that bit? You're not going home, Sammy, no get out of jail free card with this charge. Attempted murder is a biggy.' She opened her file and took out a photograph. 'I took this picture while watching you, so there's no denying your actions.'

'No comment.' He looked rattled.

'So let's start again. Who paid you? And are you prepared to go to prison for them?'

He shrugged. 'No comment.'

'Well, I hope you got your money from Quinnie before our lads turned up, because you're never going to get it now. He's going down as well, you know,' she said, her tone almost conversational.

He gave a brief snort of laughter. 'You'll have to find him first.'

'Oh, I will. Tell me about him, this Quinnie. He a newcomer to Sheffield?'

It suddenly dawned on Sammy he had virtually admitted to knowing Quinnie, and he blanched. Quinnie seemed to know everything, and it wouldn't be good for him if the man found out he'd admitted to anything at all.

'No comment.'

'What's his name? Quinnie is obviously a street name, so what's his real one? And what persuasion did he use to get you to try to kill me?'

'No comment.' Sammy ran a hand around the neckline of his T-shirt. He was starting to sweat.

'A judge won't listen to your "no comment" litany, you know,

Sammy. He'll just get fed up and send you down.' Karen gave a silent apology to all members of the judiciary.

'Look, I know nowt.' Sammy was starting to panic. He knew he was bang to rights, and had imagined Quinnie would have got him out of the place by now, but it suddenly dawned on him he'd been left to sort himself out, and he'd actually refused even the duty solicitor.

'You've done a couple of stretches, Sammy. You want that again? Third time around, the key disappears for a lot longer, you know. Is it worth it? Help us, and I can put in a good word when it comes to trial. Because it is going to come to trial, I promise you. When we've finished our little chat, you're going to be charged. And this isn't just attempted murder, it's attempted murder of a police officer, so you're definitely not getting bail.'

She knew it all boiled down to which he was more afraid of – Quinnie, or a long stretch in prison.

'No comment,' he said.

She stood. 'I'll give you till tomorrow morning to think about it. And think carefully, Sammy. It's a big charge, carries a hefty sentence. You'd do that for him?'

'You can only keep me for twenty-four hours.' There was a slight show of confidence as he spoke.

She looked him in the eyes and laughed. 'Already applied for the extension, Sammy. You're with me for some time yet. Do the right thing, Sammy, look out for yourself, and tell me who this Quinnie is, and where I can find him. Any judge will look favourably on that, especially with my recommendation in front of him.'

She stood to leave the room, and Phil picked up his own empty file folder. He leaned across the table until he was close to Sammy's face. 'Do the right thing, Sammy, tell her what she wants to know. She'll get the answer one way or another, so you might as well tell her and help yourself into the bargain. One time only offer, though. Tell her next time we come in here, but remember we won't be asking again. See you later.'

'Can I have a fag?' Sammy coughed, deep and long.

'Sorry, mate, no smoking in here. You'll thank me for that one day,' and Phil grinned at him as he left the room.

* * *

By the time Karen and Matt had sorted everybody's cars out, it was almost four o'clock, and Karen decided to head back to the office to get any reports of anything. 'It all seems to have died down. It's like we're waiting for the next thing to happen, and when I left, there had been no mention of anybody admitting to knowing either Quinnie or Dickie Bird. Is it fear, or do they genuinely not know anybody by those names?'

'That's what it's like most of the time, but then suddenly something is said and you know it's important. It's the ones who recognise that, and not the ones who bring you the information, who climb the ladder. You're good at knowing when something needs further investigation, so go with your gut instinct. Has DI Armitage started showing his true worth yet?'

Karen shrugged. 'No idea, I've hardly seen him. Neither has anybody else, come to think of it. He seems to spend most of his time with Davis. I'll be so relieved when they've both gone.'

'I'll follow you to the station.'

'No need, it's not me they're after, is it? They want the Hartner notes so they can destroy them. I'd rather you stayed here. You and Steve can protect Hermia and those notes. I'll be back later, and it won't be that late, trust me. I've had a crap couple of days, and I need to chill with my favourite feller, not the ones who are at Moss Way police station.'

They disconnected after Matt had extracted a promise from Karen that she would text him as soon as she was sitting at her desk.

* * *

Hermia was listening to one of the recordings Hartner had made once again, worried that she had missed something first time around; the cutting of the brake pipes on Karen's car had rattled her more than she was saying, and she knew that none of them would rest until this was all cleared up, and she was possibly the key to it. Hartner's notes and verbal interviews seemed to be what Quinnie was after, but she also knew that even if they had been at her flat, she wouldn't have given them up without a fight. The project had been so important to Eric, so worrisome to him because he had confided in her several times that the council had no idea how bad it was getting.

36

Steve had disappeared for an hour to meet up with Rob to discuss taking on two extra staff with the busiest time of the year approaching, and to go through the work sheets, even if it felt like a token job to keep Rob doing what he was doing so well. His main concern was keeping Hermia safe, and having to disappear, even if only for an hour, didn't feel good.

They discussed Rob making more decisions instead of having to check everything with his boss, and Steve explained to him he was taking on a new role with Matt, and would be more of an overseer to his landscape business until he knew how much he would be required in his new undertaking.

Steve left Rob and drove home, pleased that Rob hadn't displayed any signs of being unwilling to take on the extra responsibility that had initially been on a temporary basis until Steve returned to work. Diaries had been produced, and a series of monthly meetings for the rest of 2022 had been agreed, and Steve felt that both men had left their impromptu catch-up feeling happy with all the arrangements they had organised.

He walked through into the lounge, not in the least surprised to find Hermia still listening to the recording.

'Listen,' she said, before he'd even had chance to take off his coat. She rewound slightly, and played it with considerable volume.

The voice was slightly crackly and definitely rough, as if the speaker smoked twenty cigarettes an hour. He also sounded marginally drunk. 'Yeah, I know a feller. Big boss round here. Best not to wind him up, I've heard.'

She stopped the recording. 'Now, listen to this next bit. I didn't hear it first time I listened, but this time around, I've played it backwards and forwards that many times I'm sure I'm hearing it correctly now.' She pressed for the recording to continue.

'Quinlan.' There was a choking sound as if the man was trying to clear his throat, and then he said, 'Quinnie.'

'This is somebody called Sammy. Sammy Sutherland. Isn't that the chap Karen arrested for the damage to her car?'

'It is. Play it again.'

Steve listened carefully. 'He's saying Quinlan?'

'I think so. That's what it sounds like to me. Which would explain the shortening to Quinnie. But at least it gives Karen something concrete. This is what Quinnie was afraid of, I reckon. That somebody would dish out his true name. He'd obviously got something planned and he didn't want his name, hitherto unknown, to be bandied around to some oddball professor who was trying to find stuff out about the criminal fraternity in Sheffield. I think he's unknown to the police, no record, and he wants it to stay like that. Is that a big enough reason for him to take these drastic measures?'

Steve nodded. 'I would say so. He killed your dad and Johnny. He'll not see the light of day for that if they catch him. You need to pass all this on to Karen.'

'As soon as she gets here.'

* * *

And that was exactly what Karen was doing – leaving work to go home to her current housemates. They were up to four in their little community, and she hoped it wouldn't grow any larger; eventually Matt would run out of room. She put on her coat and her phone rang.

'It's Rosie.'

'Hi, Rosie. You're still at work?'

'I might say the same to you, Karen,' she said with a laugh, 'but you're going to thank me for working this late. And I'm only here at this ungodly time of day because of you. Too many bodies, Karen. Cut it out, will you?'

'I'll try. I managed to save you having my own on your table.' Karen quickly explained what had happened to her car.

'Good grief, I'm glad I've got my job and not yours. At least they're already dead when I get them. You've got to live with the baddies who aren't dead in your job.'

'So, you got something for me?'

'Sort of. You know I said I was going to test that bloody T-shirt because it was quite possible there was more than one blood type on it? There were three. One, obviously, was Terence Taylor's, another one has been matched to a Richard Bird, and this sample was taken from the blood on the victim's face... Bird removed one, if not both, of his eyes but cut himself. They really went to town on this poor lad, and it was almost a frenzy of bloodletting, which is why I thought they could have cut themselves. However, there's a third one that didn't have a direct match on our system.'

'No direct match? What's that mean? An indirect match?'

'A familial match.'

'He's related to someone on our system? That's fucking brilliant! Excuse the language, but it's time I received some good news. Tell me more.'

'The sample was taken from the area under Taylor's chin, and I want you to imagine cutting out a tongue – not an easy job to do, and I think he nicked himself with the scissors. I ran the DNA result through the database as soon as we realised we had a third piece of blood splatter, and it came back with no direct result, but a familial link to Andrew Clive Beardow.'

Karen sat down with a thud. 'Shit.'

'I'll excuse that language as well.' Rosie laughed. 'I'll send you the full report now. I'm assuming you'll know what to do with it.'

'Of course.' Although she couldn't say the words, the inference was obvious to Rosie. It would be with Matt within a matter of minutes. 'Can we tell how close a familial link?'

'They share a mother, not a father. Half-brothers.'

'So why the hell don't we know about him?'

'I can't answer that, but it's possible they didn't share a life. What if he lived with his father? What if they didn't meet up till later in life, sought each other out? Can be any number of reasons, Karen. Let me know when you find out, familial matches are quite fascinating.'

'Both share the killing gene, you mean?'

'Seemingly so. I'll let you go now and take care. Whoever this chap is, he's evil.'

'Both Hermia and I have first-hand knowledge of this.'

After thanking Rosie, Karen ended the call. She was tempted to immediately ring Matt, but decided to wait until she got home when she could discuss it with the three of them – everybody had an investment in these crimes.

* * *

The roads were quiet as Karen drove home. She had sent Matt a text to say she was on her way, and assumed the ping on her phone was his reply. She hoped he was busy in the kitchen cooking up something delicious, under supervision by Hermia.

Thinking about Hermia made her thoughts go towards Steve, and the way he cared for Herms. Matt had explained how long Steve had treated her almost as a sister, with the hopes that one day the relationship would change, but it had really only been the past fortnight, since their father's death, that Hermia had woken up to the good-looking friend of her brother's and seen him not so much as a brother, more a lover.

And Steve had grown daily in his love for her. Karen couldn't begin to imagine how he must have felt when Hermia was thrown over that balcony, and he was clearly a very distraught young man when she had arrived at the scene of the crime.

It had been such a stressful two weeks all round, and even though she had a modicum of information about Quinnie now, it didn't help with tracking him down. She reached to click on her radio, and switched it to CD, knowing the music would be gentle piano music. It soothed her, and she needed soothing. Tomorrow would be a busy day in view of the information gleaned from Rosie Masters, and it was imperative they get Quinnie and his sidekick Dickie Bird inside a cell before they killed anyone else.

Karen drove and thought. It was a plan to get through the following day with minimal stress, and she was going to push hard with Sammy Sutherland. He had the information she needed, and she was going to scare the living daylights out of him to get what he knew out of his brain and onto the recorder. She smiled to herself. She could use torture by taking in a packet of cigarettes and deliberately leaving them on the table. She could even add a cigarette lighter to the mini tableau and watch his eyes water at the thought of a cigarette.

The CD track changed, and became a piano version of 'Even Now', and she wondered if Barry Manilow had ever envisaged how many of his creations would be played in so many different formats. Her thoughts drifted along with the music, and she realised that the evenings were really getting lighter now. Summer must be on its way, and Matt had told her about the plan to take Harry to Florida for his birthday present. It was a place pretty close to the top of her bucket list, and she thought they should maybe firm up on the plan, so she could get some holiday dates booked in at work. Whether bloody Quinnie was found or not.

She felt sick at how nice thoughts brought about by the beautiful music floating around her head could change so quickly and so dramatically by one name. Quinnie.

It would have to be a priority finding out his proper name; she could do nothing without that. Did it refer to his surname? His Christian name? Nothing very Christian about a man who killed indiscriminately, and in such a brutal fashion. She thought about Threesome's missing eyes, and the horror and pain he must have experienced. He was alive when they were removed. She hoped he was unconscious when they removed his tongue, even though she knew he had been alive by the amount of blood in his mouth and around his chin.

She approached the track leading down to Steve and Matt's cottages, and switched off the music. The silence inside the car felt a bit unearthly. Steve had parked his Audi over towards his own house, and the Porsche and Matt's Land Rover were in front of Matt's cottage, so she decided to park hers down the side of the house.

The only problem was that there was already another car in that spot. One she didn't recognise, but wasn't too worried about it. She didn't really know Matt's friends and relatives. Yet. She parked at the back of Matt's car, picked up her briefcase and headed for the front door.

37

Karen opened the door quietly, just not quietly enough. Matt heard the noise of the door closing behind her, and he yelled at the top of his voice, 'Karen! Run!'

She heard a scream, then a clang of metal, and she hesitated a fraction too long. The kitchen door burst open and one of the men from the pictures she had been touting around for a couple of days stood framed by the door jamb.

'In here, bitch,' he said. He was swinging a baseball bat in his right hand. 'Come and join the party.'

With her eyes firmly on the baseball bat, she clung on to her briefcase and walked towards him.

'Mr Bird, I believe,' she said.

'Don't get cocky with me, bitch, or you'll get what he got.'

She felt the blood drain from her face, and she pushed past him. Matt was tied to the radiator, his arms behind his back and slumped over, quite clearly unconscious, with blood pouring from a head wound, probably sustained when he had called out her name in warning, telling her to run.

For a few seconds, she was aware of nothing else, she just

wanted, needed, to get to Matt, to make sure he wasn't dead.

A voice from behind her said, 'Get down by his side. Dickie, tie her up as well.'

She felt a push in her back and she stumbled forward, falling over Matt's legs. He didn't move. She felt the rope being tied around her wrists and then passed under the radiator post. Steve had been treated in the same fashion at the other end of the radiator, and he looked at her, before nodding towards the table.

Hermia was seated at the table, tied to a chair. Standing by her side was the man featured in the other picture. Quinnie. He had a gun held to Hermia's head. She had fought back at some point, because a bruise was already starting to form on her cheek.

'Okay, let's take it I'm in charge here,' Quinnie said. 'Glad you've arrived, DS Nelson. That completes the group. Now, here's what's going to happen. Hermia is going to hand over the interview memory stick, all the notes that Hartner made, and we'll leave you alone. If she doesn't, I'm going to shoot you one at a time. We'll see how long she lasts then. And I'll start with her ever-loving brother, might as well tidy up the whole family.'

He raised the gun slightly and pointed it towards the slumped over body of Matt. Karen tried to cover his body with her own but was tied so tightly she could hardly move.

'No...' Hermia's voice cracked as she said the word. 'You can have everything. The papers, everything. But you'll have to take me to get it; I can't drive with the cast.'

Quinnie grinned. 'Oh, yeah... sorry about that. I meant to kill you. You wouldn't have had the pain then, would you? So where is it? The memory stick.'

'Locked in the safe at the university. I'm working from a stick I copied it to, but the original is there.'

'It's not downloaded anywhere?'

She shook her head, pain showing on her face. 'No, I worked from the stick.'

'Where's the laptop?'

'In the lounge on the coffee table. The copy stick is in the side of it.'

Quinnie nodded towards Dickie. 'Go and get it, and smash that laptop with the big stick you've got. If she's lying, it'll do her no good if the laptop is in bits. Bring the stick to me, then we'll head off to university, get ourselves a bit of an education.'

Dickie headed out of the kitchen, taking the baseball bat with him. He'd wanted to bring a gun, but Quinnie had said he couldn't trust him to point it at the right person, so he'd brought his baseball bat instead. It'd done a good job on that ex-copper.

They heard the sounds of the laptop being smashed to smithereens, and Bird's shouts of joy as he turned it into pieces of unusable plastic.

'Right,' Quinnie said, releasing the final knot at the back of the chair. 'Stand up and we'll go.'

He was a second too late telling her to stand up. She launched herself from the chair, swinging her arm with the cast on towards his face. His nose erupted in blood, which cascaded all down the front of his clothes, and he dropped to his knees. She used the cast once again, this time repeatedly on the back of his head until he groaned and fell to the floor. Hermia grabbed at the gun as Bird came back through the door, his face wreathed in smiles until he saw the prone body of Quinnie.

Hermia pointed the gun at him. 'Untie them.'

'Not fucking likely. I'm off...'

Hermia shot him in the foot. 'I said untie them.'

'Stupid bitch,' he moaned, dragging the badly bleeding foot behind him as he reached Steve first. He untied him and Steve went immediately to Hermia to take the gun from her. 'Can you untie the other two?' he said. 'I'll keep an eye on these two bright sparks and ring for help.'

She crumpled. 'I can't,' she sobbed. 'Give me the gun, I can't move my arm to do anything. It was okay while I was hitting him...'

Steve rushed across to Matt and Karen, who was quietly tearful. 'Tell me he's not dead, Steve, please.'

Steve felt Matt's pulse. 'No, but he's out for the count.' He dialled 999 and explained everything, before releasing Karen. Then together they dealt with the comatose Matt.

'What about me and my foot?' Dickie Bird whinged, and Karen trod on it.

Hermia had retaken her seat at the table, nursing the re-injured arm, aware that the cast looked a bit worse for wear. 'Tell me he'll recover,' she said, her voice a whisper.

'The ambulance will be here in a minute,' Karen said, stroking his face. 'They'll sort him out.'

'I'll go and look out for it,' Steve said, and went to open the front door. The ambulance was just pulling onto the driveway, and he waited, waving them towards him.

Matt was taken first, shadowed by Karen following behind in her car, followed by two further ambulances who whisked away a still unconscious Quinnie and two accompanying police officers, while Dickie Bird was loaded into the final ambulance accompanied by his very own pair of officers. 'She shot my foot,' he was heard loudly complaining as he was wheeled out of the cottage.

Hermia refused to go, saying she would attend A&E the following morning as they would be at the hospital to see Matt anyway. Steve quietly handed her two painkillers to help with the pain, but when she saw her battered laptop, she cried.

'I won't stop,' she said. 'I'll pursue this report to the end, and I'll name him properly. None of this Quinnie malarkey, it'll be Quinlan.'

'And Karen doesn't know yet,' Steve said. 'We all seem to know bits and bobs of the whole story, but when we get together again, we'll sort out who knows what, I'm sure.'

* * *

DI Armitage arrived on scene as the ambulance carrying Dickie Bird pulled away. He entered through the still open front door, and saw Hermia sitting at the kitchen table, instructing Steve who was standing behind her how to get the sling more comfortable. She looked up and frowned.

'DI Armitage. Long time, no see. What can we do for you?'

'I understand things have come to a head...'

'They have. That's all you need to know. You've not been there for the rest of the investigation, so Karen will report to you when she's been checked over and when she's made sure my brother is going to live.'

Armitage stood, unsure what to do. 'So it seems we have solved the murders of our two ex-colleagues...'

'You mean my father and my uncle Johnny? And Emily George? And Terence Taylor? And me being thrown over a balcony? Get out, DI Armitage. Leave us to recover without hassle.'

'Maybe you can come in tomorrow to give statements...'

'No. You want a statement, you make an appointment to come see me, and don't bother until I'm absolutely certain Matt is going to make a full recovery.'

'Look, I understand you feeling angry...'

It seemed as if Armitage would never complete a sentence. 'Angry? You've seen nothing yet. You've spent the whole of this investigation buttering up Dickhead Davis, accompanying him to the golf course, generally always having something else to do while Karen has been run ragged, had her car vandalised on orders from this bloke whose head I smashed in, so don't come around here pretending you know anything about what's going on. You don't.'

He started to open his mouth again and she held up a hand, palm towards him in the universal language of shut your face, I don't want to hear another word from you.

'And I'm telling you now, Inspector, if it takes me the rest of my life, I am going to use the work started by Professor Eric Hartner – who, by the way, needs his death properly investigating this time, and I'm going to start the ball rolling on that one tomorrow – and I'm going to produce my report for the council, which will indicate where improvements and changes need to be made. Sheffield is my city, and the police have allowed thieves, rogues, vandals and murderers to take over an entire half of the city. This is my home, and I'll make damn sure I put everything in to cleaning it up, and make Sheffield a place to attract the right sort of people and not the ones here now, the wrong sort of people. So up yours, Inspector, and get out of my house now, before I say something I'd be ashamed of.'

Armitage walked out of the kitchen, and they heard the front door close behind him.

'Good lord, Herms. What have I fallen in love with?'

'Me,' she said with a smile, 'just me.'

EPILOGUE

SEVERAL DAYS LATER – SUNDAY, 3 APRIL 2022

Steve and Hermia stayed home, waiting until Karen's car arrived in the parking area. They rushed out, keen to help Matt into his house.

He looked older, but Hermia put that down to his having been unconscious for four days, to allow the swelling to subside. Yesterday they had been assured there would be no lasting damage, he just needed to rest quietly and in a couple of weeks he would be back to his old self.

They led him inside and he sank slowly onto the sofa. 'God, this feels good, to be back home. What did he hit me with?'

'We said we wouldn't tell you anything until you were recovered,' Karen scolded him.

'I am recovered, and if you don't tell me, I'm going to yell the place down.'

Karen sighed. 'I knew you'd be like this. You've been trying for the last two days to get the details out of me. Look, let's make a pot of tea, give you your medication and we'll tell you the lot. Will you shut up about it then?'

'Possibly.' He smiled. 'I don't need medication.'

'No medication, no story.'

He held out his hand.

Steve went through to make the drinks, and they made Matt comfortable with his legs up, quite enjoying being waited on, but not admitting to it.

Steve handed out the drinks, and Karen, seated next to the man who had given her sleepless nights over the past week, took hold of his hand.

'Okay. Here's the story. It seems from Steve's account in his statement that the back door was breached by the two men who waved a gun around and managed to get you all disabled. Fully understand that – you don't argue with a gun. I missed all of this fun and games, the first thing I really knew was hearing you scream out for me to run. I arrived home from work, expecting at the very least a fish and chip supper, but I saw an extra car here that I didn't recognise. It made me a bit wary, but I had to temper that with not knowing any of your family and friends, so I came in quietly. Then I heard you scream; there was a sort of clang which I assume was the bat hitting the radiator, and he'd bashed you on the head with a baseball bat. You were out for the count, missed all the following activities. There was significant blood, I might add.'

She looked around at the other two. 'It was scary, wasn't it?' and they both nodded.

'Hermia was tied to the kitchen chair, and Quinnie was standing by her side, holding a gun to her head. Steve was tied to the other end of the radiator. Quinnie, whose real name, by the way, is Victor Quinlan, finally identified from the interviews by our very own Hermia, told Dickie Bird to tie me up, so he tied me next to you. I couldn't move, didn't know what the hell to do. My hands were behind my back, so I couldn't even touch you.'

Matt's face was rigid. He was reliving the story through the telling, and feeling angry he hadn't been able to protect them when they needed him.

'He then started on Hermia, who it seemed had already taken a punch to the face because she had a bruise on her cheek, and I didn't reckon Steve had done it. He was asking her about the memory stick, so, smart youngster that she is, she told him the original was in her safe at the uni, and he'd have to take her there to get it back. He sent Bird into the lounge to get the copy she said she was using, and to smash up the laptop in case she'd down-loaded it as well. He made a proper mess in here, I can tell you. Then he untied Hermia and before he'd properly finished untying her, she swung that arm up with the cast on, bashed his face in, teeth fell out and his nose exploded. Blood everywhere again, and he dropped to the floor. She hadn't knocked him out, just caused severe pain, so while he was on his knees, she whacked him with the cast on the back of his head. Then she got the gun.'

'Dad taught Herms and me how to use a gun properly,' he mused. 'Guess he saved the day.'

'He did. She told Bird to untie us, and he wouldn't, so she shot him in the foot. He untied us pretty quick after that.' Karen's head dropped. 'I didn't accidentally step on his foot...'

'Oh, good,' Matt said, with a smile. 'I'm glad you didn't do anything like that.'

'After that, it was all over bar the shouting. Ambulances, three of them, our lads arrived in bulk, and everybody was despatched. Scariest drive of my life following your ambulance. You could have been dead for all I knew, but I figured they wouldn't want me in the ambulance if they needed to work on you.'

'And that's it? Nobody else dead?'

'He's surfaced, Quinlan, arrested on multiple counts of murder, and Bird also. He's had his foot put back together but he'll never walk properly on it again. There is something I need to tell you, though, all of you. I've kept this to myself up to this point because I thought it was just one issue too many until the four of us were back together again.'

Suddenly the welcome home and the lightness of the afternoon knowing Matt was back with them disappeared. Karen's face showed it was big news.

'It's about Quinlan. We had some information, and he's done a bit of talking, but not much. Just confirmation of our guesses about some things, so take the stuff like that with a pinch of salt. However, science plays a part in this, and that's spot on. He admitted it as soon as we asked him about it. When Threesome was brought in for post-mortem, the facial injuries had been caused by really sharp instruments, and Rosie crossed her fingers and hoped there would be blood from the killers as well as massive amounts from Threesome. They did a minute tiny square by tiny square of the T-shirt and hit lucky. Three different sorts of blood. They DNA tested all three and came up with answers. Threesome's own blood and Dickie Bird's blood were on file, but the other one only showed a familial match.'

'Andy Beardow?' Matt said. He looked round at them. 'Just proving he's not bashed my brain doolally. He has a look of him, and it was only when I saw him in the flesh in my kitchen that I realised. I hadn't started to verbalise it, to ask him, before I was knocked out.'

'They share a mother but not a father. They're half-brothers. We questioned him about it, didn't get a lot out of him because he knows he's going down for life with no chance of ever getting out, but he did confirm they hadn't grown up together, met up in their teenage years. We've always wondered what happened to Beardow, and it seems he went off to Spain immediately, before we'd chance to lock down ports and airports. He'd a private plane waiting to take him from somewhere local, but he had a stroke while on the plane, and basically was a cabbage for about four years before dying. He was never officially in Spain, so when he died, his loving half-brother buried him in a field in Spain. We're hoping he'll give us details as we talk to him more. He's giving us details bit by bit. I might have said it will go better with a judge, but I think as he feels better, he'll clam up. I need as much as possible out of him before that happens. He's not very well, but he's not going to die. And of course it was self-defence what Hermia did to him, so he's keeping very quiet about the fact that a woman managed to floor him.'

'And that's all of it? It was just revenge because Beardow had a stroke which basically killed him immediately after he thought he'd killed my dad?'

'It's the biggest part of it, I think. He needed Herms written off because he thought Hartner had more than he had, but he didn't know how to get to her. He must have been crazy to think Dave Forrester would ever give up his daughter, but he clearly did think that. He knew she was in the research department, a secure building that requires passes and all sorts of stuff to get within a mile of its occupants, so he needed to find out how he could access her without it being at work. Dave was the obvious target for that. There are some things we'll never know, like why your dad lost all those files, but I don't actually believe whatever happened there was anything to do with what happened later.' She sighed. 'It's been a busy week. Somebody upset DI Armitage, but we'll gloss over that.'

Matt sank back into his seat. 'I'll relax when I have proof he's dead, Andy Beardow. But now we follow Dad's dream. The Forrester Agency, back in business.' He looked around at his little group surrounding him. 'Is anybody not injured? Because we're going to need some walls building.'

ACKNOWLEDGMENTS

My first thanks go, as always, to the team at Boldwood, who worked hard to make this book what it is – Tara Loder, Cecily Blench and Candida Bradford. Thank you, ladies, excellent job as always.

I have several people to thank for lending me their names – Ray Ledger, Anthony Dawson, Andy Beardow, Karen Nelson and Becky Davis. I hope you all enjoyed the parts you played, no matter whether you survived or not! The most important mention, of course, is Oliver the cat. The real Oliver left us in June 2022, during the writing of this book, so very much loved.

I also have massive thanks to give to Sheffield Wednesday for beating Cambridge United 6–0, and giving me the perfect start to any book. Up the Owls!

My gratitude, as always, goes to my beta reading team of Marnie Harrison, Tina Jackson, Alyson Read, Nicki Murphy and Denise Cutler, and my ARC group for their prompt and speedy responses to anything I ask of them. You make the life of this author so much easier.

Anita Waller
October 2022

MORE FROM ANITA WALLER

We hope you enjoyed reading *Fatal Secrets*. If you did, please leave a review.

If you'd like to gift a copy, this book is also available as an ebook, large print, hardback, digital audio download and audiobook CD.

Sign up to Anita Waller's mailing list for news, competitions and updates on future books.

https://bit.ly/AnitaWallerNews

Explore more gripping psychological thrillers from Anita Waller...

PREVIOUSLY PUBLISHED WORKS:

Psychological thrillers

Beautiful published August 2015

Angel published May 2016

34 Days published October 2016

Strategy published August 2017

Captor published February 2018

Game Players published May 2018

Malignant published October 2018

Liars published May 2020, co-written with Patricia Dixon

Gamble published May 2020

Nine Lives published April 2021

Supernatural

Winterscroft published February 2017

Kat and Mouse series

Murder Undeniable published December 2018

Murder Unexpected published February 2019

Murder Unearthed published July 2019

Murder Untimely published October 2019

Epitaph published August 2020

Murder Unjoyful published November 2020

The Connection Trilogy

Blood Red published August 2021

Code Blue published November 2021

Mortal Green published March 2022

ABOUT THE AUTHOR

Anita Waller is the author of many bestselling psychological thrillers and the Kat and Mouse crime series. She lives in Sheffield, which continues to be the setting of many of her thrillers, and was first published by Bloodhound at the age of sixty-nine.

Visit Anita Waller's website: https://www.anitawaller.co.uk

Follow Anita on social media:

 twitter.com/anitamayw

 facebook.com/anita.m.waller

 instagram.com/anitawallerauthor

Boldw⚭d

Boldwood Books is an award-winning fiction publishing company seeking out the best stories from around the world.

Find out more at www.boldwoodbooks.com

Join our reader community for brilliant books, competitions and offers!

Follow us
@BoldwoodBooks
@BookandTonic

Sign up to our weekly deals newsletter

https://bit.ly/BoldwoodBNewsletter

THE
Murder
LIST

**THE MURDER LIST IS A NEWSLETTER
DEDICATED TO SPINE-CHILLING FICTION
AND GRIPPING PAGE-TURNERS!**

**SIGN UP TO MAKE SURE YOU'RE ON OUR
HIT LIST FOR EXCLUSIVE DEALS, AUTHOR
CONTENT, AND COMPETITIONS.**

SIGN UP TO OUR
NEWSLETTER

BIT.LY/THEMURDERLISTNEWS

Printed in Great Britain
by Amazon